IRON MAN

STARSHIP JERICHO UNIVERSE

WAR FOR LIBERTINE
BOOK 1

TOBY NEIGHBORS

Iron Man

Copyright © 2025 by Toby Neighbors

ISBN: 978-1-968189-00-6 ebook

978-1-968189-01-3 print

Mythic Adventure Publishing, LLC

Idaho, USA

Nobody wants him
    They just turn their heads
    Nobody helps him
    Now he has his revenge

IRON MAN - BLACK SABBATH

CHAPTER 1

A MAN REFLECTS on a lot of things when he's falling from sixty thousand feet. It was hard not to wonder if I had made a mistake. My name is Hugo McManus. I'm a Sergeant in the Space Defense Force Marine Corps, or at least I was until my last mission ended. It left me stranded in space just beyond the planet Libertine, a primitive world in the legendary free systems of the Milky Way galaxy. Like most everything else in life, there was good news and bad news. The good news was that I wasn't alone. Corporal Albert "Rip" Van Winkle, was with me. The bad news was that hundreds of Ashi escape pods were streaking through the thin atmosphere toward the surface of Libertine.

Below me, the mottled desert landscape seemed to be rushing toward me. It was almost time to activate the MECH jetpack and boosters. There was a fight coming, and that was just fine with me. If there was one thing I was actually good at, it was combat.

Above me was the space shuttle my friend Rip called

Condor. "How's it hanging, Iron Man?" he asked, which was his codename for me.

I didn't think we needed codenames, but Rip's enthusiasm was hard to ignore. Plus, I was only alive because he had abandoned the spaceship *Renegade*, absconding with the *Condor* so that we could make it to the surface of Libertine alive after my suicide mission had left me trapped in a MECH suit in outer space.

"Very funny," I told him. "Just keep an eye on things."

"Don't worry. When the Ashi kill you, I'll make sure I note where they leave the body."

We didn't have a plan. I had volunteered for a mission with no way to return to our ship. Taking the only MECH armor on the *Renegade* into space to dispatch some of the Ashi battleships that were attacking our vessel from the rear was straightforward enough. Unfortunately, the *Renegade* was racing back home to the Sol system, which meant I had no means of returning to it. The MECH armor was designed for space and planetary combat, but it wasn't strong enough to survive an atmospheric entry. Which means I was doomed to run out of air and die alone in space.

Sometimes, it felt like I had been chasing death since I was a child. Living, especially with other people, had always been difficult for me. The moment I realized there would be no return from the mission, I volunteered. Actually, I took the MECH without permission while my master sergeant, Remmy Steel, was busy saying his goodbyes. I figured he had a lot more to live for than I did. So, even though he had volunteered to pilot the MECH in the mission of no return, I took the space suit and got through the airlock before he could stop me.

Then, to my surprise, just as I'm wrapping up my attack on the Ashi ships, Rip arrived in the area with a shuttle. It was packed full of supplies, mostly ammunition, but knowing Corporal Van Winkle, there will probably be all sorts of things in the shuttle.

That's how I got into Libertine's airspace. We might have just landed normally, had the Ashi not launched their escape pods. All around us, the flaming-hot emergency pods plummeted toward the ground. There were hundreds of pods and we had no idea how many Ashi warriors might be crammed into each one. What we did know was that the people of Libertine, a wide mix of aliens from across the galaxy, weren't ready for them. So, I reloaded the MECH and bailed out of the shuttle.

"Do you know where we are?" I asked.

"In reference to what?" Rip asked.

Below me, all I could see was brown desert sand. Libertine was a hot planet with a thin atmosphere. There was liquid water, but it was mostly underground. The colonists had settled on the two polar continents. Instead of oceans, Libertine had seas of sand.

"In relation to the colonies," I said.

"We're about a hundred kilometers from the nearest one," Rip said. "I'm still working on that. The radar is a bit sketchy."

"What do you mean?" I asked as I hurdled toward the ground at over two hundred miles per hour.

"Everything is upside down," he said.

It took me a minute to figure out what the problem was. In space, a person's position is relative. We had thought we were entering the planet's atmosphere in the northern hemisphere, but with no way to tell which way was up or down, we had come in on the southern hemisphere. Which meant we were a hundred kilometers north of the nearest settlement.

"You came into the planet on the wrong side," I told him.

"No, I didn't," Rip argued. "It was the top. I swear it."

I didn't think 'top' was an actual aeronautical term, but I decided not to bring that up at the moment. Rip wasn't really a pilot. He had only flown simulators and games. We were Space Marines, not Navy pukes, which made it easier to forgive Rip's little mistake. He had sacrificed his future to save my sorry tail after all.

"We're in the southern hemisphere," I told him. "It doesn't matter now. Get to that settlement and warn them. They should have communications working. Sergeant Oliver and Ricky Thompson were down here delivering supplies."

"I thought you did that?"

"I was with Master Sergeant Steel in the northern hemisphere," I corrected him.

From my height, I could just make out where the brown sands turned into the dark green grasslands. In the north and south poles of Libertine, there was water, milder temperatures, and settlements. The original colonists had been planetary engineers. They had spent decades terraforming Libertine, but it was a long, slow process. And during that time, most of their equipment had worn out and broken down. They didn't even have transports capable of reaching the opposite poles until the *Renegade* had given them several.

Communications had been limited, too, but with equipment from our ship and new communication satellites, they should be talking. Of course, there was only one subject they should be talking about.

"Alright, I'm going," Rip said. "Are you sure you don't need backup?"

"That rig doesn't have weapons, does it?"

"No," Rip said. "Not yet."

"Then no, I don't need you to fly down here, get killed and turn over the shuttle to the Ashi."

"Good to know you're looking out for me... Iron Man."

"Someone's got to," I complained half-heartedly.

It was time for me to fly, only I had never worked the MECH suit outside of the *Renegade's* training hangar. If the armored suit didn't have some sort of flight-assisting computer controls, I could be in real trouble.

CHAPTER 2

"BOOSTERS ON," I said. It was a habit. Space Marines rarely ran solo and it was standard procedure to alert one's team of everything they were doing.

Only, on Libertine, there was no one to hear me.

The MECH had a jet pack and boosters as well as flaps to help control descent in gravity. I was certainly in gravity. And the ground was pulling me toward it at lethal speed.

My former Lieutenant, Micky Colt, had designed the MECH armor. It was a one-of-a-kind combat armor suit. Lieutenant Colt had laid out the design and the ship's computer on the *Renegade*, which had been built by an advanced space-faring race called the Arodoni, did the heavy lifting. It also manufactured the suit in the ship's three-dimensional printing facility. The interior was tight, at least on me. Lieutenant Colt had built the armor with his physical dimension plugged into the computer. I was taller and thicker than the LT. What can I say, I like to lift heavy objects and eat. It can be a good combination.

The armor was made of a special alloy that was both hard

and heat-dispersing. It wasn't designed for the high heat of planetary reentry, but it could take a standard laser blast, as well as most projectiles. A diamond-tipped bullet, or depleted uranium, could punch through if the bullet had enough force behind it. But there was more than a single layer of armor between the inside and outside of the MECH suit. Behind the metal alloy plating was a honeycomb layer that was ideal at absorbing impact energy. And inside the honeycomb layer was a Kevlar weave over standard insulation. The interior was molded to fit a human pilot. I sat on a rectangular seat, working pedals that activated the legs of the MECH. My arms were in movement control sleeves and my hand had access to a variety of controls.

Eye level was a HUD or Heads Up Display that fed all the MECH's information, including her exterior cameras, which were both forward and rear-facing. There was also a narrow transparent window that allowed the pilot to see out in the rare case of a power outage. The entire suit was loaded with weapons, from the lower legs to the head unit. The entire suit measured twelve feet tall by five feet wide. It was both a fighting platform and a protective armor suit for the pilot.

"Extending flaps," I said, continuing to speak to no one at all.

The flaps were, in reality, aerodynamically designed armor plates that could be pushed out from the rest of the suit. They served to slow my descent and help me control my fall. There were boosters at the elbows and feet, which had enough natural weight to pull me downward in an upright standing position. I bent my elbows and held the legs of the suit stiff as I gave the boosters a short burn.

"Activating boosters," I explained. At the very least, the suit was probably recording my efforts. If I died from a crash, someone might discover that I was at least trying to fly the MECH when I met my end.

It's easy to joke about death, but harder to face it. I had done exactly that numerous times in my career. But in all those instances, I had duty to focus on. Usually, I was fighting an enemy and trying to achieve mission parameters. As I fell through the air on Libertine, all I had to focus on was the MECH suit's controls.

The boosters fired like weapons. They pushed me in the opposite direction of my fall, slowing me in much the same way that an opening parachute slows a paratrooper. It wasn't a complete stop, but it was enough to allow me to utilize the jetpack without overtaxing the mechanism and using up all the power in the suit's battery compartments.

"Jetpack activated," I said. "Power at fifteen percent."

The jetpack brought me to a complete stop. I could hear it running. It was a bit like having a huge engine on my back. I knew that if I lost my balance, things could get ugly, but I was strong. Most people who spend a lot of time in the gym are more interested in how their body looks. They do core exercises in order to have a narrow waist and well-defined abs. My focus was more about functionality. And the core muscles are essential to all the other muscles functioning well. Needless to say, I had the core strength to stay upright.

"Activating flight controls," I said as I powered on the suite of apps built into the MECH's central processing. On my HUD, a variety of helpful information flashed before my eyes.

Altitude was holding at just over a thousand feet. Flight speed was zero. I activated the small radar built into the suit's scanners. A map stretching ten miles in all directions appeared on the HUD. It was easy to make out, and yet I could see through it too. On the map, small icons began to appear. The computer labeled them Lima One and counting.

I didn't need a closer look to know they were the escape pods from the Ashi invaders. I didn't have as much experience fighting them as some of the other members of my former platoon. But I knew enough to understand that just one of the aliens was a major threat. In the MECH, I stood twelve feet tall, but I still wasn't as tall as the average Ashi warrior. They were like massive, hulking humans in their basic physiology, but their skin was green and their internal organs were different. For instance, they had two separate hearts to pump blood through their massively muscled bodies. Instead of rib cages, they had bone plates that protected their vitals. The only way to really hurt them was through the stomach.

Their heads were completely different from humans. The Ashi had wide lower jaws, with big tusks on each side that curled upward and ended in sharp points. Their lips were thick and many had flappy jowls. Their teeth were pointed and some protruded from their fleshy lips. They had wide noses with slits for nostrils. Their eyes were wide-set and narrow. Above the eyes was a massive brow bone and mostly bald heads with only small tufts of hair. I didn't know if that was a style choice or just the way their hair grew. Otherwise, their bodies seemed hairless.

The Ashi were the founders of the Galactic Imperium, serving both as the supreme rulers as well as the defenders of their kingdom. Their home planet was part of the galaxy's inner core. Five other powerful worlds from the core elected representatives to something called the Prime Council. Their job was to govern the galaxy, or at least that part of it controlled by the Imperium, which was mostly everything. The Free Worlds, like Libertine, had been outside the known hyperspace network. Everything within that network had been subject to the Imperium for thousands of years.

Of course, I was less concerned with galactic politics than I was about the fact that my new planet of residence was being invaded by a very hostile alien race. I can't honestly say I was concerned for the locals. I really didn't know them yet. But I did feel some responsibility for the planet being invaded. The Ashi had followed the *Renegade* to the Libertine system. And while I wasn't the captain of that ship, and had no real say in the command decisions that were made, I had been part of her crew. On top of that, it had been my mission to stop the Ashi battleships that were in the system. I had done my duty, which was to keep them from attacking the *Renegade* from the rear, where she was most vulnerable. While my mission had been a success, it had also allowed the aliens to escape their damaged vessels and descend on the planet. So, it was kind of my fault, depending on how you looked at things.

I suppose it's possible to say the Ashi couldn't be blamed for the invasion. They were merely trying to survive. There were no other options for them. But that didn't mean they were innocent either. They had terrorized the galaxy for thousands of years. They attacked the *Renegade* without cause and chased her through several systems. My gut told me they weren't going to be looking to make peace with the locals either. Which meant I needed to stop them before they could hurt the innocent beings trying to scratch out a home on the rugged planet.

You may wonder why I care so much about Libertine. The truth is, I'm drawn to the isolation of it. I don't care what it stands for or that it is inhabited by a wide variety of alien species. What I found interesting about the place was the possibility that a person could carve out a life for themselves on that world without depending on anyone else. All my life, people have found me to be strange, different and hard to get along with. For my part, I feel the same way about other people. I can count on one hand the number of people who saw past my rough exterior and made the effort to really get to know me. It was one of the reasons I always volunteered for the most dangerous missions. It's why I threw myself into combat, often at the consternation of my fellow Marines. What can I say? That's just the kind of person I am. When everyone else is running for safety, I'm running toward the danger.

Case in point. Lima Four on my radar app was directly below me. I eased off on the jetpack and let the MECH drop toward the ground in a controlled descent. Looking down, I could see the Ashi escape pod. It was big, easily the size of Rip's *Condor*. My initial guess was that four, maybe five Ashi warriors could fit inside. Smoke was rising from the scorched escape pod. I'm no engineer, but there were no parachutes or wind sails to slow the craft down. It probably had some sort of jet engines, but I couldn't be sure.

Call me what you like, but I hoped it crashed and killed everyone on board. It would save me the trouble. But of course, I'm not that lucky.

Landing was a treat. I came down a bit too hard, but the legs of the MECH absorbed the momentum. I immediately engaged the rotating machine gun on my right forearm. It popped up from the armor plating and began to rotate as it drew the belt-fed ammunition into the firing chambers.

"Rip, do you read me?"

My MECH armor had a comlink signal booster, but Rip was probably forty or fifty miles away, not to mention several miles up. There was communication gear in the settlements that might reach me, but he wouldn't be there yet.

I powered on the suit's exterior speakers and increased the volume. When I spoke, my words would be translated and projected from my armor.

"To the warriors in the escape pod. You are surrounded. Lay down your weapons and surrender, or you will be killed."

The words sounded strange to my ears. The Ashi language was rough and guttural, mostly barking and growling sounds. They boomed from the MECH's speakers. I was standing on sand-covered ground. Not the sea of sand, but gritty, hard, rocky terrain. It was baked from the Libertine sun, with cracks in the dry soil. It was dull gray, with a tinge of red. Had I been the type to care about such things, I could have taken samples of the dirt. But it didn't look like much to me — not as iron-rich as Mars, and less nutrient-dense than the soil on Earth.

"Come out, now!" I ordered.

There was no response from inside the escape pod. I began to walk around it. The MECH armor was heavy, but had a surprisingly easy tread. The hydraulics in the legs used shock absorbers and struts to make each step a bit like walking in soft sand. Not that I was actually walking. I drove the MECH, which operated a lot like a hoverbike. I wagged the pedals, which had full three hundred and sixty-degree movement capability. The MECH took a little time to get used to, but it was surprisingly dexterous, and the controls were intuitive. I had mastered walking and running back on the *Renegade*.

"Last chance," I said.

In response, there was a boom from the door, which burst out from the pod almost like a bullet. Not with explosive charges, but compressed air or gas. I wasn't near the door, having moved halfway around the object. Not that I had noticed the door. The sides of the escape pod all looked the same to me. Suddenly, a huge green form appeared. It had bent over double as it slipped out of the pod, which was half buried from its rough landing. I could see over the top of the emergency craft and spotted the warrior before he sprang up with his laser weapon in hand.

The Ashi fought in battle with bulky laser rifles. They were effective shooters, but not as powerful as I thought the enemy would use. They were behemoths and could have easily used much larger firearms. In fact, when I had fought them on the planet Casasil, they carried high-capacity laser cannons. But the warrior from the escape pod had the scaled-down assault rifle. He brought it up over the top of the vehicle he was sheltering behind. It took him a full second to spot me and try to target me. I already had him in my sights. The round machine gun spewed thick metal slugs in a swarm before he could fire a shot. Some of my bullets hit the escape pod and ricocheted harmlessly away, but at least half a dozen found their mark. Blood and tissue formed a blue mist as the Ashi warrior was knocked off his feet. I moved around to the other side of the pod cautiously. The last thing I wanted was to run into another of them without warning.

But there were no more Ashi in or out of the pod—just the single warrior, who had fallen under my barrage of bullets. Four had hit his upper chest and were stopped by the thick bone plate under his bulging pectoral muscles. Another had ripped a gash in his fleshy face and splintered the Ashi's tusk on that same side. But the real damage was the bullet that impacted the narrow, fleshy throat. The Ashi didn't have much in the way of a neck, but there was a narrow space between the upper limit of his breastbone and the thick jaw. That bullet had driven deep and with catastrophic damage to the flesh and blood vessels found there. The alien's weapon was cast aside, and his hands tried in vain to hold back the tidal wave of blood from the wound in its neck.

I kicked the weapon out of its reach, then peered into the escape pod. There was room for four warriors inside, but none were there. Three of the four seats had gone unused. I hoped it was a sign of things to come. Turning back toward the dying alien, I looked down at him. The wretched creature was sputtering as the blood from his wounds soaked into the dry ground.

"This world is not yours," I said, the MECH suit's language app translating my words into Ashi.

"All... will... die," the creature managed to say.

His choking growls were displayed in words on my HUD.

"Not if I have anything to say about it," I replied.

The MECH had a sharp, dagger spring mounted into the armor on my left forearm. I triggered it. The blade punched up under the dying warrior's wide lower jaw, piercing through tissue and splitting his brain before sticking the hardened point into the top of his skull. The Ashi warrior died instantly. His pain and suffering in this life was over, what awaited him beyond was no concern of mine.

I jerked the blade free, wiped it on the alien's kilt, and locked it back in the MECH forearm. The suit was packed with weapons. They were nearly all part of the armor suit itself, hidden in the MECH's design and readily available when they were needed. I had to appreciate the armor's capacity for deadly force.

Lima Four was dealt with, but there were fourteen other escape pods within the range of my suit's radar. That meant there was plenty of killing left to do and it was high time I got on with it, before the Ashi survivors found a defensible place to thwart my efforts.

CHAPTER 3

LIMA SEVEN WAS the closest pod on the ground, but there were still more coming down. I had run to the site of the escape pod, which used less of the MECH's power supply than flying with the jet pack. (If I'm being honest, I was more comfortable with my feet on the ground.)

The aliens were already out of their pod. There were four Ashi, all armed, but clearly suffering some type of trauma. I couldn't tell what it was at first. But as I got closer, I realized the heat on Libertine was wearing the big aliens down. My MECH armor registered the temperature at 136° Fahrenheit (57.7 Celsius). I said a little prayer of thanks for the MECH's environmental controls.

I approached the group slowly. They must have seen me coming, but they seemed unconcerned. Three were slumped onto the ground against the side of their escape pod, trying to keep the sun off their exhausted bodies. The fourth was on his feet. He had a laser rifle in one hand and a bottle of some type in the other. I saw him tilt his head back and pour the drink into his wide mouth, gulping it down greedily.

"Throw down your weapons," I ordered.

The growling translation boomed across the otherwise quiet landscape. None of the three exhausted aliens moved. They had weapons but weren't holding them in a menacing fashion. In fact, it appeared to me as my HUD zoomed in on the aliens that lifting their weapons might be too much for them.

The fourth Ashi raised his rifle with one hand and fired at me. The distance between us was nearly seventy-five yards. His shot wasn't even close. I raised my right arm, spinning the machine gun into action. The Ashi warrior fired again. The laser blast ripped into the ground between us. I fired a small volley. I was a pretty good shot, but the MECH had aiming assistance, making it even easier to find the target. My bullets ripped into the alien's stomach and tore through his bowels. He died before his huge body hit the ground. The bottle of vital liquids fell, too. What little was left inside spilled out onto the parched ground.

The other aliens didn't even make a sound. They didn't complain or move to help their comrade. As I got closer, I could see the cuts and bruises. They had fought amongst themselves, probably for the water the victor had been guzzling down before he died.

"Put down your weapons and I will let you live," I ordered.

"Do you have water?" One of the aliens asked.

I had water for myself, nothing I could share with the aliens, even if I had been willing, which I wasn't.

"No," I said.

"Then kill us now. It will be a kindness."

I won't lie, killing helpless soldiers is not something I would do under most circumstances. But the truth of the situation was starting to dawn on me. The Ashi were big. Their bodies were made for war, but they required certain conditions. Cooler temperatures, it appeared, were necessary for the Ashi to thrive. I knew that with the right supplies, they could make a go of things, perhaps cross the hundred or so miles of desert to reach the grasslands where liquid water could be found. But the warriors in Lima Seven had turned against each other. Not only did three of the four lose the right to drink what little water was in the escape pod, but the fourth had been so dehydrated from the fighting that he couldn't drink what he won fast enough.

I saved my ammunition and killed each of them with the dagger. It was dirty work. And to be honest, after I killed the first of them, I expected the other two to come to their senses. They didn't. Nor did they seem to fear death. I knew Marines who didn't fear dying. They always fell into two categories: either they had tremendous religious faith or they hated themselves so much that they were eager to die. I sometimes fell into the latter category myself, yet my time on the *Renegade* had been some of the best experiences in my life. I might have been willing to die, but I wasn't anxious for my life to end. The aliens seemed less inclined to see the possibilities on Libertine. Of course, they may have thought that the world was nothing but desert. It was an understandable presumption. From orbit, it looked like a dust-ball. And the aliens had come down in the arid border between the vast sand dunes that wrapped around the center of the planet and the polar continents, where the temperatures were mild and the terraforming was making the biggest impact.

I had encountered five Ashi warriors since landing on Libertine and killed all five. But it was a waste of time and effort, not to mention my MECH suit's battery power and our limited ammunition. The aliens wouldn't survive. They were not built for the intense heat of the desert world, and didn't have adequate supplies in their escape pods to facilitate their survival. Those that landed more than ten miles from a water source wouldn't make it unless they hunkered down, rationed their water and set out across the desert at night.

Turning south, I started to run again. It was another benefit of the MECH suit, which could run for hours without getting tired or winded. I wasn't the type to trust a robotic suit to do the work for me, but running in the specialized armor was almost like using an elliptical cardio machine; that is to say, the momentum from one step did a large part of the work for the next step, and so on. It allowed the user to keep up a run in the MECH much longer than they would have been able to do otherwise. Plus, the environmental controls kept the interior at a cooler temperature and held water that I could sip on through a straw. It even had little adrenaline injectors that could pump enough of the fluid into my system to keep me going no matter what. Not that I needed it or would have used it for the run. Don't get me wrong, a hundred miles is still too far to travel on foot even in a MECH suit, but I didn't want to waste any more time.

I got about twenty-five miles before the comlink in my suit chirped. It was Rip, no surprise there.

"Yo, Iron Man, do you copy? Over."

"I read you," I said. "Now come get me."

"You sweep up the trash already?"

"No," I admitted. "But I learned a thing or two. The heat is killing the Ashi out here. What's the radar look like?"

"I had to get it set up. Seems like the folks around here weren't in too big a hurry to use their new tech."

"I'll bet they're enjoying the animals we brought them, though," I said.

"Maybe, this place is really something, Hugo. I've never seen anything like it."

That wasn't what I expected to hear. I had been to the settlements in the north. They were tiny, squalid villages. The aliens all seemed nice enough, but they were barely surviving.

"And the escape pods?" I asked. "Any of them a threat to the people where you are?"

"No, they're all south of here. Only a few came down in the green zone."

"That's good news," I said. "Come and get me."

"Roger that. On my way."

I slowed the MECH to save energy. The locals living in the villages at the poles were industrious and smart, but they didn't have much in the way of physical resources. I knew the only ammunition Rip and I would have was what remained on the shuttle. There were a few Casians we had trained on the *Renegade* to use cannons similar to the one on the MECH. They were big, six-legged pachyderms who wore their weapons on their back. They had a few crates of belt-fed ammunition, probably twenty thousand rounds or so. But that was for the protection of the villages from native predators, not an invasion. Rip and I would have to ration everything we had until, hopefully someday, more humans might arrive. I never thought I would long for more people, but stranger things have happened.

CHAPTER 4

GETTING out of a MECH is never easy. Climbing out of one that's crowded into the back of a shuttle is no fun at all. But I managed, then joined Rip in the cockpit. The ship was a hybrid aircraft capable of flying in atmosphere and in space. I thought of it as a shuttle because it was generally used to shuttle manpower and supplies from orbit to the surface of a planet. The one we were in was completely designed and built on the *Renegade*. That was one of the perks of the advanced alien technology: you could build just about anything. We had found dozens of shuttlecraft on the *Renegade* when we took control of her, along with hundreds of drones for all sorts of purposes, from spy birds to attack drones.

The *Condor* was pretty much standard issue, with very few bells and whistles. What it did have was human-compatible seating in the cockpit—two very comfortable captain's chairs. The autopilot was very good, which meant that Rip didn't have to do a lot as we cruised south toward the settlements.

"How was it back there?" Rip asked.

"Hot," I replied. "The Ashi can't take it."

"Must be aggravating to have your ship shot to pieces, but you manage to escape, only to land on an inhospitable world."

"The smart ones will survive," I said. "And then we'll have a problem on our hands."

"You think so?"

"When they have a lot of warriors together, they're predictable and easy to fight. They're kind of stupid, really, bunching together, coming straight ahead all the time. But a few of them will realize they can't beat us with overwhelming strength. They'll have to fight smarter."

"Maybe they won't want to fight at all," Rip said.

"I just saw four of them fight nearly to the death over a bottle of water," I said. "It makes me think that maybe fighting is all they know."

"They're certainly built for it," Rip said.

He rubbed his arm. An Ashi laser blast had nearly blown it in two on Casasil. He had been rescued and the medical team on the *Renegade* had rebuilt the bone in his upper arm. There was a pretty nasty scar, but otherwise his arm was as good as new. But of course, that was never really the case. Whatever medical polymer they used to replace the bone wasn't meant to be inside a human body. At best, it wouldn't feel exactly right; at worst, it would ache for the rest of his life.

We flew over rolling hills that were covered with a hearty grass that was a deep green in color. Unlike the settlements in the north, there were tall mountains in the south polar region. Rip flew us toward a settlement just inside the mountains, about a third of the way up the steep slope where a few trees dotted the green landscape. A plateau opened up and I saw a gorgeous lake. You might expect evergreens and aspens in such a place, except on Libertine, the south pole was a warm, tropical environment. There was a bright, sandy beach along the shore of the lake and lots of palm trees swaying in the evening breeze. Most of the structures were simple huts, some were nothing more than platforms with thatched roofs and no walls to speak of.

"This is different," I said.

"But not so bad, right? I can see myself spending some time here."

"There are no other humans on this planet," I reminded him.

"For now. A few pictures of this place and the girls back home will be lining up to make the trip."

We landed on a natural stone platform and shut down the shuttle. From where I sat, the cockpit had a sweeping view of the surrounding land. It was spectacular. Best of all, it was strategically sound. I could see the mountains, of course, but I also had a nearly one hundred and eighty-degree view of the open grasslands. Nothing could get close to the settlement without being seen.

"We need a radar right here," I said.

"The ship's will work for now," Rip said. "You need to meet the colonists. Be prepared for a very cool reception."

We left the ship and were immediately met by a tall alien with a bald head and milk white skin. Its anatomy was similar to a human's, two legs, two arms, but the body was much thinner, with no real defining features other than a series of small, round lumps that stood out from the being's chest to its stomach, eight in total. It had four fingers on each hand, which were long and delicate, with tiny cups on the tips that could squeeze closed. The alien wore a long, flowing garment that was little more than a strip of gauzy fabric, probably made from the same grasses used to thatch the roofs on their buildings. It was thin enough that I could see through it.

"You have returned," the alien said in a strange, almost musical language. Our comlinks were designed with hundreds of languages built into the tiny devices. There was a small speaker that we kept clipped to the collar of our fatigues that provided a translation of our own language.

"As I assured you I would," Rip said. "This is Sergeant Hugo McManus."

"It's a pleasure to meet you," I said, even though I didn't normally enjoy meeting people. I knew it was the proper thing to say even if it wasn't true.

"I am Eldona, Mother of this settlement," the alien replied.

It was hard to read the alien body language. Her voice sounded sweet, almost serene. Her language sounded like musical notes instead of words. Yet her body was rigid, and she didn't extend a hand or make any sort of welcoming gestures.

"Were my fellow Marines here a few days ago?"

"There were visitors like you," Eldona said. "They pushed their technology on us."

"I'm certain there was no ill intent," I said.

"And yet, your kind assumed we were in need. They foisted their machines on us without even considering that we might not desire it."

"You don't want to connect with the rest of the colonists here?"

"You know very little of our history," Eldona said. "Are we in danger?"

"Not right at this moment, but there is a possibility that the Ashi warriors who landed on Libertine might make their way here."

"I take it you will see that they do not harm us," she replied.

"For that, we shall share our shelter and food with you. But I would prefer that you do not interact with my children. We have no need of your technology and no desire to take part in whatever warmongering the Imperium has been up to."

"I think I understand," I told her. It was another lie, but I did understand the desire to be left alone.

"Come then. We shall feed you and I will tell you the history of our commune."

Rip gave me a doubtful look, but we were Marines and, as far as I know, we have never turned down a free meal. We followed Eldona. She moved like a dancer, graceful, with long strides across the grassy expanse that led toward the lake. The settlement was built around the water, with dozens of small huts standing on pylons several feet above the ground. In the distance, I saw aliens gathered around small fire pits and lounging on hammocks. It was a beautiful place. The water was clear. Even from a distance, I could make out the fish swimming in it. There were a few aliens with round nets. They expertly tossed them into the lake, then pulled them out a few moments later with small but substantial catches.

"We are not in need here," Eldona said as we reached a small hut with no walls. She waved a hand, and we sat down.

"It's very beautiful here," I said.

"On that, we are agreed," she replied as she bent over a stack of wood. It was neatly arranged, with small sticks and dry grass on the bottom below the thicker pieces of neatly cut wood. She used a bit of stone and a metal rod to cast a shower of sparks onto the dry grass, which kindled easily. "Wood is more common higher in the mountains," she explained. "We save it by burning only a few fires each night and sharing the warmth."

"Smart," I said.

"Life here is good. We are not slaves to the accumulation of goods."

"Including the tech we brought down," Rip said.

"We have it," Eldona said. "But we have no real use for it."

"I thought the colonists here were trying to terraform the planet," I said. "To make it habitable for more people."

"You're looking for Solace," she explained. "There are still some there who want to manipulate the planet for their own gains."

"You make it sound sordid," I told her.

She stood between the lake and the fire. It wasn't dark yet, but the sun was low. I was shocked to find my eye drawn to the curve of her hip and her long legs. It had never occurred to me that I might find an alien attractive. Perhaps it was the setting, or her lack of proper garments, but the discovery was unsettling.

"Not everyone who migrated here came to build a new world for billions of people," she said. "Some of us were looking for a way to escape the trappings and snares of modern civilization. My people just want to live. They share their lives. What work needs to be done is done, but we do not slave our lives away to pay mortgages and buy all the latest tech, only to have the government steal what we earn to enrich the politicians in the Core."

I had to admit, I agreed with everything she was saying. Just days before, I had said something similar to Master Sergeant Steel. All I wanted was room to be myself without other people clinging to me or judging every decision I made. There was room on a planet like Libertine, even with only a fraction of the surface habitable, for a man to be alone and build something with his own two hands.

"What happens when the Ashi show up?" Rip asked.

"They never have. Before you came, they did not know we existed," Eldona said.

"And we're sorry," I told her. "We didn't mean to bring trouble to your people. Rip and I will do our best to make sure you aren't bothered by the Ashi warriors who survived the desert. And we're happy to pull our own weight."

As I was speaking, a man came with two large fish already on spits. They had been cleaned and scaled, their innards removed, and the cavity filled with herbs.

"It is not our way to turn those in need back from our hospitality," Eldona said. "But we do not wish to have your war here. We are people of peace."

"Alright," I said. "We'll leave soon. Do any of your people know where the other settlements are?"

"Loutar has a very excellent, woven map," Eldona said. "I will see that he allows you to study it. You should rest here tonight. Enjoy our hospitality, then go do what you must do."

Rip and the newcomer with the fish set up the spits over the open flames. Soon, the smell of the roasting meat made my stomach growl. An older woman brought us bowls filled with a soft, cooked vegetable. It was starchy and delicious, a bit like potatoes but with a more earthy flavor. We ate our fill and had fish left over. The sun didn't drop completely below the horizon. Long shadows draped over the lake and a cool breeze kicked up. Hammocks were hung in our small shelter. We activated the radar on the shuttle, syncing it to our comlinks to alert us of any movement in the valley below. Then we slept.

The next morning, we ate fish dried over the fire from the night before, and drank spring water. It was a nice way to start the day. We were given a bowl of berries, which I tested before eating, rubbing a little of the juice from one berry on the inside of my lip. The food was good, filling and nutritious. We had rations in the shuttle, but nothing that could compare to the fresh food from the village.

There were not many beings of the same species in the commune. Just like the settlements in the north, it was populated by beings from a wide variety of worlds. A few were even aquatic-type creatures, who seemed more at home swimming in the lake than walking on the shore. Children laughed as they played by the gentle waters. I saw craftsmen working on projects but no one seemed rushed. A few of the younger men left at dawn and returned in only a couple of hours with loads of firewood. I saw others leave with woven baskets made of some type of reeds. They returned with fruits and greens foraged from the wilderness around the lake. It was, without a doubt, a very rich and accommodating area.

After breakfast, a short alien approached with what looked like a rug rolled up under one arm. He had a round head with short, pointed ears on top, and a pug nose that moved as he sniffed the air near us. I didn't have to ask if he could smell us; that much seemed clear. He had small, watery eyes and didn't speak until he had a good grasp of our scent.

"You need directions to the other settlements?" He asked.

"Yes," Rip said. "That would be a big help."

"I have something," the alien said. "I'm called Loutar."

"I'm Hugo," I replied. "This is Rip."

"You are soldiers?"

"We are or were," I said. Then I pointed up toward the sky. "Our ship was attacked. We volunteered to stay and fight."

The short alien snorted. It was something between a chuckle and a whimper; I couldn't be sure which. He walked to the edge of our small building and unrolled his tapestry on the floor. I was surprised at how detailed the weave was. It was dusty brown at the edges, but showed a large circular landmass with green at the edges, and mountains in a long line from east to west across the center.

"Solace is here," he said, pointing with a split hoof instead of a finger at the center of the map. "Right at the southern pole. It never gets dark there. They live high up. The air is thin there. It's cold too."

He shivered and then pointed at a golden dot. "This is Lake Tyconda and our commune."

There was no way to tell the scale of the map or how far it was between the two settlements, but there were several mountains between them. My guess was it would take days, maybe even weeks, to hike from one settlement to the other.

"These dots were all villages," Loutar continued. "But they aren't all fixed. Some move, depending on what forage is available."

"Are they like your village?" I asked. "Or would they have communications?"

"It is doubtful," Loutar said. "Who would we need to speak to?"

"You don't have any communication with the other settlements in the north?"

"The scientists at Solace did," he said with a nod of his round head. "But that was many cycles ago. I have not been to the high mountains in a long time. Maybe they still seek to continue their work ... or perhaps not."

"Can we photograph your map?" I asked.

"Yes, of course," Loutar said. "I am honored."

Rip used his helmet to record the map. He put the map into an app that recreated it in conjunction with lines of longitude and latitude from orbital surveys. Together, they gave us a better idea of where everything on the southern continent was located.

"This is a huge help to us," I told Loutar. "How can we repay you?"

"Gratitude is all I seek," he said. "But if you go to Solace, would you be able to carry letters to our friends there?"

I looked at Rip. "I don't see why not," he said. "There's plenty of room on the *Condor*."

"What is a condor?" Loutar asked.

"It's a bird from our planet," I said.

"Bird?"

"An animal that flies," I said. "Condors are big birds with feathers that fly."

Loutar nodded and smiled his piggish lips. "I like this condor," he said. "I hope our paths will cross again."

He bowed, and we returned the gesture. I had gotten used to bowing while we were on the *Renegade,* which had several Dudonus volunteers. They were big on bowing, too. It seemed to be a universal gesture.

Loutar rolled up his tapestry and trundled off. We watched him for a moment, then gathered our things. We didn't have much. Every Marine carried a few basic toiletries in their kit, such as a toothbrush, soap, and deodorant. It crossed my mind that in about a week, we would both begin to smell. There were some very basic things we would need to come up with on our own. There would be no more runs to the commissary or weekend furloughs that would allow us to stock up on supplies.

As we walked back to the shuttle, I finally asked the question that had been on my mind since the attack in orbit.

"Rip, why are you here?"

"Someone had to save you," he said. "I was the most logical choice."

"But you understand we'll probably never leave this planet,"

I said. "You're stuck here, probably for the rest of your life. And we may be the only humans on the planet."

"Yeah, I thought about that," Rip said. "The truth is, I felt like a fifth wheel on the *Renegade*. It wasn't so bad before everyone left, but after that... it just felt like I was the odd man out."

"But the *Renegade* is on its way back to the Sol system. It's probably almost there."

"Sure, but then what?"

"Find a nice girl, settle down, live your best life," I told him. "Isn't that what everyone says life is all about?"

"Never had much luck in the nice girl department," he said. "Besides, look at that view."

We were standing near the shuttle, looking out between the mountains at the wide grassy plains below. It was a spectacular vista. Puffy white clouds were drifting through a light blue sky. Libertine's star shown warm and bright. There was just enough breeze to keep me cool, and I understood what Rip was saying.

"It's a hell of a view," I said.

"Not many of those left on earth," Rip said. "And we could never afford to live in a place like that back home."

"Agreed," I said.

"Besides, how could I get lonely?" he quipped. "I got you, ain't I?"

He laughed as I turned and walked away. We had work to do and I was keen to get started.

CHAPTER 5

"THERE'S ANOTHER ONE," I said, pointing through the canopy over the cockpit.

Rip had the *Condor* on a long, slow turn. He tilted the ship sideways so we got a better view of the ground. There was a pair of Ashi warriors moving slowly across the grassy plain. We had spent the better part of a day hunting down the Ashi who survived the desert. It wasn't a difficult chore. Once we spotted the big aliens, Rip would put the shuttle into a hover about a kilometer away. I went to the back of the ship and used a Hemlock Stinger to dispatch the Ashi survivors. The Hemlock was a widely used sniper rifle. It fired laser bolts via a heavy external battery supply. The weapon itself was long and light, little more than a long barrel through which the laser focusing array could fire beams of energy. It was a simple point-and-shoot weapon. Even at long distances, the laser fired true. There was no need to calculate distance, or anticipate drag, or any of the things a projectile shot would require. Whatever a person could see through the Hemlock's two-hundred-times digital zoom scope, it could hit. A time or two, the Ashi fired back, yet we stayed out of range of their laser rifles. Some traveled in groups and tried to find cover once the shooting started, but with the shuttle, we could easily move around any obstacle and hunt down the enemy.

I moved into the cargo bay. It was crowded with supplies. Most were crates of ammunition and missiles for the MECH. But there were other supplies too. Looking at all the gear on board, I had my doubts that Rip's explanation to come and save me was accurate. But everyone had their secrets. He had saved my life and didn't owe me an explanation. Maybe he just didn't want to go back to the Sol system. If he wanted to tell me those reasons one day, that would be fine and if he never did, that was okay too. I wasn't going to look a gift horse in the mouth.

After climbing over the MECH, I opened the rear hatch and spotted the aliens. There were two of them, just a little over a mile from our position when you factored in our altitude. I lifted the Hemlock to my shoulder and slid the barrel through a cargo loop hanging from the ceiling to steady my shot. The shuttle was in hover mode and was surprisingly stable. Still, it was a long shot and holding my aim wasn't easy. The aliens must have spotted us, but they didn't run away. Through the scope, they looked exhausted. That was an issue with big, muscular bodies, I knew that firsthand. We had a greater blood volume, which required more oxygen and expended more energy doing the simplest tasks. The Ashi weren't built for marathons and that's what the survival situation they were in required. They were in a desperate search for water and it seemed that nothing else mattered, not even an enemy aircraft. I doubted they could see me, or what I was planning.

With the rifle locked in, I fired my first shot. It hit one of the Ashi warriors in the side of his head. He dropped flat on his face.

There was something horrific about the way a person fell when they died. They did nothing to stop themselves or break the fall. It was just a sudden collapse. I watched the dead warrior fall, his face smacking straight into the ground and bouncing once before lying still. His companion saw him die, then turned and howled at us. He raised his rifle, shooting without really aiming and with no hope of hitting us. We were too far out to be in danger, but the alien wasn't trying to escape either. He was defiant in the face of mortal danger. I couldn't help but admire his valor, even as I took aim and fired. The laser blast hit the Ashi warrior in the face. I saw the tissue around the shot blacken just before he dropped to the ground beside his friend.

"Two more," I said over the comlink.

"That's a total of twenty-seven today," Rip said. "I've got nothing else on radar."

"Let's head for Solace then," I recommended.

"Roger that."

I made my way to the cockpit as the ship turned and started climbing toward the mountains. We had decided shortly after leaving and spotting the first of the Ashi survivors on radar to deal with as many of the aliens as we could. I couldn't help but wonder how the settlements in the northern hemisphere were faring. But I knew the Casian Marines that we had trained were ready for danger. They dealt with a menacing predator that came up out of the desert. Dealing with the Ashi survivors wouldn't be much different.

We flew straight to where Loutar had marked the location of the Solace settlement. It was nearly perfect, only off by a few degrees. Unlike at Tyconda Lake, an entire group of officials approached as Rip landed the shuttle. I was surprised at how well he was flying the aircraft. Of course, I couldn't tell him that.

"Some landing," I said.

"Every one you can walk away from and all that business," Rip said.

"Good thing the computer does most of the work."

"I should have left you drifting in outer space."

"Come on," I said. "Time to face the music."

"You'd think we had done something wrong instead of supplying the settlements with goods and protecting them from the Ashi."

"I guess they think they were pretty well off before we came and brought the Ashi with us."

"I can't argue with you if you're logical about everything," Rip said with a chuckle.

We left the ship and were greeted by a group of aliens. There were times when speaking to the aliens seemed almost as natural as having a conversation with another human being. But there were other times when the aliens were so different, both from humans and even from each other, that it was impossible not to think of them as aliens.

"We are the Solace Colony Council," a fat alien with tall eye stalks and a gaping mouth that was devoid of teeth that I could see, said. His voice was like the screech of a bird of prey. "I am Uggar, the Colony Premier."

"I'm Sergeant Hugo McManus," I said. "This is my companion, Corporal Rip Van Winkle."

"Why have you come?" Uggar asked.

"As you are probably aware, the Ashi have landed warriors on Libertine," I said. "We're here to help you defeat them."

"We have seen no threat," Uggar said. "We are not militant beings."

"I understand that," I replied. "But there is a threat. We spent much of the day hunting the survivors down, but there will be more. Some may even reach Solace."

That caused the Premier to quiver all over. His body reminded me of a slug. Behind him, the other aliens chirped and twittered like nervous insects.

"Do you have any word from the northern settlements?" Rip asked. "They're in danger, too."

"Your people came and set up equipment, but we have little use for those beings in the north."

"What about your efforts at terraforming the planet?" I asked.

"They are surely continuing," Uggar said. "That is outside my purview. I am responsible for the colony, not the sandy seas."

I could hear the animals bleating and lowing nearby. It seemed they were being taken care of. It was also apparent that the locals weren't interested in having us stick around any longer than we needed to.

"What of your defenses?" I asked.

"Weapons are not wanted in Solace. The Casian soldiers were disbanded and sent away," Uggar said. "We have lived in peace here for generations. That will not change."

I knew the Ashi wouldn't see it that way, but it wasn't my job to convince the Premier of the danger. They could use our help or not.

"I would like to contact the colonies up north," I said. "Would you allow us to use your communication equipment?"

"If you must," Uggar said. "It is this way."

He led us to a prefabricated storage building that was older than me by at least a decade. The roof was sagging and the door didn't latch closed any longer. When we stepped inside, we could smell some type of chemical solvent.

"You don't have things set up?" Rip asked.

"Haven't gotten around to it yet," Uggar said. I couldn't tell if he was smirking or frowning. "I trust you can see to the equipment. I have other things to occupy my time."

"We're good," I told him. "We have letters from Lake Tyconda."

I pulled out a small bundle of letters tied together with a piece of twine. Most of the letters were very small. I had never written a letter on actual paper. All my messaging had been electronic, but the villagers on Libertine took advantage of small luxuries like paper. I gave the bundle to Uggar. He took the letters in one hand that looked more like a flipper.

"A Premier's toil never ceases," he grumbled before waddling away.

Turning back to Rip, I could see the frustration on my companion's face. "This isn't Marine standard," he said.

"No, it isn't," I replied. "Looks like everything's here, though."

"Including the weapons for the Casian volunteers," Rip pointed out. "I didn't see any of them in the village."

The colony wasn't that large. It was mainly two sections, one with housing, the other with work buildings and shops. From the air, it had appeared to be an industrious place, but once we landed, it seemed sad and depressing. Most of the buildings were constructed of prefab materials. Someone, at some point in time, had invested a lot into the place. There were several garage or warehouse-type structures. And a few interconnected office-style buildings. The big cargo containers had been emptied and remodeled into stores or shops. There were even a few that looked like taverns, although when we arrived the town seemed mostly deserted. I couldn't tell if that was true or if the residents had been ordered into their homes by Uggar. The colony's Premier had a pretty lofty view of himself. It seemed tyranny was a universal phenomenon.

"I didn't either," I said. "In fact, I didn't see much of anyone."

"Can't say I blame people for moving on," Rip said as he pulled the top off a crate of solar panels. "There's nothing in this settlement worth dealing with the council over."

"Safety, maybe," I suggested, opening a crate where the battery terminals were kept for the solar energy banks. "Looked to me like all the animals ferried down from the *Renegade* were kept here."

"Why is that not surprising?" Rip said.

"Up north, they divided everything. They were happy to have us."

"Looks like we landed on the wrong side of the world," Rip said.

It took us an hour to get the equipment set up. Solar panels were opened and pointed at the sun. They would be mounted to the roof of the building at some point, if the structure was sound enough to support them. Inside, we set up the communications equipment. Once we had power flowing, it only took a few minutes to ping the satellite in orbit that would bounce our signals from the southern pole to the northern pole of Libertine.

I left the squawking to Rip. He didn't seem to mind talking to people. Instead, I began inspecting the weapons. If the locals didn't plan to use them, I had ideas. There were several Casian harnesses, six in all, each with twin sets of multi-barrel rotating cannons. They fired .50 caliber rounds from belt-fed ammo boxes that were mounted between the two weapons. A Casian could easily carry the heavy machine guns and several thousand rounds of ammunition on its back. The machine guns could be swapped out of the harnesses for missile launchers, of which there were a couple for each of the six rigs I found in the shed. There was also a crate of Marine-issued laser rifles. The beauty of those guns was in their durability and adaptability. They could be used for hunting or for defense. The grips, firing mechanism and shoulder stock could all be easily modified, which was essential for the alien species who were expected to wield them. But the locals seemed to have no interest in the weapons. I hoped that maybe that was a good thing. Maybe war wasn't part of life on Libertine. There was nothing wrong with that.

"Any word from the north?" I asked when Rip pulled off the headphones he had been using with the communication equipment.

"They tracked the Ashi in their vicinity," Rip said. "Most of 'em got baked. Those smart enough to travel at night were attacked by the predators up there."

"Sand Vipers," I said. "Very nasty.

"Seems like it. The being I talked to called himself Elder. He's the leader in a colony called Free Town."

"I remember him. He and the Master Sergeant were pretty friendly. He used to be a scientist."

"They've still got guards in most of their settlements," Rip explained. "They aren't ready for a real invasion, but they don't seem to need us."

"That's good," I said, not quite sure why it felt as though it were a letdown.

"So, what do you think we should do?"

"Whatever we want, I suppose."

"Seems odd," Rip said. "I thought things would be different."

"How so?"

He shrugged his shoulders. "I guess I thought we would be heroes."

"If that's what you wanted, you should have stayed on the *Renegade.*"

"I'm not saying it's what I wanted, just what I expected.

Everyone here seems bothered that we've come. Sure, we brought the Ashi with us, but they aren't nearly the threat we expected."

"There are still plenty of them out there," I said. "And none of the settlements down here have any real protection."

"They don't want any," Rip pointed out.

"No one wants it until they need it," I said. "Let's get comms gear set up in the primary settlements. If we're needed, they can reach us that way."

"And then what?"

"And then we can do whatever we want," I said. "I think I'm going to build a house, do a little exploring. Look around you, Rip. There's an entire world here and we have the run of the place."

"True," Rip said. "You could never do this back home. It takes weeks just a get a permit to visit a park and then it costs a fortune."

"We'll take advantage of our freedom here," I said, trying to sound reassuring. That wasn't really my strong suit. Usually, I just kept my mouth shut and did my job. But I felt a sense of obligation to Rip. He was the reason I was alive and I was the reason he was stuck on Libertine. The least I could do was help him to see the possibilities that were ahead of us. "We'll be the first humans to explore this planet."

"Never thought of myself as much of an explorer, but that sounds kinda cool," he said.

"At some point, humans will return to this world," I said. "Maybe not for many years, but if you know anything about the SDF, it's that they'll be sending Marines to any place they think could be strategically important."

"A huge portion of this world isn't hospitable," Rip pointed out.

"It's not worse than Mars," I said. "It's hotter, but the air is breathable."

"Yeah, I can see us building some dome colonies out in the desert."

"And mining," I added. "There's no telling what sort of minerals and fossil fuels they could get out of this place. For all we know, there could be gold just lying on the ground in these mountains waiting for us to pick it up."

"Or diamonds," Rip said. "Can you imagine finding a diamond as big as the ones on the *Renegade?*"

"No, but those had to come from somewhere."

"I think I get it," Rip said, "the appeal of what could be. I'll explore this world with you, man. Sounds like it could be fun."

"Beats running sim drills all day on a cramped SDF ship," I insisted.

"No doubt. I hate them stinking barracks on an interstellar ship."

"Stinking is right."

"It's like the stuff they use to clean it makes it smell worse."

We both laughed. The conditions on SDF starships for Space Marines were cramped and unsanitary. It was almost impossible to avoid foot rot and fungal outbreaks. Above all, what I hated the most about life onboard a military ship was the lack of privacy. I'm the kind of guy who enjoys solitude, which was one of the reasons I thought living on Libertine would be a good fit for me. But I was more than willing to spend time with Rip. Despite my personal feelings about being alone, it was good to know I wasn't the only human on the planet. Someday, that would change. Until then, I planned to enjoy myself.

CHAPTER 6

WE FELL into a groove setting up the communications relay huts in the villages we visited. It took about a day to get things up and running with solar power, radar scans and syncing the comm units to the communication satellites in orbit. We also constructed a small shelter so that the equipment was protected from the worst of the weather. The crates used to transport the gear were easy to break down and reuse to build the huts. And even though the equipment was made to be used in almost any weather, it was better in the long run to protect it from the worst of whatever weather Libertine had to throw around.

For three days, we went from village to village, setting up the communications equipment and teaching the locals how to utilize it. None of them seemed enthusiastic about the high-tech gear nor did they show any interest in connecting with the colonies on the northern pole. Still, the aliens had friends and acquaintances in the other settlements. The idea of sending them messages and passing along news was interesting enough that a few beings in each little village volunteered to learn to use the gear we set up.

I didn't make a big thing of it, but I did set the radar to sound an electronic ping if it picked up movement. Most of the villages were deep in the mountains, which hindered radar, but I felt better knowing they would at least have warning if the Ashi approached. Should the locals choose not to care enough to keep tabs on the radar, that was up to them.

On the fourth day, we returned to Lake Tyconda only to find my worst fears realized. We saw the smoke from another settlement and left in the *Condor* immediately to help, but it was already too late. The huts had been burned, the residents slaughtered.

"Oh, geeze," Rip said. "That's... that's..."

"As bad as it gets," I said.

He was flying low and we could see the scorch marks on the naked flesh of the villagers. Some had been hit with laser fire, others caught in the burning structures. It was a terrible way to die.

"What do you want to do?"

"Land, look for survivors," I said. "Once that's done, we hunt down the bastards responsible."

"Ooo-rah! Now that's a plan."

Rip landed the *Condor,* and we went to work checking the bodies. It was gristly work, but a few were still alive. Rip had medical supplies on board the shuttle. It was mostly first aid for human physiology, yet it worked on the aliens, too. We sprayed burns and wrapped bandages. There was nothing we could do for smoke inhalation or internal injuries. I knew some of the survivors wouldn't make it through the night. Still, we had the means to get them from their isolated village to Solace, where help might be available.

"I think it's best if we split up," I said. "I'll take the MECH and start hunting down the Ashi."

"That'll give us room in the *Condor* for the wounded. I'll get 'em to Solace as fast as I safely can, then double back to give you air support."

"Sounds like a plan."

One of the survivors was the leader of the commune, Eldora. I found her lying on her side. One of her arms was broken, and there was a laser burn on her hip. There were also burns on her hands and arms from where she had tried to help others in the burning buildings. She moaned as I rolled her onto her back. The thin wrap she had worn to meet us was ripped to tatters. I was just relieved that she was alive.

"Eldora," I said. "Can you tell me what's hurting?"

Her face was bruised. One eye was swollen shut, the other was barely a slit. Tears leaked out of it, and I could tell she was struggling to see who I was.

"It's Hugo," I told her. "Sergeant Hugo McManus, from off-world."

"Oh," she managed to say, her voice tinged with pain. "Hurts... breathe..."

The translation was clear enough to me. Her left side was already bruised and swelling.

"Try not to move," I told her. "It's going to be okay. I'm here now, and nothing else will hurt you."

It was a bold promise, but I felt it was true at that moment. I had a deep compassion for her, even though she was an alien. My feelings both surprised and confused me. Affection for people was dangerous in my experience. It left a person open to harming me if I cared too much for them. Over the years, I had built up strong walls to insulate myself from people. On the other hand, Eldora had slipped right through my defenses and struck a chord within me that I didn't think was possible.

"Rip, I've got a live one."

"Copy that," he replied via our comlink. "On my way."

We had first aid supplies, but nothing that would help Eldora. She had been beaten and clearly had broken bones. The only thing I could do was give her pain medication and there was no way of knowing how it would affect her alien physiology.

We moved the survivors, eight in total, to the *Condor* after salvaging some blankets to pad down the metal deck.

In every village we stayed in, our first priority was setting up solar panels and a wind turbine to charge the *Condor's* power supply. In turn, it had recharged the MECH. Getting back inside the armored suit wasn't easy, but once I managed that, it powered right up. The armored suit's hydraulics made carrying the wounded simple. Rip rigged up a harness that allowed me to lift them off the ground in one of their own hammocks.

When the shuttle lifted off, I was left behind with the dead. There was no way of knowing if any of the survivors would live very long. The Ashi had been brutal. They attacked with their laser rifles, their big knives and their brute strength. The village was completely destroyed. It made no sense to me. No one in the village was a threat to them. They simply killed for the sport of it. Perhaps they couldn't help themselves ... yet, that was about to change.

"Iron Man, you copy?" Rip's voice sounded crystal clear inside the MECH.

"Loud and clear, Condor," I replied.

"I have your targets on radar. They're in a valley seven klicks from your location," Rip explained. "Sending you data now."

"Receiving," I said, already starting to move.

"I'll make a wider circle before heading for Solace."

"Don't waste any time," I said.

"Copy that. I just want to make sure you haven't got any surprises waiting for you. I'll be back as soon as I can."

"Don't worry about me, Rip. I've got this."

"Five armed warriors are not a joke, Hugo. Watch yourself."

"Always," I replied.

It was true, and then again it wasn't. I did have a habit of throwing myself straight at the enemy. On the other hand, that was before serving on the *Jericho*. Since then, I was more willing to work with a team rather than just wildly attacking. But, despite the lessons I had learned serving with Master Sergeant Steel, I could feel myself wanting to charge straight ahead.

Instead, I activated the MECH's rocket pack and braced myself for flight. It wasn't an easy decision. I greatly preferred keeping both feet on the ground, or at least both of the MECH's powerful feet on the ground. I could move pretty easily in the large armored suit. I had a good grasp of every function except for the flight controls. Or rather, while I understood the flight controls, I had no experience in actually piloting the suit. I knew what it was supposed to do. I also knew that Lieutenant Micky Colt, who designed the MECH and spent more time in it than anyone, had nearly killed himself trying to fly it.

There was no disputing that if I could fly across to the next mountain, I would have a tactical advantage over the Ashi. By getting ahead of them, I could choose where we fought. And I would have the high ground, which had been an advantage in every battle where it was utilized. That's not to say that five hulking Ashi warriors couldn't overcome terrain obstacles, but I had to fight smarter, not harder, than my enemies.

Holding the MECH's arms and legs stiff, I activated the jet pack.

"Here goes nothing," I said out loud. "Engaging jet propulsion, now."

I shot straight up into the air like a rocket. The G-forces were strong and yet it felt exhilarating. I let the rocket pack boost me over eight hundred feet straight up into the air. It took two seconds. Then I cut the rocket booster.

"Extend flaps," I said, activating the MECH's voice controls. "Engage boosters."

I had used the boosters before. They could slow my descent, which began almost as soon as I cut the jet pack's thrust. Not only did it slow my fall, it allowed me to control it. I wasn't flying exactly, but I was able to propel myself forward with relative control. It wasn't hard to know where to go. There was a huge mountain in front of me. Finding a place to safely land was more challenging. The mountains on the southern pole of Libertine weren't covered with trees. Nor were they barren, arid and craggy. They were covered in grasses and small bushes with clumps of trees popping up here and there. The ground was mounded and in many places very steep. What I needed was a relatively flat place to land and reconnoiter my enemies from. It wasn't as simple as just looking down. I was seeing everything via the MECH's external cameras, which were fine most of the time. Yet it created a two-dimensional image and I couldn't make out the contours of the ground below me.

Fortunately, the MECH's computer system had an app that overlayed the ground with topographical lines of elevation. The tactical app lit three different places with good cover from which to fight from, and the flight app showed good landing spots on the steep mountainside. I also had data from the *Condor,* which showed where the Ashi were in the valley and which direction they were moving in. There was no doubt that they could see me high above them, moving down the mountain. Whether they knew who I was couldn't be assumed, but if their actions at Tyconda Lake were any indication, then I had to believe that every living creature was their enemy, especially me. But that was just fine in my book. I loved a good fight and I was ready to take it to the Ashi. There was a score to settle. I planned to settle it.

CHAPTER 7

I LANDED PRETTY WELL in a clearing ringed by shrubs and some moss-covered boulders. I immediately got as low to the ground as I could. Time was on my side. Not that I was patient. Waiting for a fight was the hardest thing I had ever experienced. It was tougher than boot camp, harder to endure than special forces training, and even worse than aggressive interrogation exposure. I didn't mind pain, not that I liked it or got some sort of emotional high from it, but it didn't bother me. The threat of death didn't haunt me. I had made peace with my maker a long time ago. I wasn't religious, but I also didn't figure on death being worse than someone flipping my switch. At least if I were dead, I wouldn't struggle with making connections with people.

Lying flat on my stomach in the MECH was extremely uncomfortable. The safety harness held me tight while those straps dug into my body with all the weight of gravity pulling me down. Instead, I rolled onto my back, with my feet downhill. A quick systems check showed everything was ready, including a handy high-altitude drone, which I launched immediately. It really was small, hardly larger than a bumblebee. It took off into the clear sky where it flew alone. Libertine had no aerial life-forms, no birds, only flying insects.

I already had a good map of the terrain around me for several miles in all directions. Plus, I knew where the Ashi were headed. Not their destination, but their direction. What I didn't know was their purpose. A downed human flyer was focused on survival until rescue came. If a pilot had to put down behind enemy lines, they had a much harder task of getting back to their own side or to a safe LZ for pickup. But the people of Libertine weren't anyone's enemies and there was no Ashi presence on the planet for them to be trying to reach. That left me with just one conclusion: they wanted to do as much damage as possible until they were rescued. Only the last part of my assumption didn't hold up. I had seen the aliens in battle. They didn't bother helping their wounded. If a warrior went down, even with a minor wound, they were disregarded. If that sort of attitude held up, it was probable that no one would ever come to Libertine on a rescue mission for them.

Of course, that didn't mean no one would come. Perhaps, the survivors just wanted to show that they had been busy slaughtering the free people on Libertine when their betters came back to check out the planet. I didn't know much about galactic politics, but I had heard enough to know that Libertine had been unknown to the Imperium. So, it made sense to think they would probably come around at some point to enforce their will on the free people who lived on the planet or to establish their own colonies if that was something they did. Humanity would have, and might still, I considered. Humans loved the idea of going places, especially places where no other humans had been before.

The drone linked with my suit and used thermal imaging to

quickly pick up the enemy. I could run several apps at the same time with the MECH's computer and interact with them on my HUD. I used the mapping application as a base layer. It showed the valley and mountain I was situated on. On top of the map came the terrain lines, and on top of that was the app that showed the location of my enemy. They appeared as a red dot on my map, with tiny hashes showing where they had been and an arrow that showed the direction they were currently moving. On the sides of the display, I could see the wind direction and how many hours of daylight were left. There was plenty of killing time left in the day.

I was only a couple of kilometers from the group, less than a mile in a straight line, although they were several hundred feet lower than I was on the mountainside. If they were smart, they would have split up. They had to know I was going to fight them. Why else would I be there? Like I said, there had been no way to hide my flight from one mountain to the other. They should have marked my position when I landed. It was something anyone could do, even without drones and computer apps. If the enemy was ahead of me, I might want to move around and flank them ... or avoid them altogether. But the Ashi didn't think like that. They were big, brutish creatures who went straight at their target with no thought of their own safety.

"Iron Man, you copy? This is the *Condor*."

"I read you, *Condor*," I said with a smirk. "Where are you?"

"Still about eight miles out from Lake Tyconda. What's your position?"

I read off the coordinates that my suit showed me. "But don't come this way yet," I warned Rip.

"Why not? You don't want air support?"

"They're coming right to me," I explained. "You'll probably just spook them off."

"There are five of them, Hugo. Don't play games, man."

He was right. I should have just launched a few of the short-range missiles that were part of the munitions in my suit. I had six in each of the MECH's shoulder compartments. I could program a couple with the enemy's position and launch them where I lay. With no trees or other obstacles to contend with, the missiles would easily find their targets. Even just a pair or maybe three of the missiles would be enough to kill the enemy, but I was also aware that we had no way of getting more munitions. It was better to save the missiles for a more dire situation. Besides, I was spoiling for a fight.

"I'm not," I said. "But I want answers."

"I don't think I even know the questions, bro. Just blast those big, green aliens and let's move on."

"Don't worry," I said. "They won't get away."

"Yeah, well, make sure you do. I didn't sign up for a solo mission."

"Just watch and learn," I told him.

The boulders near my feet were half buried in the thick soil. I spread my arms wide, or the arms of the MECH, to brace myself, then extended my feet. It would have taken hours of digging and long pry bars to wrench the rocks free without he armored suit, but it was built with heavy-duty hydraulic servos in both the arms and legs of the combat platform. As I pushed out with my legs, the rocks tore free from the ground and started rolling down the hillside.

At the same time, I sent the drone diving down for a closer look at the enemy. They weren't traveling in a straight line. The mountainside was too steep for that. But they were making their way up, moving almost horizontally from my position. They were spread out slightly. The boulder went crashing down hill fast, kicking up more rocks and soil.

I jumped up, amazed at how responsive and powerful the MECH suit was. I hit my mechanical feet running. Dust was forming a cloud straight downhill, making the perfect camouflage. Normally, the MECH's heavy footsteps would have been heard, but the rumble from the landslide was masking them.

The Ashi warriors saw the danger coming. The boulder was bouncing and spinning. The moss had all been knocked off. Dirt and smaller stones were kicked up every time the boulder hit the mountainside. I half watched them on the video from the drone. It was well within the effective range of their laser rifles, but none of the aliens noticed the small drone. All their attention was on the landslide and getting out of its path.

Just as I had suspected, the group of five aliens split. Three moved to my right, advancing in the direction they had already been traveling. And two moved left. I angled toward the two. The boulder raced past them, bouncing between the two groups at high speed. Then came the smaller debris. It wasn't really a threat to the aliens, but it did leave a thick cloud of dust, and out of it, I charged straight at the two surprised Ashi warriors.

Even the MECH suit wasn't as tall as the green-skinned aliens. They were massive. They wore only short kilts with wide, leather belts. Both of the aliens had laser rifles although neither was held ready to fire. They were caught completely off guard and like most people who find themselves suddenly under attack, they hesitated for just a second. It was all the time I needed.

Triggering the spring-loaded, double-edged sword that was built into the MECH's left forearm, I slashed the blade hard across one of the aliens and sent him staggering back. The blade had cut deep into his shoulder and across his chest. Blue blood flowed from the wound and the alien couldn't lift his right arm. The laser rifle he had been carrying dropped to the ground. In the same charge, I used my momentum to drive the point of the blade straight into the second alien's stomach. His breath was expelled in a heavy puff as the blade punched through his body and severed his spine. For a moment, I held him upright. The Ashi warrior was face to face with the MECH's primary camera. I could see the pain and shock in his eyes. Holding him upright should have been difficult, but the MECH wasn't strained. Unfortunately, I was still moving downhill. The fingers of my left hand worked the controls that retracted the blade. The alien fell dead and slid further down the hill as I spun around. The metal feet of the MECH dug into the soft soil and stopped my descent.

The wounded alien was howling in pain. There was no way to know if the others could hear it over the rumble of the landslide. But I jumped toward him. The Ashi warrior, weak and clearly in shock from his terrible wound, still managed to draw his own blade. I grabbed his arm in the MECH's metal hands, twisting the weapon so that the tip of his point went up under the alien's wide jaw. Then I shoved it hard. It wasn't like a real fight. It was more like a simulation; only the armored MECH arm moved and I could feel it. Still, the strength of the alien was lost on me. Maybe because he was weakened from the gash across his chest, or maybe, compared to the MECH, he wasn't very strong. I didn't know, but the knife drove up through the alien's throat and into his brain. He fell to the ground and I spun around, expecting danger. But there was no sign of the other aliens through the thick dust cloud. I glanced at the small video displayed on the corner of my HUD. It showed the trio of Ashi warriors standing together as they watched the rocks and boulders in the landslide crashing down into the valley.

I've never been one to hesitate, so I stormed forward. Old habits die hard, they say, and I suppose it's true. More to the point, I almost died. The aliens were farther out from the dust cloud than I expected. They saw me coming and had just enough time to react before I reached them. Once more, I had triggered my forearm blade. It stuck out over the MECH's hand. I still had a lot to learn about the armored suit. It was big and powerful, but my coordination was off. I slashed at the first Ashi and missed. To his right and a little bit behind the alien, a second warrior shot me. The laser blast hit the MECH's shoulder and sent me spinning down the hill. There were just a few seconds between my fall and the aliens' follow-up attack. I was off balance and fell onto my back, sliding several feet downhill from the aliens, who looked as interested in my attack as one might be in seeing rain fall on a cloudy day. They weren't surprised and certainly not scared. Fortunately for me, they weren't all that careful with their aim either.

One blast flew over me and another hit the ground just beside my hip. One thing I learned in that fight was to trust the armor. I didn't yet, but I also had a reckless attitude in battle. Without any concern for my own safety, I opened the shoulder compartment with a voice command. There are alarms going off inside the MECH. I didn't care. I fired one mini-rocket straight at the aliens, who, to their credit, dodged out of the way. Two jumped to their left; the other went right. My missile, even at close range, gave them a split-second warning of the danger. It shot between them and impacted the hill. That's when things really got dicey.

CHAPTER 8

A HUGE CHUNK of the hillside blew up and out in spectacular fashion. There was fire and smoke. The shock wave knocked the Ashi warriors off their feet.

"Hugo!" Rip called over the comlink.

The shockwave missed me, but the ensuing landslide did not. All around, and even underneath the MECH, the dirt and soil began to slide downhill. I was moving involuntarily. Warning alarms were ringing in the MECH and even though I tried to get back up, it was like being in soft sand. There was no support for the heavy metal armored suit.

"No traction," I said, panting, my mind spinning for a way to get free.

"Get out of there," Rip ordered from his shuttle.

"Trying," I replied.

I was sliding down hill on my back, with my head lower than my legs, but I still managed to sit upright. The dust around me was so thick I couldn't tell what was happening or how close I was to slamming into the valley and being buried alive.

"Activate jet pack," I said. "Engage!"

Suddenly, I was no longer sitting. It was as if a huge, invisible hand had plucked me out of the dirt and tossed me through the air. Only I wasn't flying straight up like before.

"Hugo! Watch out!" Rip cried.

I was left to my own devices. The MECH had all sorts of components and abilities, but an autopilot wasn't among them. I had been falling down the mountainside. When I fired the booster, I didn't shoot up. Instead, I shot sideways, over the valley safely, but straight toward the mountain on the opposite side. Twisting onto my side, I activated the boosters. I saw the far mountainside getting dangerously close before the boosters on my right side set me on an arcing curve. I might have made it into the air if not for a cluster of palm trees. I slammed straight into them. The thick wooden trunks snapped and my boosters all cut out at the same time. My feet flew up over my head and I hit the ground in a bouncing roll.

The next thing I knew, everything was still. A buzzer was sounding in my ear and my HUD was off. I peered through the narrow slot between the breastplate and the armor that concealed the core of the MECH. I could see clear sky.

"Rip, you there?" I asked.

The comlink was down too. The MECH was completely powered down. I pressed the emergency release button. Compressed gas vented, pushing the armor that covered me apart. Still strapped in, I could feel the hot air of Libertine tinged with dust, wafting inside the MECH. After unfastening my safety straps, I climbed out. Nearby, the roar of the *Condor's* repulsers could be heard. I was on the far mountain, opposite from where I had started. Dust was still billowing up across the valley, concealing everything I was concerned about from view.

"You maniac!" Rip chided. "What were you hoping to accomplish with that stunt?"

"I was trying to escape," I said as I walked slowly into the open rear hatch of the shuttle, where Rip was waiting for me.

"You need flying lessons."

"Tell me about it," I said.

"Is the MECH totaled?"

"Power's out," I said. "I don't know what else. Any sign of the bad guys?"

"No," Rip admitted. "It's impossible to see through the dust."

"We have to be sure," I argued.

"We will be," Rip said. "Thermal will pick them up once the mountain settles down. Or if they hike out of the dust cloud."

"They could be dead," I pointed out.

"True. They might have gotten caught in the landslide."

"Buried alive. That's a hell of a way to check out."

"Works for me, though," Rip said. "Dead is dead."

"Speaking of, did the villagers make it to Solace?"

"I lost two before I got there. Two more were borderline. They don't really have medical facilities on this world. Not even at the primary colony."

"Not enough of one race, maybe," I said. "But the survivors are better off there for now."

We didn't find any trace of the other three aliens. The Ashi warriors, it seemed, had been buried in the landslide. Meanwhile, Rip and I discovered that moving the MECH wasn't easy. Fortunately, it wasn't damaged too bad. One of the replaceable armored plates that covered the MECH rear section was crumpled, probably when I fell onto my backside and then slid down the steep embankment. That also happened to be where the MECH power core was located. We found a power connection had been knocked from the terminal. After reattaching the cable, the suit of armor powered back on, and I was able to pilot it into the shuttle.

"Let's not take any more unnecessary chances," Rip said.

"I was trying to save the ammunition," I told him.

"It won't be much good to us if you're dead," he pointed out.

"True."

"Besides, we've got crates of extra ammo. If you're going to conserve anything, save your ground-to-air missiles. We've only got two full sets of replacements. Everything else we've got plenty of. Especially ammo for the machine guns. We've got that in spades."

"Noted," I said, feeling a bit sheepish.

We circled the valley for nearly two hours, scanning for survivors. There was nothing to be found, so we headed back to the village by the lake. There wasn't much left but smoldering ruins and dead bodies. We set up the solar chargers to capture as much power from the late afternoon sun as possible, then went to work digging a mass grave. The MECH suit made the task much easier. It also made moving the bodies less odious. We salvaged everything we could but there weren't enough blankets or hammocks left to wrap the bodies. After laying them all side by side in the grave, we buried them in the darkness. A fire might have been appropriate, although it didn't seem that way with so many of the villagers having been killed in their burning huts.

There was no shelter left standing, but we didn't need much. Rip and I slept under the stars in emergency bags from the shuttle. Not that it was cold, but the emergency bags had self-inflating sides that were meant to give the sleeper insulation from the cold. They also made a softer bed than sleeping directly on the ground.

"Hell of a day," Rip said.

"How did the officials in Solace take the news?" I asked.

"Not good. They seemed more put out than scared."

"We should head back tomorrow," I said. "I want to be sure the survivors are getting proper care."

"How are you going to ensure that?" Rip asked. "We're not doctors and our portable med bot won't be much use to aliens."

"I just want to be sure that everything that could be done for them is being done," I said. "I feel like we owe them that much."

"Maybe. In my book, we don't owe anyone anything."

"You're probably right," I said, but I didn't feel that way. I knew the truth of the matter, although I still felt a sense of shame that innocent lives had been taken by aliens who followed us into the Libertine system.

"It's crazy to think we're looking at stars that might also be visible back on Earth," Rip said.

"It seems like an impossible distance."

"And yet, it isn't anymore."

"How long until more people show up here?" I asked.

"My guess? A couple of years," Rip said. "The SDF will want to build ships capable of hyperspace travel right away, but they'll be cautious about it too."

"Seems like Libertine would be a good place to start with," I said. "Lots of available land."

"No one group can claim it as their ancestral home either," Rip pointed out. "You know how people feel about that sort of thing."

"Good point. I kinda wish we had more time."

"You think that now. Who knows how you'll feel in a couple of years? You might be ready for something different."

"Like what?"

"Civilization, maybe," Rip said. "I can see you with about a dozen little Hugos running around trying to knock down walls with brute force."

"Very funny," I said.

"Yeah, I'm hilarious. What took you so long to figure it out?"

"I don't think I'm the domestic type."

"Maybe you'll be itching for a real fight then," Rip suggested. "You might find the peaceful life boring."

It was a good point. One that I feared might actually be true.

The following day, we flew back to Solace. Five of the nine survivors had died. I was greatly relieved that Eldora wasn't among the dead.

"You came back?" She said. The tall, willowy alien was lying in a hammock in the makeshift medical center. I saw a few short, multi-legged aliens scurrying about. They were like big caterpillars, but they moved much faster than I expected. It was clear they had been tasked with looking after the survivors from Lake Tyconda.

"Why wouldn't I?"

"Honestly, I thought you would be killed."

"I'm not that easy to kill," I said softly. "We took care of them that attacked your village."

"Buried the dead, too," Rip added.

"I can't stand to think about it," Eldora said, turning her swollen face to the side so she didn't have to look straight at them.

"We're sorry," I told her.

She lifted a hand, reaching for me. I felt suddenly very self-conscious. Rip nodded for me to take her hand. I could charge straight into battle, but my own hands shook as I took hold of Eldora's long, delicate hand. It was similar to my own, but also different. Her hand was longer, the fingers longer still. Holding it reminded me of holding a baby bird. You couldn't squeeze it for fear of hurting her. The skin had a very light blue coloring. My own calloused hand felt clumsy in hers.

"You've done all you could for us," Eldora said. "I will be forever grateful to you. Both of you."

"Just doing our job," Rip said, which wasn't really true. We didn't have jobs anymore. We weren't officially Space Marines. If not for Rip taking the *Condor* from the *Renegade*, I would be dead. And we had no way of returning to duty. If the SDF expected us to build a base on Libertine, they would be disappointed.

"It's the least we could do," I added. "What are they saying you need?"

"Time, and rest," Eldora said. "I was one of the lucky ones. My injuries are self-healing."

"I'm glad you made it," I told her.

Was it strange to have such strong emotions concerning an alien? Yeah, it was. But Eldora, who seemed so strong when we first met and so delicate in the Solace medical center, was different than any human I had met before.

Rip and I were friends brought together by the Corps. We were both Marines first, and the proximity of our duty and the shared mission we fought for had forged a bond. That was one of the things I loved about the Space Marines. It had helped me get past the awkward social conventions normally required to make friends. I was no good at social situations. Human women mystified me. But for some reason, my feelings for Eldora were stronger than those I had for my own kind. I wouldn't have said it was attraction in the romantic sense, but more of a kindred spirit.

"Me too," she said. "I want to go home."

"There isn't much of a home left for you to go to," Rip said softly. "I'm sorry."

"It'll have to be rebuilt," I said. "With your permission, Rip and I will make a start of it."

"You do not need my permission," she said. "Do as you wish."

"We'll come back," Rip said. "In a few days. If you're well enough to travel by then, we can take you where you want to go."

"I would like that," she said.

We left her to rest. The other survivors were worse off than Eldora, but the three that remained alive had very good odds of making a full recovery. That fact helped as a deep depression threatened to engulf me. I think maybe Rip was feeling some guilt about the attack, too. We both threw ourselves into the work of clearing the rubble from the village. Two of the structures had been damaged, but not destroyed. We saved them, replacing the thatched roofs with sturdy materials we found unused and forgotten in Solace. Much of the original colony's resources had been left abandoned in favor of natural resources. I understood the desire to use what the planet offered, especially renewables like wood and grass. The new roofs on the tropical style buildings were ugly in comparison to the thatched grass roofs that had been in place. But they weren't flammable and were more structurally sound than a thatched roof.

Rip spent a great deal of time repairing the ground-based radar system that should have warned the villagers of the approaching danger. Not that they would have known what to do if it worked. The settlement was unprepared for danger. It was a topic no one wanted to think much about and during the long, sun-drenched days we spent in the village, I came to understand that a type of laid-back unconcern could easily invade a person's mind. The crystal clear waters of the huge lake lapping at the shore created a sort of mesmerizing effect on me. We both stripped down in the warm sunshine and cooled off in the waters of the lake when we grew too hot. In the evenings, we lounged around a small fire, watching the stars above and listening to the fish jumping in the lake. It was easy to forget about the Imperium or the human race in faraway Sol. In fact, I felt myself losing sight of the rest of Libertine. What else was of importance when a person was surrounded by such incredible beauty?

After three days, there was nothing left of the old village but the two remaining structures with their ugly roofs, and a few scorch marks on the ground that couldn't be covered. Grass had already begun to sprout up over the mound of dirt that covered the late villagers. A short way down the mountainside from the village plateau, Rip had rebuilt the solar charging station, complete with satellite communications and ground radar with a loudspeaker that would sound if the radar picked up anything the computer didn't recognize as native wildlife.

There were animals in the mountains. Most were small, like field mice and tunneling moles. There were other animals that preyed on the smaller variety. One looked a lot like Earth's foxes, but with dusty brown fur. The alpha predator in the mountains was a large bear-like animal. It had no fur, and its thick, brown hide made it hard to spot when it wasn't moving. They looked like rocks when they were stationary, which was most of the daylight hours. At night, they hunted the smaller animals in the hills and mountains.

Halfway through the third day, we went back to Solace. Only to be greeted by an irate Premier. Uggar's eyes bulged with outrage as he fussed at us.

"You took colony goods without permission," he said. "You're no better than thieves!"

"You weren't using them," I said. "The structures at Lake Tyconda needed new roofs."

"You can't just go around taking whatever you want!" Uggar demanded as I started for the medical center. "Those materials are valuable."

"So valuable, you just left them out to rot?" Rip said. "I'll bet you can't even tell us what we took."

"That doesn't matter," Uggar said. "I'm not the colony quartermaster. I am the Premier."

"Alright, so what do you want?" I asked.

That shocked Uggar just as much as when we argued with him. He wasn't sure what to say. He clearly hadn't expected to get any sort of satisfaction from us. What he had been longing for was a chance to complain.

"What I want is... for you to respect our property."

"Done," I said. "We won't take anything else without your permission."

"Good!" Uggar said. "Because you clearly had no right to what you stole."

"We can pay you for it or return it," Rip said, getting irritated with the feisty alien.

"We do not want it back," Uggar said. "Your kind is quick to dismiss an offense."

"There was no offense intended," I said. "We were just doing what we could to help the village that was attacked by the Ashi."

"So you say," Uggar said. "For all we know, you are the ones who attacked the village."

That set Rip off. He started to grab the short alien by the front of his robes, but I managed to keep him from doing it by pushing Rip back.

"That's a dirty lie," Rip shouted. "We aren't murderers."

"So, you say," Uggar snapped. "None of us has ever seen a Human before. You are clearly a violent species."

"And you're a lying little slug. Let me go, Sarge. I'll show this pathetic little creep what happens when he insults us."

"Let it go," I told him. "He's just trying to get under your skin."

"He's already there," Rip said.

"We're here to see about the villagers," I told Uggar. "If there's nothing else, we'll be on our way."

"Do so," Uggar said with a snide look. "And make it quick."

The short council member hurried away. I could see other aliens watching us from the shadows of their homes and the open doorways of the shops in the colony. We were the outsiders and the locals didn't trust us.

Fortunately, we found Eldora and the other three surviving members of the little community waiting for us at the medical center. The swelling on her face had gone down. It was a sickly green shade. At first, I felt a sense of alarm, but then I realized it was the effect of her milky white skin and alien blood. She stood wrapped in a quilt made from many bits of discarded wool fabric.

"You look much improved," I said.

"I'm eager to go home," she replied. "Is your offer still on the table?"

"That's why we're here," I told her.

"The ship's warmed up and ready," Rip added. "All we need to do is get you to it."

"This is Lucern, and Braydell. I think you know Loutar."

The short alien who had helped us with his map had a distressed look on his piggish face. One fleshy jowl was puckered around a vivid scar that was covered in thick, transparent cream. Under one arm, he had a crutch. His left foot was heavily bandaged.

"Good to see you survived, Loutar," I said.

"I was foraging when the Ashi attacked. I returned too late to stop them."

"And he paid a heavy price for his bravery," Eldora said.

I couldn't help but wonder what the short, plump little alien might have tried. Most of the aliens I had encountered in my relatively short time outside my own star system were not fighters. Most wouldn't even resist an attack, much less try to defend others. Our bravery and experience in combat were among the things humanity had that could benefit other species. Of course, I knew it could be turned against them as well. But I felt my respect for Loutar rising.

"Too little, too late," Loutar said glumly.

"They were lucky you didn't have the means to defend the village at your disposal," I told him. "That won't be the case any longer."

"We are not a people of violence," Eldora said.

"You don't have to be," I assured her. "Rip and I have that part covered."

We moved slowly through the colony to the landing area where the *Condor* was waiting. The MECH was still in the village by Lake Tyconda, which meant there was plenty of room in the rear compartment for the survivors. They limped on board without so much as a single resident of Solace wishing them well. I realized there was a lot I still had to learn about living among the aliens on Libertine.

"Weather's good," Rip said from the cockpit, his voice coming through my earpiece comlink. "Should be a smooth ride."

"Take it slow and easy just in case," I urged him.

"Roger that. Slow and easy, here we go."

CHAPTER 9

THE FLIGHT WAS OVER QUICKLY, but I could tell the changes in altitude and motion were hard on the survivors. We got them off the shuttle quickly in the hopes that having their feet on solid ground would help. But the sight of their missing homes was hard to take. We had cleaned up the village, but the pylons their homes had been built on were still in the ground. Most were scorched from the fires. They seemed like the bones of a long-dead creature half buried in the sand near the shore of the lake.

"Sorry," I told Eldora. "I know this must be hard."

"A bit like having someone tear out my heart with their bare hands," she said, her big eyes brimming with tears. "I should sit down."

She sank into the sandy beach and wept for the people who had died. The other survivors soon joined her. Rip and I gave them space. It was the beginning of a new phase of life for us. Rip and I stayed in the tiny community while the survivors finished healing. We fished, gathered firewood wherever it could be found and foraged for berries and greens that grew wild.

We turned over both of the remaining structures to Eldora and her people. Rip stretched out a tarp from the side of the *Condor* and we made our camp under it. I was experienced in rough camps. It was part of being a Marine, and both Rip and I had slept in far worse conditions. In time, we began to feel like the settlement was our home too, even though we had to use language devices to be understood. In the evenings, Loutar taught us to spin plant fiber into thread, which he wove expertly into blankets and clothing.

We spent most of our days either keeping tabs on the security of the settlements or foraging away from the camp. I found a deep sense of peace in the mountains. They were unlike anything I had ever known before — a sparse, tropical environment that was almost like a vacation spot on Earth, only without the crowds of people. In time, more aliens joined the four survivors. More structures were built using materials from Solace, which Rip and I pleaded with Premier Uggah to donate to the village. There simply weren't enough trees growing on the mountains to provide proper lumber to build with. So, the new structures were made from prefab materials with big openings for windows, and thatched grasses for rooftops.

I spent most of my days with only a baggy pair of shorts for clothing. My skin tanned a golden brown color, and my hair grew long. I even let my beard grow. Rip did the same, and it didn't take long for the pair of us to look like a couple of beach bums. In a way, that was what we were. But we were also explorers. I didn't find gold in piles by the mountain streams, but we did discover that the mountains were rich in valuable ores such as lithium and rhodium. I was no geologist, but we had portable scanners from the *Condor* that could penetrate deep into the ground. There was no doubt in my mind that if humans ever discovered the rich ores available on Libertine, they would stop at nothing to exploit them.

But humanity was a long way off. Perhaps Libertine could be reached in a starship, but none appeared. Using the *Condor's* satellite controls, we took scans of the system from orbit. The *Renegade* had left the people on Libertine with an array of tools in orbit, including instruments that detected energy surges at the hyperspace portals, which is why we should have discovered the slave galley as soon as it arrived in the system. But the long days had lulled us into a sense of complacency. We had started neglecting the communications and satellite equipment. The Ashi threat had faded away. No new reports of sightings had come in for weeks, nor were there requests for help. Rip and I still carried pistols for protection against the larger predators, but without realizing it, we had let our usual vigilance drop. And it nearly cost us our lives.

I had never seen an interstellar ship breaking through orbit, but the slave galley charged through Libertine's atmosphere like a fiery demon bent on destruction. It seemed large from my vantage point on the mountain. Rip noticed it first, and we stood side by side as the ship progressed toward us. Smoke billowed around it and left a trail in its wake.

"This isn't good," Rip said.

"What do you think it is?" I asked.

Neither of us heard Eldora approaching behind us. Over the weeks since she arrived, her body had healed. The friendship between us and between her people had grown. They were grateful to us, but also scarred by what had happened. The once open and unconcerned aliens had become quiet, reserved and fearful.

"Slavers," Eldora said with a note of distress in her voice.

Rip and I turned and looked back at her. I hadn't even heard her approaching. Years of guardedness and practiced self-awareness had faded in the beauty and serenity of Lake Tyconda. It was something I regretted at that moment. It seemed like I had let the enemy in because of my carelessness.

"How do you know?" I asked.

"I know," she said. There was a deep sense of loss in her voice. Over time, I had even begun to understand her musical language, although I couldn't replicate it.

"Do they come often?" Rip asked.

"Never," Eldora replied.

"Any chance they're here to sell and not take?"

"No," Eldora said. "We have nothing they want. They will sell us to the highest bidders in the core worlds."

"Unless someone stops them," Rip said.

"I guess this vacation couldn't last forever," I said, suddenly angry.

I honestly can't say if I was more bothered by the idea of slavery or by the interruption in the idyllic pace of life I had grown comfortable in.

"They never do," Rip said. "Time to suit up, Iron Man."

I turned to Eldora. "Will they have slaves on board already?"

"I do not know," she said. "But they won't land. They'll take us from the air."

"Not if I have anything to say about it," I replied. "Get everyone inside. Rip and I can handle this."

"There's just two of you," she said. "Stay with us. You don't have to die trying to protect Libertine."

"Who said anything about dying?" I asked.

By that point, the smoke was clearing around the ship. It was a big, oval-shaped vessel with a colorful insignia painted on the side.

"That's a licensed slave ship, Hugo. It will have defenses."

"I understand that," I replied. "But I have to do something. It can't be a coincidence that it's here now."

"It isn't," she said. "The Imperium knows of our existence. The hyperspace lane used to reach this system has undoubtedly been added to the navigation networks. It was only a matter of time before the slavers came."

"All the more reason to send them back with their tail between their legs," I said. "Don't worry about me, Eldora. Fighting is the only thing I've ever been good at."

"That isn't true," she said. "Come back to us."

She turned and ran toward the collection of huts near the water's edge. For a few seconds, I watched her. Eldora had long legs, and as she ran, I could see her muscles flexing beneath her pale skin. We were different species and incompatible physically. I hadn't even really let myself consider anything more than friendship with her, but since her return to the village, she had become a very dear friend. I couldn't imagine my life without her in it, which was a completely new circumstance for me. I had never been that close to another human being. In the Marines, I learned very quickly that people could be taken from me. In combat, people died. The Marines combated the inevitable bouts of grief by constantly moving people around to new units and new posts. There simply wasn't enough time for people to grow very close, and I, for one, had never spent enough time with any platoon or special forces unit to get attached to them until my cruise on the *Jericho*. That mission had changed everything for me.

Likewise, my weeks on Libertine had been the first of my life away from the rigid structure of the military. In many ways, it had been difficult, but growth normally was - and I felt that I was growing, or at least improving in my social skills. It helped that Eldora and many of the other aliens in the village didn't need to talk much. They were comfortable in silence, just as I was.

When I reached the *Condor* Rip had already pulled down the tarp over our little camp. He was in the cockpit going through the preflight checklist and powering up the shuttle's computer systems. I went into the back and began feeding belts of ammunition into the two rotating cannons we had mounted to the top of the aircraft. There was plenty of ammunition. Rip had constructed two massive hoppers inside the *Condor's* passenger compartment. Each one held ten thousand rounds of soft alloy metal bullets and tracers.

"Your toys have ammo," I said, letting my comlink carry the words through the ship and into the cockpit where Rip was preparing to fly.

"Good. Suit up. That slave ship is headed right for us."

"Eldora said it would have defensive systems."

"Is that code for guns?"

"Probably," I said. "They like to fly in low and snatch people up. I'm guessing they have some kind of gravity beam generator."

"What's our plan of attack?" Rip said.

"Get them on the ground. From there, we can deal with them on our terms."

"Roger that. You take point, I'll follow."

"Get us into the air," I ordered. "A couple thousand feet over their altitude if possible."

"Copy that. *Condor* is clear for takeoff. I suggest you hold onto something."

I grabbed an overhead support bar just in time. The shuttle rose up on her repulser lifts, then shot forward like a bullet from a gun. The G-forces were intense. I heard Rip shouting with excitement as the ship raced upward in a curving arc. He began relaying information to me as the shuttle leveled out and I could climb into the MECH armor.

"We're at twelve thousand feet," Rip said. "This baby scoots, huh?"

"I'm more interested in the slave ship."

"It's sixty miles out and still descending," Rip said. "Air speed is two hundred and sixty knots and slowing. Looks like she's headed straight for Solace."

"It's the biggest colony in this hemisphere," I pointed out.

"Would it be wrong to let them take a few people before we intervene?"

"Very funny," I said. "I'm suited up. All systems online. Open the rear hatch and bring us around in a looping turn that puts us behind their ship."

"Roger that, opening rear hatch."

The cockpit was sealed off, and the big rear door lowered. All the air was sucked out of the shuttle, but that was okay. I was in the MECH armor, hunched over, but close to the rear hatch. One jump and I would be out of the aircraft, but I didn't want to do that yet. Instead, I tapped into the shuttle's scanners and external cameras. I brought the information on the alien ship up on my HUD.

"It's big," I said.

"The bigger they are, the harder they fall."

"Just so they don't kill everyone on board," I said. "There could be innocents on that vessel."

"Roger that. I'll try not to kill everyone."

The shuttle was built with Arodoni technology. The Arodoni were a highly advanced race that hadn't been seen in the galaxy for hundreds of years. They left behind a massive ship called the *Renegade*. And from that ship, Rip and I had traveled through space and fought in a few battles against slavers, both authorized and pirates. The shuttle had excellent scanners and the onboard computer system quickly identified the ship's components. It pointed out the weak spots on the big, oval-shaped vessel.

"Looks like we'll need to get under her," I said. "Take out the repulsers. Without them, she won't be able to climb back to orbit."

"What's this we business," Rip said. "The last place I want to be is under a humungous ship when you shoot out the components that made it fly."

"True, I guess you get to be the distraction."

"It's a good thing I'm an ace pilot," Rip proclaimed.

"I believe this is your first combat mission."

"There you go being logical again. There's no need to bring that up now."

"Just be sure you're around for a lot more flying, Corporal."

"I can't believe you just pulled rank on me."

We were curving back toward the alien ship. If it took any notice of us, there were no visible signs. No weapons appeared and the slave ship didn't alter course.

"She just passed ten thousand feet," Rip said. "Looks like she's leveling out."

"What's the altitude of Solace?"

"Seventy-five hundred feet up, maybe," Rip said. "I never really paid attention."

"Alright, I'm going after it. You keep circling around."

"Roger that. Watch your six, Iron Man."

"Right back at you, Condor."

I pumped both pedals down and suddenly I was out of the ship, falling through the air.

CHAPTER 10

"ENGAGING BOOSTERS," I ordered the suit. "Open flaps."

The MECH suddenly bristled with wide, flat armor plates shifting to create more drag on the big armored suit as it fell through the air.

I could see the alien ship just a few kilometers from my position, but below me. The upper section glistened in the relentless Libertine sunlight. It was moving past me, a huge mechanical behemoth.

"I'm clear, Iron Man," Rip called over the comlink. "Do your thing, brother. I got your back. Weapons hot. The *Condor* is ready to rock."

"Roger that, *Condor*," I replied.

Everything was happening fast. We were moving over the grasslands, and the mountains were close. I dropped down past the midline of the alien ship. The boosters on the bottoms of the MECH feet were firing, but nothing else. My goal was to cripple the alien ship, not destroy it, which meant I needed to fire my missiles at operational components that wouldn't cause a chain reaction.

"Targeting app online," I said, bringing the computer program to life on my HUD. "This baby is a target-rich environment."

"Be sure you do enough damage to keep it from returning to orbit."

I continued falling, but at a controlled pace. The bottom of the massive ship was different from the top. I could see trap doors and what looked like long, articulated arms for snatching things up. In a lot of ways, the slave ship reminded me of the *Renegade* because it seemed so clean and new. Human ships were thick metal, with massive welds and bolts that held everything together. The slave ship was sleek. It had a dozen repulsers that looked almost like round targets that one might see on a shooting range. I let the targeting app in the MECH do its work.

It sometimes felt like I was running a sim rather than in actual combat. I could feel the G-forces from my fall, but the MECH was doing all the real work. All I had to do was activate the right systems. From my shoulders, ten mini-rockets shot out toward the alien ship. Their exhaust left little contrails as they raced toward their targets. The first of them hit the ship's nearest repulser and exploded. It was underwhelming with no fiery blast and no resulting buck or shift on the slave vessel itself. Still, the MECH suit registered a loss of function from the alien ship's repulser, which was rapidly followed by more impacts.

"That did it," Rip called out. "She's losing altitude."

"Seems too easy," I said.

But Rip was right. The ship was falling. It suddenly passed me, and as it turned, the main engines engaged. I was hit suddenly with a visible wave of thrust that sent me tumbling backward. Alarms sounded and I was reminded how little I knew of actual flying.

"Watch yourself, Iron Man," Rip warned. "You're passing five thousand feet."

The suit was in a tumble. My HUD showed flashes of the ground and the sky as I spun through the air. My stomach suddenly cramped and threatened to revolt.

"Trying to regain control," I said.

"Focus on your instruments, not what you see," Rip suggested.

He had no idea my eyes were squeezed shut. It took a lot of effort to open them and start regaining control of the MECH. It wasn't an aircraft. The big armored suit was shaped like a human but also had flaps and boosters to help me regain control. I was able to stretch out the suit's arms and legs, then used the boosters to slow the spin down. But my fall was happening too fast. An alarm lit up on my HUD.

Impact Imminent. Terminal Velocity Warning. Impact Imminent.

My only option was to fire the jet pack to gain altitude. But in the back of my mind was the incident on the mountainside the last time I had used the jet pack. I wasn't in the right posture and the boost from the jet pack had nearly slammed me straight into the opposite mountain. If I fired it at the wrong moment, it might send me down instead of up.

Fear could be crippling. I had certainly frozen a number of times in social situations. Women could stop me in my tracks with a teasing remark. I've been told it's a way they flirt and I should be flattered, but I always feel flabbergasted instead. In combat, I didn't let fear stop me. Firing the jetpack while in an uncontrolled spin was a bit like playing Russian Roulette. But there was a part of me that was fine with dying. In fact, I had to hold back the desire at times as it threatened to overwhelm me and cause me to commit self-harm. I hated the thought of being weak, so I had never cut my life short, but I had a bad habit of rushing headlong into danger.

There wasn't enough time to gain full control of the MECH. So, as the heavy metal suit plummeted toward the ground, I took a chance and fired the jetpack. I wasn't lucky enough to go straight up, but I wasn't unlucky either. I shot up and over, toward the slave ship. In fact, I narrowly avoided colliding with it. The big slave galley was going down. Its main engines were firing, but couldn't keep it aloft without the repulsers.

As I managed to slow my own descent, the alien ship landed hard.

"It's down!" Rip said, his voice so close I almost turned to look for him.

"I see it. I'm landing nearby. Let's stay alert. There's no telling what the slavers might do."

"Roger that," Rip said. "Keeping my distance. But you call if there's trouble and I'll come running."

It took all my concentration to land. I wasn't fully in control of the MECH. It was like trying to walk on a loose rope over a gaping chasm. I managed to get one foot down, but then the MECH flopped onto its side.

"I'm down," I said.

"Down as in injured?" Rip asked.

"Negative."

"How's the MECH?"

"Everything is fine. Stop fussing," I snapped as I got the MECH upright again.

Controlling the heavy armor suit was becoming easier for me, yet I was very glad to be on the ground where I felt I could utilize the armor to its greatest advantage. In the air, I was always one mistake from losing control.

"They have to come out of their ship to repair the damage," I said. "When they do, I'll take them out."

"Piece of cake," Rip said. "Man, that just made my mouth water."

There was no cake on Libertine. We lived on fresh meat and vegetables, mostly wild greens. It was a big change from the hyper-processed food on board SDF vessels. We were both feeling the change, but occasionally we craved food from our old lives.

"Stop daydreaming and pay—"

I was only half joking with Rip, but my statement was cut off suddenly as the MECH shut down.

"Rip!" I said. "Rip, can you hear me?"

There was no reply. It felt like I had suddenly gone deaf and blind. The HUD and camera feeds went dark. Worse yet, I couldn't move. Or rather, I could still move, but the MECH wouldn't respond.

"I'm down," I said, even though I knew Rip couldn't hear me. "I'm leaving the MECH."

I hit the emergency eject button. It was designed to withstand a power outage. The plates opened slightly and I pressed hard to open up the compartment where I was seated. There was no time to worry about Rip. I didn't know if whatever caused my power failure had also caused the shuttle to fail. If so, he would probably crash and die. It was hard to compartmentalize. Rip and I weren't the kinds of people who had deep conversations or shared our intimate thoughts with others. But we had become partners. We had left the past behind and were focused on our lives in the new world of Libertine. We worked together, camped out, joked and shared meals. That bond had become important to me. The thought of losing it, of losing Rip, was painful to contemplate. So, I pushed it down deep and focused on the task at hand.

I climbed out of the MECH and looked over my shoulder at the alien ship. Air was venting from several exhaust ports. There was no way to know who or what would come out of the ship. But I knew they would come. They had to fix the ship, and they had to deal with me. It wouldn't do them any good to fix one problem and leave the other. I would sabotage them again and again, which meant they would have to neutralize me. And they were slave traders, which meant they would certainly have the means to take me down.

I, on the other hand, was in my compression fatigues with no armor and no weapons. The MECH had weapons, but I had nothing. It had never occurred to me that I might need them. And if there were any usable weapons on the MECH, I didn't know about them. Having not been involved in the design and development of the fighting platform, there were plenty of things about it I didn't know.

Left with just my wits and bare hands, I sprinted toward the ship. It had come down near the foothills just shy of the actual mountains. The wide, grassy plains left little cover for me to shelter in. And if I was going to have a prayer of stopping the slavers, it would happen up close, not from a distance.

The ship was big and up close I could see that it wasn't as sleek as it appeared to be from a distance. There were components that stuck out of the hull, conduits and exhaust ports. It was shaped like a giant egg, and on one side, a ramp was opening. Going down on my knees, I tried to make myself as small as possible. All those hours in the gym building muscle suddenly seemed like a bad idea. I knelt in the grass and stayed as close to the ship as I could while maintaining a view of the ramp.

It didn't take long for the slavers to come out and I was caught completely off guard when they did.

CHAPTER 11

THE SLAVERS WERE a mix of species. There were two monstrous beings with long arms like a gorilla, but with horns from their flat heads and down either side of their spine. There was a creature that looked like a mix of a horse and a goat with three heads. It had bags of gear strapped to its back. There was an alien who looked exactly like Uggar, the Premier of Solace. But what shocked me the most was that a human seemed to be in charge of the group. A human woman with long, black hair. She had dusky skin, thick shoulders and legs. On her feet were tall boots. Even from a distance, I could see a livid scar running down one cheek. Behind her came three short aliens that hopped like grasshoppers.

The woman barked orders at the others. She was clearly speaking a guttural language but it was gibberish to me. My language device had stopped working, along with the MECH. The good news was that only the woman seemed to be armed. She carried a slender laser rifle and had the vigilant look of a fighter. I had seen many such women in the SDF Marines.

Finally, a humanoid alien came out. He had three eyes and six arms, but stood on two legs like a human. He went straight to work on the nearest of the repulsers. Most of the damaged components were under the ship. There would be no way to get to them unless the ship could be raised by a few of the repulsers. I watched the group as they spread out. The six-armed alien worked on the ship, assisted by the hopping trio and the goat/horse alien. The woman with the laser rifle and the two big-horned beings stood watch.

I knew it was only a matter of time before they spotted me. The woman immediately took note of the MECH but didn't seem concerned about it. Which was more than enough evidence to convince me the power outage had been initiated by the slavers. There was no sign of Rip in the *Condor,* which was worrisome. It was possible he was still maintaining some distance, although I feared the shuttle had crashed. Just the thought of losing my friend made me feel ill and full of rage at the same time.

The memory of my encounter on a slave ship in the Casa system was weighing heavily on my mind. The Marine platoon from the *Renegade* had been sent to stop the slavers. We got on board and were immediately attacked. Fortunately, our armor saved us, but the energy weapons used by the aliens rendered us unconscious. I didn't have armor of any type or a weapon. There weren't even any stones or sticks to use against the slavers. But if I waited, I would be discovered and attacked with no hope of recourse. That left only one option. I started running.

It might have been smarter to run away. I could have used the alien ship for cover and run for safety, but that was against my nature. Charging toward danger always felt right to me. Maybe I wanted to shock my enemies, to make them fear me. Or maybe, as most people thought, I had a death wish. Whatever the reason, my instinct was to challenge whatever foe I faced directly. So, I ran toward the aliens. They saw me coming, of course. The woman could have shot me with her laser rifle, but she seemed unconcerned. After barking an order to the horned creatures, one of them moved to meet me.

Call me crazy, but I love a good fight. It's unnatural, maybe, I don't know. I can't even say why I love it, I just always have. A grin spread across my face as I closed on the alien. It wore a dingy, stained set of coveralls with a belt around its thick waist. Up close, the alien was just as big as me and thick with muscle, especially in its long arms. I lowered my shoulder and rammed the creature. I fully expected to blast right through him. My goal was to knock the horned slaver off his feet and continue straight toward the woman with the gun. But the long-armed alien was tougher than I expected. Running into him felt like throwing myself against a stone wall.

The horned slaver grunted at the impact, but didn't fall. I bounced back, staggering a little from the collision. The alien swiped at me with one long arm. I saw short, thick claws on the ends of his fingers. It was an elementary attack. The powerful alien probably didn't need to do more than slash at his opponents. Had the claws struck, there was no doubt I would have been terribly wounded. But I easily ducked under the swipe and, moving close, I drove my elbow into the creature's side. It was like hitting a heavy bag. The blow landed hard, although it had little impact on the big creature. He started to reach for me, but I lashed out with a heel kick to the side of the creature's short leg. That had a much more advantageous reaction. The leg bent inward and the alien roared in pain. It dropped forward, using its long arms for support like a gorilla. I moved around behind the alien and chopped at his neck with the edge of my hand. The impact sent pain radiating up my arm. The blow had hurt me more than my opponent.

The alien spun around, swinging another clumsy slash at me. I caught his arm and threw my hips into his midsection. At the same time, I rotated, just as Master Sergeant Steel had taught me during the long cruise on the *Jericho*. The alien flipped over my body and crashed onto the ground. I looked up in time to see the woman raising her rifle. I dropped to the ground just as one laser blast sizzled over my head. Rolling to the side, I avoided a second shot. It hit the ground, burning a swath through the thick grass. The third shot hit the horned alien, who was struggling to get back on his feet. The slaver stiffened, then fell.

If you spend enough time fighting, you get to know the ebb and flow of conflict. Without really thinking, you learn to react. It's a situation where a split second's hesitation can cost you dearly. I wasn't thinking about what was happening, but the instant the horned alien stiffened under the impact of the woman's laser, I launched myself forward. Her shock at accidentally shooting her own companion caused her to hesitate. Still, she was several yards away, and I had to dive to avoid getting shot as she raised her rifle back to her shoulder.

Time seemed to slow down as I jumped toward her. I threw myself forward and low, aiming for her knees. I heard the laser blast shoot over me and felt the heat down my back. It crossed my mind that maybe she wasn't firing stun blasts. And then I smashed into her legs. My shoulder caught her just above the knee of her right leg. I felt it stiffen, then flex backward. She screamed as she fell. I rolled the instant we hit the ground, moving up her body and snatching the rifle from her hands. There was a look of shock on her face as the pain scrambled her brain for a moment.

The other alien with long arms and horns was charging at

me. He vaulted himself on his arms like a simian and lowered his head like a bull. I got the laser rifle up and fired three fast shots without really aiming. It was all instinct and muscle memory. The first shot missed, the second two didn't. The slaver stiffened before falling headfirst into the ground like a crashing ship. I started to get up when the woman grabbed me. She slid one arm around my neck. I grabbed it and, for a brief moment, wondered about her. The arm was rock hard, solid muscle. Then I found her thumb and twisted it hard. She screamed, releasing her hold on my neck, but found my hair with her other hand. Normally, I kept my hair cut very short, although the weeks on Libertine had allowed it to grow longer. She got a handful and cranked my head back. I leaned back instinctively, which turned out to be a mistake.

As you might expect, I was a very experienced hand-to-hand combat specialist. Most Marines spent time sparring regularly and I was no exception. But there were unspoken rules when sparring. Pulling hair and biting or pinching was frowned upon. Sparring was for honing techniques and building muscle memory. Yet, in a real fight, anything was possible. I felt a rush of hot air on my face just before the woman bit my ear.

It was my turn to shout in pain. I drove my elbow into her stomach and felt the whoosh of air as it was blown from her lungs. There was no time to waste in getting clear of her. If I had hesitated, she would undoubtedly have latched onto me again.

Sitting upright, I turned just as she lunged for me. I drove the butt of the slender, laser rifle straight into her forehead. It snapped her head back and I saw her eyes rolling upward before they closed. There was a wave of relief as I got back on my knees and started to get up. The woman had been ferocious. I glanced down, checking the alien weapon. It was a habit reinforced by years of military training. A gun was only as good as the person who maintained it. The laser rifle seemed too delicate for field use. I would have guessed that it was a training weapon or maybe a target rifle, but not a tactical gun.

As I was looking down at the rifle, the goat horse alien closed in from behind me. I should have heard it coming. In fact, I should have covered the other aliens with the rifle before checking it out. Hindsight is twenty-twenty. The alien kicked me with both of its rear hooves. I went flying face-first into the grass. How I managed to stay conscious and not have whiplash is a mystery to me. After hitting the ground, I rolled up and, with the rifle still in hand, fired at the large alien. It went down on its knees, then flopped over, its tongue hanging from the goat-like mouth. I watched it just long enough to notice its side still rising and falling as it breathed. So, it wasn't dead. And the impact from the laser blast hadn't left a nasty hole, just a scorch mark over the dull brown hide of its chest.

The trio of smaller aliens was already back inside the ship and the six-armed being was rushing after it. I was suddenly uncertain what I should do. Part of me wanted to stay with the beings around me. They were still alive and needed to be restrained. The ramp into the ship was starting to rise off the ground. Instinct kicked in and I sprinted forward, rushing past the fallen human woman, whose presence mystified me.

We had discovered humans on a pirate ship and on an illegal slave trade station. But Eldora had said the oval-shaped craft was an authorized or regulation slave vessel. So, how could it have a human on board? It made no sense, but I knew there was a lot to the workings of the galaxy that I didn't understand. The woman was unconscious and, for the moment, not a threat. I wanted to stay with her, to restrain her and ensure I could question her. There were so many things I wanted to know. Who was she? How had she become part of the slave ship's crew? Were there more humans on board? Where had she come from? But there was no time to see about the woman. If I didn't get on board before the ramp closed, I might never get the chance again. I wasn't about to let that opportunity slip through my fingers. So I charged toward the ship, leaped onto the ramp, and followed the six-armed alien into the gloomy interior.

CHAPTER 12

THE SMELL HIT me like a physical blow. It was the worst
stench I had ever encountered, a mix of rotting flesh, sewage and
sickness all contained inside an unventilated area. I gagged and
nearly retched, but managed to hold myself together as my eyes
adjusted to the dim lighting. There was movement. The small
aliens, more than the original three, but the same species, were
hopping away. I couldn't see the six-armed person. There were
cables and what looked like scaffolding around me. There were
also big, boxy compartments that I guessed were where the articulated grappling arms I had seen on the bottom of the ship were
housed. There were big cages hanging from the ceiling, and
several support pillars with steps that fanned out from them with
no railing.

I hurried toward the nearest pillar and climbed up it. The
stairs spiraled around the pillar, which had several maintenance
compartments on it. They were labeled in strange lettering, the
paint faded, but clear enough. On the next level, I discovered the
source of the odor. Hundreds of beings were crowded into

compartments divided by open walls that looked to be made from some type of chain links. I stepped out onto the deck plates and saw liquid beneath me. It was blood, water and sewage; a thick, viscous sludge that seemed to have built up over time. The beings in the locked compartments looked at me with large, frightened eyes. They were slightly shorter than me, bipeds with shaggy hair and long, drooping mustaches. Their mouths were small, their noses large and hooked like an eagle's beak. They had big, dark eyes that were surrounded by folds of thin, wrinkled skin. They made strange sounds, something of a mash-up between owl hoots and dove coos. They wore long, baggy garments, but I saw feathers and fur on their necks and arms. Their bodies were big and they had long, multi-jointed arms that folded up against their sides.

I had seen slaves before and, while I had never seen that species of alien, I had no doubt they had been taken from their home world against their will. But they weren't my concern yet. I would eventually come back to them, although not before I ensured there were no more slavers to worry about. I continued up the stairs, winding my way past another level of captives. There were less than the bird people below and a wide variety of species. They huddled together in segregated groups inside the locked compartments. Once more, I left them and hurried upward in my search for the slavers.

On the fourth level, there were aliens with weapons. It still amazes me that beings so clumsy and uncoordinated could capture untold numbers of intelligent beings. They opened fire with laser-based weapons as I emerged from below. But either through fear or inability, they failed to target me. I ducked back down, bending low so that my head barely cleared the deck. The fourth level of the ship was clearly living space for the aliens. I saw a strange galley, a sitting area, shelves with various entertainment options, but mostly open space for the crew to move around. There were three aliens firing at me from behind what looked to be some type of exercise machine. I fired back and easily drove them to safety. They were merely firing their weapons in the general direction of the stairs without really taking aim.

My fear was that the delicate laser rifle I was using would run out of power. Without it, I had no way to fight the alien slavers. But it was easy to move around and flank my attackers. They were overly concerned with their own safety. I might have ordered them to drop their weapons and surrender, yet without my language device, it was an impossible task. My only option was to take them down, which I did. One managed to fire back at me as I raced from the stairs toward the sitting area. It was the most valiant effort of the trio, but they weren't fighters. I gunned them down where they cowered behind the exercise machine.

And that was the lot of them. The three cowards were small aliens, with delicate features and big, oval-shaped heads. I had seen similar images of them back in the Sol system, where some people claimed to have been visited or even abducted by mysterious grey aliens. After searching the fourth and fifth levels, I went back down to the first. It was empty. A hatch on the opposite side of the ship was left open. When I went to it, I could see some of the slavers hopping away. I could have pursued them, but it seemed unnecessary. They were not a threat, at least not to me. Going back to the far side of the ship, I found the controls that opened the other hatch. To my dismay, I found the human female missing from the aliens who lay stunned on the ground. I took the time to tie up the hands of the long-armed, horned aliens. They certainly seemed like the most dangerous of the slavers. I also bound up the legs of the goat horse. It was breathing long, deep breaths and showed no signs of regaining consciousness. I found that a bit surprising, as the alien was at least twice the size of its companions. Yet the same stun beam had put it down and out, just as it had the horned slavers.

To my relief, the *Condor* landed next to the MECH after making several slow circles above the alien ship. The guns we had mounted onto the shuttle's hull weren't really suited for firing at targets on the ground from close range. Rip came out of the *Condor* in full space armor and armed with his rifle, an Ambrose Hill XOR with a fully automatic machine gun upper barrel, and an eight-round grenade launcher underneath. It was a heavy weapon that packed a powerful punch, but Rip could handle it. He looked ready for anything in his Marine armor.

"All clear," I said in a loud voice.

"What happened? Why'd you cut comms?" Rip asked.

"I didn't. They knocked out all my electrical systems."

"Damn, Hugo. You're not even in light armor. How'd you clear the slavers?"

"The only way I know how," I said calmly. "Trust me, they weren't fighters. But get this, they had a woman with them."

"A woman?"

"A human," I said. "Female."

I held up the delicate laser rifle. "She came out with this. The only one of them that was armed."

"You kill her?"

"Negative," I said. "We fought. She nearly bit my ear off."

"Nice," Rip said. "Sounds like a real charmer."

"Still human," I pointed out. "I hit her with the rifle and she went out cold. But when I finished clearing the ship, she was gone. Couldn't have gotten far, though. I hyperextended her leg, taking her down."

"You don't pull any punches," Rip said.

"Not when I'm outnumbered with no weapons," I said.

"Why didn't you secure her?"

"Didn't have time. The aliens were sealing up the ship."

"You could have waited for me," Rip pointed out.

"I had no way to contact you. I didn't know if you had been hit with whatever zapped my power. For all I knew, you were dead in a fiery crash."

"Have a little faith in me, would ya?" Rip complained.

"I'm just telling you my state of mind."

"Is it empty then?"

I chuckled at his unintended double meaning. He didn't notice.

He was pointing at the ship. I shook my head. "There's a couple hundred prisoners on board that thing," I told him. "If your translator is working, you can set them free."

"Set free on a low-tech world with no prospects of ever getting back where they came from may not be much of a conso-lation," Rip said.

"The way I see it, they at least have some choices. And trust me, they're going to want to get off that ship."

"That bad?"

"Oh, yeah, the worst."

"At least I've got air filters in this monkey suit," he said, refer-ring to his space armor and battle helmet. "Let's get your MECH back online first, then we can see about freeing the slaves."

It didn't take Rip long to get the power back on the MECH. He wasn't a wrench spinner, but he was pretty good with tech-nology. I, on the other hand, wasn't really much use with any kind of mechanical work outside of basic weapons maintenance.

Rip joined me beside the MECH. He had to pull a set of fuses. They weren't burned up, but the EMP or whatever tech the Slavers used to knock out my power tripped their internal circuits, which kept the power surge from frying the MECH's electronics. Rip replaced the fuses and reinserted the device. The power came back on, and I climbed inside, sealing the heavy armor up and bringing up the radar systems.

"Looks like we're clear," I told Rip via the MECH's comlink.

"Roger that, I'm going in."

He entered the alien spaceship, and I kept watch, going through the MECH's weapons systems as I did. Most of it was either too small to use against a spaceship or too big to use against a small number of fighters. The MECH was designed for combat situations, just not conflict on a small scale. It would have been ideal in a full-fledged war, although at times, I felt like it was overkill.

It didn't take Rip long to come out of the alien ship, leading a group of aliens. They were the shaggy aliens in baggy clothes with dark eyes and beak-like noses. They reminded me of both goats and birds somehow, as if they were a combination of species.

"What's the plan?" I asked.

"These are Musclars," Rip said. "Lots more coming."

"What are we going to do with them?"

"How should I know?"

"They need shelter, supplies, probably even medical attention."

"I suppose that's up to them," Rip said. "I doubt the city leaders up in Solace will help."

"I guess they can utilize the ship for shelter. It's not going anywhere."

"It could, though," Rip said. "We could probably fly this thing back home."

That thought had never crossed my mind. It was partly because I felt like Libertine was my home, as much as I thought of any place as being a home. Since joining the Space Marines, I had given up any sort of permanent residence. I liked our place at Lake Tyconda in the mountains, but it felt more like a camp than a home or even a military base.

"You think?" I asked.

Rip shrugged. "I'm just saying, it's possible. We may not want to go just anywhere in a stolen slave ship, but it is a viable, interstellar vessel. I don't think we can afford to leave it down here too long."

"It needs fixing," I said. "I ruined most of the repulsers."

"My guess is they have replacements on board," Rip said. "I'll see that the slaves are all freed and the resources on board are utilized. But I don't want the replacement parts to be wasted, or the fuel for that matter. She'll probably need all the power she can get to break orbit again."

"I'll find a place where they can shelter for the night," I volunteered. "And see if I can lay eyes on the human female while I'm at it."

"If you find her, try not to kill her," Rip said with a chuckle. "I'd like to know how she got here."

"You and me both," I told him. "Be back soon."

"Copy that," Rip replied.

To the North was nothing but open plains and the sandy deserts beyond. South of where the ship went down, just a few kilometers, were hills that led to the mountains. The entire southern continent on Libertine was like a tropical island, only with sparse vegetation and oceans of sand instead of water. The trees were tall, swaying palm-like arbors that grew in small clusters. The soil was light and sandy, the grass that grew in it was soft and thin. It felt like a young world to me, if such a thing were observable. I knew that somewhere in the vast reaches of the hot world, machines were burning fossil fuels and pumping greenhouse gases into the atmosphere. At least that was the terraforming model I had been told the locals were using. Yet those stations had been left abandoned long ago. They might still be chugging out the carbon-rich gas or they might be dead. The point was, much of Libertine was inhospitable and what small parts that could sustain lifeforms were barely capable of doing so. It wasn't a rich, vibrant world, but more of a young, sparse world. Still, it wasn't too cold or too hot in the foothills. It didn't rain much, but there were streams that flowed down out of the mountains. I was certain I could find a place where the freed slaves could make a start at a new life.

I set out at a fast jog in the MECH, moving south. Flying would have been faster, but it was harder to do and used up more power. Running was much safer. I let the MECH's radar pulse as I ran. It was designed to scour the skies for enemy aircraft although it could be tuned down to pick up movement on the ground around me. Within minutes, I had a lock on the woman. She was the only member of the Slaver crew who had fled. The others were either secured or dead.

She was moving south as well, only much slower than I was. Moving wide of her, I continued on and found a small stream about four kilometers from the slave ship. It ran down from the mountains, winding between the hills before disappearing underground. There was a good place between two of the taller hills that offered protection from the wind and plenty of room to make camp. There were tree clusters spread along the riverbank. It was idyllic, a small slice of Libertine that was almost paradise. Food and resources weren't plentiful, but I guessed there was food of some kind on the slave ship. I marked the location on my mapping app and forwarded it to Rip.

"Looks like a good spot just four klicks out," I said.

The comlink signal was boosted by the transmitter built into the *Condor* and extended the area they could stay in communication.

"That's probably as far as these poor souls can travel," Rip said. "We'll have to ferry some of them on the ship. Whatever food and med supplies they can scrounge up, too."

"Copy that," I said. "I've got a fix on the woman."

"You sound like a caveman."

"What else should I call her?" I asked.

"I suppose you should ask her that," Rip said. "Want backup?"

"She's unarmed and injured. I think I can handle it."

Rip chuckled, "Famous last words."

CHAPTER 13

THE WOMAN DIDN'T AVOID me. She saw me moving in her direction, but she didn't change course. As I closed in on her, she stopped moving. She was favoring her right leg and had a nasty bruise on her forehead that caused both of her eyes to swell.

"I surrender," she muttered. "Can't believe you got the drop on me like that."

"I'm pretty experienced," I said.

Her head shot up with a look of surprise on her puffy face.

"You understand me?"

"Five by five," I said, my voice coming from the MECH's communication speakers that were built into what appeared to be the armor's head. "I'm the guy whose ear you bit."

She stared hard, a look of anger flashing in her eyes. I've never been very good at reading body language. Women are usually a complete mystery to me. But I recognized the emotions that were playing out in the woman's mind.

"What are you waiting for? Finish it!" she said.

"I'm not here to kill you."

"Kill me or let me go," she replied. "I won't be a slave."

"I'm not a slaver," I said. "How's the knee?"

"Screw you."

I didn't have a stun beam among the MECH's many weapons. It wasn't equipped with restraints either. But I wasn't going to simply turn away from the woman and let her go.

"We have questions," I said. "You can come with me the easy way or the hard way. It's your choice."

"I'm not going anywhere," the woman said, easing herself to the ground.

"We have meds," I told her. "Some anti-inflammatory and a cold pack would be helpful, I think."

"Screw you," she said again.

I sighed. I didn't want to cause her more damage or pain, yet her attitude wasn't getting us anywhere. I decided to give diplomacy one more chance.

"I'm Hugo. I was Space Marines."

"I didn't think humans were advanced enough to leave the Sol system," she said.

"It's a recent development," I explained. "But my friend Rip and I were left here on Libertine. We didn't know there were other humans outside of Sol."

"Now, you know."

"What's your name?" I asked.

"Screw you."

"How'd you get here?"

She covered her eyes with the back of one hand, lying down in the grass gently. I was moved by her gracefulness. Maybe I just hadn't seen a woman in a while, but she seemed almost alluring to me in that moment. But she didn't answer my question.

"How did you get out of the Sol system?" I asked.

She ignored me again. With a sigh, I moved forward. She didn't try to flee. I bent down and reached for her arm using the MECH's hands. The big combat platform wasn't made to be delicate, but I had practiced picking up weapons and ammunition, along with heavier crates and supplies.

The metallic hand took hold of the woman's arm. She didn't struggle or pull away, which I was grateful for. I didn't want to hurt her and the MECH was not gentle. Pulling her to her feet, she stood up and wobbled on her good leg. I could almost see her face-to-face through the window between the armor plates.

"You're coming with me," I told her. "I'll let you ride on the MECH or I can carry you."

"Whatever," she grumbled, but when I lowered the MECH's free hand, she sat down on it.

Lifting her was not a problem. I used the MECH's other hand to steady her close to the robotic platform's chest. It reminded me of holding a newborn kitten. The woman adjusted herself a time or two, but she didn't try to flee. By the time we got back to the *Condor,* I could see that her injured knee was swollen.

"Another successful mission accomplished," Rip said.

"Looks that way," I replied. "She's hurt."

"She got a name?"

"Won't tell me," I said. "Her knee is pretty jacked."

"Set her down and I'll take a look. You mind leading these refugees out to the camp you found?"

"Sure," I replied.

In the Space Marines, I had been Rip's superior, but we had both let that rigid chain of command go in the weeks we had spent on Libertine. We had become friends; in fact, I had never been closer to anyone than I was to Rip. I suppose being the only two humans on the planet made it easier. We both knew the other's strengths and weaknesses, which made it easier to divide tasks.

"I've got a load of the sick in the *Condor*," Rip said. "We'll meet you out there."

"Copy that."

I was a little reluctant to leave the woman. There was no reason for me to be possessive, yet I felt that way. It was almost like a need to hold onto her. I hadn't thought solitude would bother me and, the truth was, I had rarely been alone on Libertine. When I wasn't out exploring with Rip, I was usually helping Eldora in the village by the lake. But there was something about the woman that sparked feelings I wasn't expecting.

There were almost two hundred refugees who had been freed from the slave ship. Most held bundles of supplies. They had taken anything and everything that could be taken from the alien ship. Some of it was obviously useful, like blankets and food. Other things seemed less practical to me, like seat cushions and bundles of metal rods that were used to link the slave cages together. Some had tools, alien clothing, a few even had small electronic devices. I didn't bother trying to find out what they were carrying. Desperate times called for desperate measures and I didn't think the refugees were wrong to take whatever they could from the abductors who had stolen their futures.

I led the way. Not that it was hard to find the valley. From the hilltops, I could easily see the slave ship even without the MECH's visual assistance. Once the refugees had reached the valley and begun making a temporary camp, I returned to the slave ship where I locked the two horned aliens into the cages on board. By the time that was finished, the sun was going down, and Rip had flown the *Condor* to the camp and back. Together, we loaded it with food from the slave ship.

"What did you do with the woman?" I asked.

"Zaya, that's her name," Rip said. "She's at the refugee camp."

"You aren't afraid she'll flee?"

"I don't think she's going anywhere on that knee. When I get a chance, I'll run the doc-bot over and scan it. Looks like you probably tore something in there."

"She was trying to kill me," I said.

"That's nothing new," Rip teased. "You certainly have a way with the females, my friend. No doubt about it."

"Very funny," I said. "She told you her name?"

"I made her tell me before I would give her a shot of painkiller," Rip said. I could hear him grinning as he spoke. "I didn't even bother trying to get any more info out of her. She's none too happy that we spoiled her party."

"She was enslaving people," I said. "Kinda hard to believe that a human being would willingly take part in that."

"I tend to agree with you, but we don't know her story yet."

"True. People do what they have to do when things get desperate."

CHAPTER 14

WE HAULED three loads of food to the refugees. I guessed it was enough to feed them all for a couple of weeks. After that, I had no idea. There were edibles growing wild, and Solace, the colony on the mountain, had livestock. But I didn't think there was enough for the sudden influx of refugees. We would probably have to separate them and take one half north. Rip and I had been talking of flying over there for a couple of weeks, although we always seemed to find an excuse not to do it.

I left the MECH inside the shuttle after we finished unloading the last of the food. Then, Rip and I found Zaya. She was resting on the ground at the bottom of a hill with the other injured and sick refugees. I counted twenty-eight aliens that were different than the Musclars. They looked completely demoralized. I couldn't blame them. At least the Musclars were part of a larger group. They probably felt less alone and hopeless than the others who had only one or two fellow refugees of the same species. I knew that being one of only two humans on an alien planet had an effect on a person that I hadn't anticipated. It was one thing to choose to be alone; it was completely different when a person had no choice in the matter. I felt especially protective of Rip. I didn't relish the idea of being the only human in the entire world.

Finding another human was surprisingly emotional. There was an instant connection, even though I knew she hated me. I still felt a strong need to be near her and protect her. It was a lot like infatuation. And even though Zaya was attractive enough, I hadn't had a crush on a woman since my teenage years. So, I had a pretty good idea that what I was feeling wasn't romantic in nature, even though it was very similar.

"The way I see it," Rip told her as we knelt beside her on the grass. "We've got two options. One, we can go get the medical supplies you need and bring them back here."

"These Musclars hate me, you know that, right?" she said. "They'll probably murder me before you get back."

"You abducted them," I pointed out. "You were going to enslave them."

She didn't respond, but there was a look of intense dislike in her eyes as she stared at me. I was reminded of the saying, *If looks could kill.*

"The second option is we take you to our camp," Rip said. "It's a short hop from here, and we've got medical supplies there. Including the doc-bot that will fix your knee up pretty quick, I think."

"Fine," she said, pronouncing the word as if she were making a huge concession to us, rather than us helping her.

"We aren't going to force you to do anything," I said. "We don't keep slaves here."

"Good for you," she remarked.

"That said, you won't be welcome if you cause trouble. The village we're staying at was nearly wiped out by the Ashi."

"Those green-skinned monsters have no concept of mercy," she said, her tone softening slightly.

"We're going to want some answers, though," Rip said. "Like how you got here."

She didn't respond, but I could see her walls starting to come down a little. We helped her up and assisted her in walking to the *Condor*.

"You are leaving," one of the refugees said as it approached us.

I couldn't tell if it was male or female. They all looked very similar to me, although they had different shades of fur and feathers. They all had the long mustachios that hung down on either side of their mouths. I had clipped the language device onto the collar of my shirt. It translated the alien's words for me. And I saw a look of surprise cross Zaya's face when she realized how we were communicating with the refugee aliens.

"We are," Rip said. "Tomorrow I will return and take a few of you to meet the leader of the primary colony here on Libertine."

"They will help us?"

Rip shrugged. "They should, but I can't say for certain what they'll do. Please consider the idea of splitting your group. We can ferry half of you to the Northern area. That will make it easier for the locals to help support your people. But keep in mind that resources on Libertine are limited."

"We are here for a purpose, that much is clear to us," the alien said. "God has ordained it."

I was a little shocked at his proclamation. Religion was not something I understood well, but it was a bit of a surprise to hear an alien speak of God. Obviously, their concept and name for God were not the same as ours. It was the translation app that made it sound familiar.

"Okay," Rip said. "We'll be back tomorrow."

The alien gave a little bow as he stepped back. I got Zaya strapped into the cargo area just inside the ramp and close to the MECH. It occurred to me that there were weapons in the *Condor*. Another human could probably find them and turn them on us. I didn't think Zaya was in any shape to do that, but I thought maybe it was best that we didn't leave her alone in the ship.

"I'll ride back here," I said.

An odd look crossed Rip's face before he nodded and started for the cockpit. I didn't know what it was. We had become good friends, but I had never seen that expression before. And it never occurred to me in the moment that he might feel jealous that I was going to spend more time with Zaya than he was. I was only staying close to keep her from finding a way to try and kill us.

We didn't speak on the flight, which only lasted ten minutes. When the ship landed, I disembarked and found Eldora waiting for us.

"You survived," she said.

"We did, most of the slavers didn't," I told her.

"You killed them?"

"Those that fought," I said. "There's a couple left alive. We locked them inside the cages on their ship."

"More will come," she said.

"Probably so," I admitted. "I'm sorry for that."

"It is not your fault. I know I blamed you at first, but this," she waved first at the burned remains of the village, and then out toward the grassy plains where the slave ship was left, "was inevitable. At least you're here now. I don't know how you took out an entire ship by yourself, but the people of this world owe you their gratitude."

"He wasn't by himself," Rip declared as he came out of the back of the ship. "I had his back the entire time."

"Way back," I replied.

"Hey, I feel pretty sure I'm an officer now," Rip teased. "And that's how they do it. Giving orders, staying away from the danger, and taking all the credit."

Eldora actually laughed. Her voice and speech were already musical. I couldn't imitate it even if I did understand her language. But when she laughed, it was a truly beautiful sound.

"There were over two hundred slaves already on the ship," I said. "They are making a temporary camp down in the foothills."

"Two hundred?" Eldora remarked, her already large eyes opening even wider.

"Mostly Musclars," Rip said. "Are you familiar with them?"

Eldora shook her head. It didn't necessarily surprise me. Libertine was a very diverse mix of alien races, but there were thousands of species across the galaxy. And most were content to stay among their own kind.

"We found one human," I told her. "She's injured, but we brought her here. I hope that's okay."

Rip and I had both a camp near the radar and communications equipment, which we ran via a solar generator, but we also spent a lot of time in the lakeside village itself. We were even working on rebuilding one of the huts that dotted the shoreline.

"Of course," Eldora said. "You must help her. Let us know if we might contribute in some way."

It was an extremely generous offer considering that the village by the lake had very recently been attacked and nearly destroyed by Ashi troops. They had nothing to offer except perhaps a place where the newcomers could build something new. The fish in the lake offered probably the best source of protein and fat that was readily available. But the more those resources were harvested, the less there were for the future. I had no idea how quickly fish spawned or grew, but Eldora and the other survivors rarely took more of them than was needed for a single meal.

"I'll let them know," I said.

Eldora left just as Rip came to the back hatch of the *Condor* with Zaya. He had an arm around her waist, and she had her arm around his shoulder. She wasn't putting any weight on her injured leg.

"Let's get her to camp," Rip suggested.

I nodded. We made Zaya comfortable and scanned her leg with the medical equipment that Rip had taken from the *Renegade,* along with other supplies, when he effectively went AWOL to save me. The medical scanner was about the size of a toolbox and had several hoses and articulated arms for cleaning wounds, removing foreign objects from a human body, and stitching up lacerations. It could even do surgery under the right conditions.

While it did its work, Rip and I had a conversation about the refugees.

"Once she's settled, we should get up to Solace," I said.

"Agreed. Uggar won't be happy if he thinks we made him look bad to the other colonies."

"If only they would man their communications," I said. "The people in the north have to know a slave ship entered the atmosphere."

"Yeah, I suppose," Rip said. He was looking past me, watching Zaya.

I guess I knew then that she was going to be an issue. And honestly, we had no obligation to the colonies on Libertine or even the refugees from the slave ship. We weren't officially representing the SDF. And, truth be told, the colonists in Solace didn't really want us around. So, it's not surprising that Rip had other interests on his mind. I felt a sting of jealousy in that moment as he looked past me toward Zaya. It came at me from both directions. Sure, I wanted the woman to like me, even though I was notoriously inept at romantic relationships. And I wasn't infatuated by her, but she was the only human female on the planet. I had certainly entertained thoughts that perhaps she might see something in me she liked. Yet it wasn't just jealousy over the woman. I was jealous for Rip's friendship, too. We had grown close over the weeks we had spent on Libertine together. In fact, I had never had a closer friend. Not that we got deep into our personal lives or shared much about our past. Still, he was my friend and I didn't want to share him with anyone else.

Jealously is an uncomfortable emotion and I usually did my best to ignore or avoid those types of feelings. So, I pretended not to notice that Rip was only giving me a sliver of his attention. Behind us, the medical scanner beeped. We walked over, and Rip knelt beside the device.

"Ooooh," he said. "Torn ACL."

"Torn what?" Zaya asked.

"ACL, that's your Anterior Cruciate Ligament," Rip said.

Zaya had a look of confusion on her face, so I jumped in. "The tendon that holds the bone in your upper leg to the bone in your lower leg."

"Yeah, it's behind the kneecap," Rip said, tapping his own knee. "The good news is that it's just a tear. You didn't completely snap it in two."

"It really hurts," Zaya said.

"You'll be fine," Rip said. "A few steroid shots and some red light therapy will have you good as new in a few days. Well, maybe not as good as new, but you'll be getting around just fine."

"I'll see if we have a brace," I told Rip.

"You want me to cut off your pant leg, or just help you take them off?" Rip asked.

"I will not," Zaya said angrily.

"Hey, cool it there, missy," Rip said. "No one is trying to take advantage of you."

The woman had a look of fear and determination on her face. She was strong, that much was clear.

"You're safe here," I told her. "We're not even going to be around for a few hours. We've got to make a trip up the mountain."

"What's up there?" Zaya asked.

"The primary colony of this world," I said.

"It's a crappy little place," Rip said as he made some adjustments to the medical device beside Zaya's knee.

"They'll need to take in the Musclars," I continued.

Zaya chuckled. "Good luck."

"What's that supposed to mean?" Rip asked.

"Musclars are good for one thing only," Zaya said. "Hard labor. You put them on a sweet little world like this and they'll infect everyone on it."

"Infect them?" I asked. "Are they contagious with some sort of pathogen?"

"I have no idea what you're talking about," Zaya said.

"A pathogen, you know, like a germ, an illness."

"No," she said, shaking her head. "Not... that. They're religious fanatics."

"Religious fanatics?" Rip asked. "That's interesting."

"Not really," Zaya said with a sigh as I removed a knee stabilizing brace from our medical supplies.

Rip handed her a pair of scissors and showed her that she needed to cut the pant leg off well above the knee. She complied, and he pulled the lower portion of the pant legs down to the middle of her shin. Her skin was pale, but I could already see a bruise forming. Her knee was swollen, but that was normal. The medical device filled a syringe with steroids and made an injection. Zaya groaned in pain.

"It's killing me," she said.

Rip was holding her leg steady. "Hang in there," he said.

The needle came out, and she breathed a ragged sigh of relief.

"See, that wasn't so bad," Rip said as he gently laid a strip of red lights inside a transparent sleeve across her knee. "Take these." He handed her a couple of pills.

"What are they?"

"Pain killers," he said.

She threw them into her mouth and I handed her a bottle of water. She drank the pills down and then covered her eyes with one hand. Her hair was splayed out around her head and shoulders. I turned away, unsure why the woman's hair made me feel strange inside.

"You can sleep for a while," Rip said. "But we need to know how you got on that slaver ship."

"The same way everyone else does," she said softly.

"Just rest," Rip said.

He headed for the *Condor* and I followed him. We didn't speak about her until we had lifted off from the village by the lake.

"You believe her?" I asked.

"Not sure yet," Rip replied. "To be honest, I'm not sure about anything at the moment."

"What do you mean?"

"It's just that things were a bit too easy today," Rip said. "You took down an entire slave ship by yourself."

"Maybe I'm that good," I joked.

"No doubt, but it's also possible that this is all a trick. Maybe someone wanted her in our camp."

"She's not faking the injury, though."

"No, you did a number on her knee," Rip said. "There's no way to fool the doc-bot about a torn ACL."

"We'll have to keep an eye on her," I said.

"And maybe question her separately. I want to know if she tells us the same thing."

The pang of jealously was back. It made me wonder if Rip was being cautious or if he just wanted to be left alone with the woman. Either way, I couldn't argue with his logic. I didn't think it had been easy to shoot down the slave ship or take out the crew. But I knew that the Imperium had outlawed weapons hundreds of years before we left the Sol system. The slavers could act with impunity because the locals had no way of fighting back. When a person doesn't have to worry about resistance, they can get lazy and lower their guard.

"Sounds like a plan," I said. "Why don't you have the first crack at her when we get back?"

"She'll probably still be groggy," he said. "The pain meds will act almost like truth serum."

"I guess we'll find out soon," I replied. "You can question her while I reach out to the northern colonies. Let them know what happened with the slavers."

Rip nodded in agreement and that's exactly what we did.

CHAPTER 15

NO ONE WAS happy about the Mulscars. I didn't know the history of Libertine, but I had heard that it was a safe haven for those fleeing the Imperium. Instead, we discovered an impoverished, barely habitable world, where every newcomer was treated with suspicion. And perhaps the Mulscars had a bad reputation, I couldn't say for certain. But what did seem evident to me was that no one in Solace, or in Freetown - which was the primary colony in the northern polar region - was happy about so many individuals of the same species.

"Perhaps they feel like one group will seize power and create difficulties for anyone else," Rip said.

"How is that we've left the Sol system and ventured into a highly advanced galaxy, only to discover that archaic practices like slavery and racism are rampant?"

"Whoa man, don't go all philosopher warrior on me, bro," Rip said. "How the heck should I know why the galaxy is full of backward-thinking species?"

After my time urging the leaders at Freetown to reach out to the other settlements and prepare to take a hundred or so of the refugees, it was my time to question Zaya. Rip had already built a fire, and there was a cool breeze blowing. Evenings were always my favorite part of the day. It felt good to kindle a fire as the heat of the day dissipated and cook our dinner over the flames. It was primal and real. I was used to eating slop on a military ship or chemical-laden, soupy concoctions that came in a sealed package for combat operators down range. On Libertine, we ate what we foraged ourselves and what we caught or killed. The food was cooked over open flames or hung to dry in smoky huts. It was both filling and satisfying on a much more basic level than walking into a chow hall and getting a tray from a culinary specialist.

I settled beside Zaya near the fire and let my tense muscles relax. It felt good to be off my feet for a change.

"How's the knee?" I asked.

"Better," Zaya replied. "Still swollen, but it doesn't hurt as much."

"That's good. A few days of rest will work wonders."

"That's what your friend said."

"We both had field medic training in the SDF."

"What's SDF?"

"Space Defense Force," I said. "Do you remember it? You were born on Earth, right?"

Zaya nodded. The golden light from the fire shone on her face. The scar down her cheek left the skin around it puckered. She had a round face, not the classically beautiful, slender oval that women sought through cosmetic means if their genetics didn't deliver to their satisfaction. Yet, there was a strength there that I found deeply interesting. She had brown eyes, thick lashes and eyebrows. Other than the long scar on her cheek, her face was unmarked.

"I was," she said. "I don't remember a lot, though."

"What happened?"

"I was taken," she said. "That's all I know. I remember nightmares about the little people. Grays is what your friend called them. I was just a kid and no one took me seriously. And then suddenly, it was like that life was all a dream. I don't know much about it."

"Trauma can have that effect," I told her as I poked at the fire with a stick.

"Maybe," she said. "It was a long, long time ago."

"You the only human?"

"No," she said, shaking her head. "There were four or five of us at first. But we were split up and sold to different groups."

"Sold?"

"Yeah," Zaya said. "That's the way things work, you know. I don't know why the two of you seem so surprised."

"You didn't seem like a slave," I said. "You seemed to me more like a slaver."

She made a sound that was part chuckle and partly a snort of derision. "What choice does a slave have? I was abducted as a child and forced to work cleaning bilge tanks. They were so rank that most of the slaves who did it died. Can you imagine being shut up in a container with nothing but waste for hours at a time? Do that for a few years, soldier boy, and tell me you wouldn't jump at the chance to do anything else, anything at all, even abduct other people and force them to do it."

"So, you were given a chance to join a slave ship?"

"I can't say how long I worked in the bilge tanks. It's not like anyone was keeping tabs on me. We worked, we washed, we slept. That was it — mostly in near total darkness. If you wanted to survive, you cleaned. And one day, I was moved from cleaning bilge tanks to cleaning slave ships. It was a rough way to grow up. Everyone was looking to get out or get something from you. I had to learn to fight and that got the attention of the slavers, too. They needed muscle. I guess humans are unique in that regard; we aren't afraid to fight."

"How long have you been slaving?"

"That's a great question. Let me just count up my birthday parties," she said, her voice brimming with sarcasm. "Oh wait, I never had one because I was a slave!"

"There's no need to get upset."

"Oh, there's plenty of reasons to be upset. Not the least of which is that you ruined my life. Do you have any idea how long it took me to carve out a place for myself on the *Subjugation*? Now, I'm stuck on this wretched planet with no hope of escape."

"What's wrong with Libertine?"

"Oh, I don't know. How about the fact that you live in a hovel with no running water," she said. "Or the fact that there is nothing to do here but eek out a living by collecting berries and smoking fish. Do you have any idea what the fish in that lake eat?"

"Worms?" I suggested.

"Sure, bugs when they get a chance. But most of the time, they eat the feces of the bigger fish."

Eldora had brought us three medium-sized fish, which Rip had cleaned. They were on spits over the flames, roasting.

"It's good protein," I said. "And fat too. That's better than just about anything you get on Earth unless you're rich."

Zaya turned up her nose and looked away.

"Why did your ship come here?" I asked after a few moments of silence.

"Do you really think the masters conferred with me before they went someplace?" Zaya said. "You and your buddy are idiots."

"They didn't tell you where they were going?"

"No," Zaya explained. "They just went wherever they wanted. We kept the slaves in line and cleaned up the ship."

"How'd you get that laser rifle?"

"I made it," she said. "They had weapons on board. Most of them didn't work. I cobbled a few pieces together and made a stun blaster."

"Pretty smart."

"What else was I supposed to do, wrestle with the Gonars? I'm not as strong as you."

I nodded. It all made sense, but that didn't mean it was true. And it didn't really give us the information we needed.

"Do you know if the officers on your ship kept a log?"

"What do you mean?"

"A log, a ship's log. You know, a record of where they went and what they did?"

"I have no idea."

"How did you communicate with them?"

"The same way I'm communicating with you."

"They spoke our language?"

"No," she was getting exasperated. "I spoke theirs."

"You spoke their language. Can you read it too?"

"No, I can't read. I never learned to read," she snapped. "I never had that chance."

"Calm down," I told her. "I just need to know how that ship found this planet."

"Well, I don't know. So, you can either leave me alone or kill me."

"I'm not going to kill you," I said.

"Everything okay?" Rip asked as he checked on the fish.

Zaya crossed her arms and rolled onto her side, facing away from us. I looked at Rip and shrugged my shoulders. I wasn't quite sure what I had done to make Zaya so angry. I couldn't understand what made her so upset at the prospect of being free. It was like she would have preferred to continue her life as a slave and I suppose that it was possible that she couldn't fathom any other kind of life. She had been a slave since childhood. Maybe her fellow slaves didn't talk of freedom or hope for a better life. Maybe the idea of living free was somehow looked down on by those who were trapped in slavery. I really had no idea but I wasn't keen on being scolded by the woman who had tried to stun or kill me just hours earlier. I guess maybe she didn't want to be friends with me, either.

I got to my feet and walked past Rip. "I'm going for a walk," I told him.

"Can't promise I won't eat your fish while you're gone," he joked.

I knew he wouldn't but I feigned as if I was going to smack him. He flinched, we both chuckled and I walked away into the darkness. Nothing was ever the same after that.

CHAPTER 16

IT WAS three days before we had the refugees settled, although to our surprise, many chose to stay in the valley we had initially placed them in. They cut sod and made communal shelters. I didn't spend much time with them, but helped Rip ferry several dozen to the northern pole, and another shuttle took a group up to Solace. In those three days, Zaya made a remarkable recovery. On the fourth day, she and Rip began repairs on the slave ship. I could see there was more between them than just teamwork, but I couldn't say why that was. Perhaps it was lack of options or maybe they were genuinely compatible; either way, they were spending more and more time alone.

It was a week before the slave ship was fully repaired and I noticed things missing from the camp where Rip and I had set up the communications equipment. Some rations taken from the *Renegade* disappeared and most of the medical supplies. I knew what was coming next and, to be honest, the only thing that really surprised me was when Rip told me their plans.

It was late in the evening. I had caught a medium-sized

animal in a snare. It had enough meat that we were able to divvy it up between the villagers and our own little camp. Rip cooked it in a pot with some root vegetables that were similar to potatoes, carrots, and onions. It made a good stew with a hearty broth. After our meal, Rip joined me for a walk near the lake shore. It was a very calm night. The surface of the water was smooth and reflected the thousands of stars visible in the night sky.

"We're leaving," he said softly. "I'm guessing you knew that."

"It seemed likely," I told him.

"She isn't happy here, Hugo. I tried to change her mind, but well... you know women."

I actually didn't. I knew some women from my time in the Space Marines, but in all honesty, I didn't understand how women thought or even how they communicated in most instances. My short time with Zaya had dashed any thoughts I might have harbored about a romantic connection. She was short-tempered, gruff and opinionated. Any time something came up that she didn't know or understand, she took it as a personal attack on her intelligence. It was hard to tiptoe through the landmines of what she retained from her short childhood on Earth and what she didn't know.

"I'm not sure she knows how to be happy," I said.

It was brutal honesty but said with some compassion. If Rip took offense, he didn't let it show.

"We're happy together," he said. "We discussed bringing you along, but—"

"No," I said, cutting him off. He immediately breathed a sigh of relief. "I'm not leaving."

"That's what I figured, man. I don't mean to leave you down here alone, but... honestly, I didn't really think things through. I didn't know how lonely it would be here."

"I think it's peaceful," I replied. "But you don't have to explain yourself to me, Rip. I owe you my life. There's nothing I would willingly do to keep you from being happy."

"Thanks, brother. That means a lot to me."

"Where are you going?"

"I'm not sure," he said.

"Earth? The Sol system?"

"I suggested it, but she's got concerns. You know how it makes her feel when she thinks people are looking down at her."

I couldn't honestly say how she felt about anything, but I knew she got angry easily and assumed that was what he meant.

"Are there other worlds you might go to?"

"Oh, yeah," Rip said. "Hundreds, I guess. Not that we're planning to settle down. But we've got options. We can sell the slave ship or maybe convert it to a freighter. I guess we could do just about anything once we get the stink out."

"Good luck with that?"

"Tell me about it," he said with a chuckle. "It'll take some time, but we've got plenty of that."

"What about the Imperium?" I asked him. "Aren't you concerned you'll run into trouble?"

"Who can say," he admitted. "Heck, we may decide it's better here than we thought. Maybe we'll come on back one day."

"Maybe," I said, but of course, I didn't believe him.

It was clear from the way he was talking with me that he was trying to make me feel better about him leaving. If I was being honest, I felt angry about it. Zaya wasn't going to make him happy, but I would never try and keep him on Libertine. That had been my wish, not his. He had given up everything to save me, and if he wanted to go frolicking around the galaxy with Zaya, who was I to stop him?

The next day, I sat on a hill and watched as the slave ship was powered up. I doubted that Zaya was much help piloting the ship. I had seen her masters. There had been three of them on the slave ship, all the same species. I was beginning to think that the galaxy was much more segregated and prejudiced than expected. It was unlikely they would have taught the young human female how to fly the ship. Rip was most likely doing that. When we were aboard the *Renegade,* the advanced artificial life form that called itself GIGI had created a program that translated all known languages, both spoken and written. With his space armor helmet on, he could read the labels on the controls, as well as the data from the ship's scanners and computer. It would most likely do most of the flying via an autopilot.

The ship hovered for nearly an hour, then began to fly. It made a looping turn, then headed north, gaining altitude. I was left alone, the only human on Libertine. But that had been my desire, to be alone, to carve out a life for myself using my own two hands. So that is what I did.

The village by the lake was growing. Two families from Solace had moved down and a few of the Musclars had moved up to the tropical lake with its sandy beaches and swaying palm trees. I maintained the communication equipment there, but didn't spend much time in the village. Still, it was the touchpoint to what little could be called civilization on the Free World of Libertine. I preferred to be in the wilder parts of the mountain chain that encircled the southern polar region on the hot planet. There were times when I went for many days without seeing another soul. Was it lonely? Sure, but it was easier in many ways than trying to get along on a ship full of people.

Solitude became my companion. I lived the life of a true mountain man, marking berry patches and the various places where edible plants grew in abundance. I ran trap lines, hunted with a bow and arrows that I made myself and fished in the mountain streams. Wood that was suitable for building was the currency of the land. Whenever I found good timber that was either knocked down by the wind or standing dead, I transported it to the village and traded it for other goods like blankets and clothing, fishing line, and food. Eldora was a master at making soft, flat bread from a type of wild plant that she cut, dried, and ground down into a flour.

I wasn't part of the village, although I was becoming part of the local scene on Libertine. People, there were all types of aliens on the planet, knew who I was and what I was capable of doing. Along with my own exploits in the wilderness, I made it my business to keep the communication equipment, shuttle craft, MECH armor and weapons in good working order. No one else seemed to care about it. The locals hardly ever used the communication equipment, even to speak to family or friends in another village. Despite the slavers who had shown up so unexpectedly, no one felt the need to look after their own defense. I saw that as a mistake but I kept such opinions to myself.

I was closest to Eldora. We were friends, although I doubt she would have considered me to be a close friend. I didn't open up and share my life story with her. Nor did she with me, but when I came into the village, she always made a place for me by their communal fire. There were other members of the village who made their disdain for me clear. The Musclars were the most vocal in their dislike for me. It didn't seem to matter to them that I had saved them from a life of slavery. All they really seemed to care about were the rules of their religion, which forbade sharing meals with people who didn't agree with their beliefs. At first, they tried to convert me, but when I resisted, they turned nasty. I found them rude and judgmental, but it was easy enough to stay out of their way.

After a year on my own, my hair was shaggy, as was my beard. I spent most of my days wearing just a small garment around my waist. Hard work in the hot sun turned my skin dark brown and left highlights in my hair. It was different than resistance training in a gym, yet I felt like I was in the best shape of my life. Hiking up and down mountains every day, hauling wood, stalking game and building things honed my entire body.

Of course, none of that prepared me for the attack. I had come to Libertine a hardened combat veteran, a Space Marine drilled in the habit of situational awareness. But months of solitude had made me less wary. And although not welcomed by everyone in the Lake Tyconda village, I had never felt threatened there, which is probably why I didn't see the pair of Musclars coming.

I was kneeling by the edge of the lake, cleaning a string of fish. Earlier in the day, I had arrived with two excellent logs for building. I used a rechargeable cargo lifter to move the heavy timber. They were tied together, their dry limbs cut and bundled for firewood that was nearly as welcome in the village as the thick logs that would be used to build more huts. In exchange for the wood, I had gotten a new belt made of woven reed fibers harvested from the far side of Lake Tyconda. The villagers were experts at peeling the thin layers of the reed, twisting it into a thread and braiding it. They used the twine for all sorts of projects, from woven blankets to lines for fishing or nets. The belt was useful and sturdy. I kept my knife on it while I worked out in the wild places, plus it held up the kilt I had taken to wearing. It had been a good trade, and included the fish I was preparing for dinner and a place by the village fire that night.

Only not everyone saw me as a welcome addition. I was

aware in a vague sense that the Musclars didn't like me. What I didn't realize was that they were frustrated by their failure to convert the others to their beliefs or that they were conversing regularly with the village in the foothills. They had named the city Mecula and built a shrine that was carved into a boulder, which they situated in the center of their village.

I was more of the live and let live type. It didn't bother me that the Musclars were unfriendly or even racist. They were at most a minor nuisance when I went into the small lakeside community. But little did I know they had other plans.

"Drop the blade, Hu-man," one of the Musclars told me as I was gutting a fish.

I still used the language device to translate the alien languages. I had picked up some of the words over time, but even in the little village, there were several languages being spoken. I did recognize the last word of the threat. The aliens knew my name, although they sometimes confused Hugo with human.

My hands were bloody and slick. There was a painful prick in the center of my back, clear evidence that the Musclars were using some type of weapon. I laid the fish and my knife on the flat rock at my feet.

"It's down," I said, the little language device translating my words in the Musclar language.

"On your knees," the voice behind me said.

I was already squatting down, but felt the jab in my back pushing me forward. It hurt. I had no idea if it was a pointed stick or a bladed weapon, but it cut the skin. I felt a trickle of blood flowing down as I moved forward and planted my knees into the sand of the lakeshore.

"You will bow before the Master of the universe," another of the Musclars said as it stepped closer. It was to my left side. I turned my head and looked up into the alien's eyes.

"Submit to God or you will face the judgement," the alien pressing his weapon into my back said.

"What's that?"

"You are an infidel," the alien beside me said. "If you refuse to worship the Master of the universe, you will either pay the tax or die."

"What tax?"

"Worship heathen!"

"Okay, okay, relax," I said.

A lot of old feelings suddenly surged up inside me. They were things that used to haunt my sleep and left me feeling like there was a void deep inside me. Over the months of peace and relative tranquility on Libertine, those feelings had grown weaker ... or so I thought. They all came surging back, chief among them was an intense fury.

I started to lean forward as if I was bowing down, but then I dropped onto my right side, rolling away from the Musclars. I felt the water in my hair. The two aliens looked shocked. One had a crude spear. The blade was metal. It was bent, but thick enough to do real damage and sharp. The alien holding it suddenly thrust it at my face. I was on my back but still moving. With a twist, I avoided the spear thrust and caught hold of the weapon just below the blade.

The aliens weren't prepared for me to fight back. The one with the spear tried to pull it away from me, but it wasn't strong enough. The other made a move like it was going to attack me, but I lashed out with one foot. I kicked hard, straight at the alien's knee. It bent the wrong direction, and the alien shrieked with pain before toppling backward.

I started to stand up and let the frightened alien's frantic pull on his weapon add to my momentum. In one swift move, I was back on my feet. The Musclars were nearly as tall as I was, but nowhere near as thick. With my free hand, I rammed my palm into the side of the alien's face. It squawked and fell backward.

"Unable to translate," the language device pinned to my new belt said.

"No kidding," I replied, twirling the spear around so that the point faced the two Musclars.

Looking around, I didn't see any of their companions. There were eight in total living in the village. I had spent almost no time with them. You make assumptions about other races almost without even realizing you're doing it. I assumed the Musclars were like humans, that there were male and female, and that they had come to the village as family units. But I couldn't tell them apart or know what they were really like.

"You are a dead creature," the alien I had hit snapped.

I started to stab him with the spear, but then thought better of that idea. It would have felt good for a moment but it might have angered some of the villagers. No doubt, the other Musclars would do all they could to drum up animosity toward me if I killed one of their own. It didn't matter what the alien was threatening to do. So, I spun the spear around and smashed the butt of the weapon across his face instead. It knocked him unconscious.

The other Musclar was thrashing in the sand, wailing in pain. It held the injured knee with both of its feathery hands. I didn't think either of the aliens was a threat any longer, so I started back toward the village proper. It never occurred to me to stop at the *Condor* and retrieve a rifle. I did, however, stoop down and pick up my knife. It was still fouled with fish blood, but a quick dip into the lake water washed it clean. I dried it quickly on my kilt and stuck it back into the sheath on my new belt, thinking there would be time to clean and oil the blade later. I was a stickler for proper care when it came to a person's weapons, but in the heat of the moment, there was no time to do more.

I was jogging in the direction of the huts that lined the shore. The sun was setting. Long shadows from the mountain peaks were spreading across the lake. It was a good time to fish. They were jumping and feeding on insects that landed on the surface of the water. I could see that wood had been neatly arranged in the village's single fire pit. When I had first come to the village, there had been easily three times the number of aliens calling the community home. They had almost twenty huts built, and several fire pits were used along the sandy shoreline. But since the Ashi attack that had wiped the village out, there were only six huts, and only eighteen villagers. Eight of those were Musclars, far more than any of the other alien races living in the lakeside community.

I was nearing the first of the huts, the latest one to be built, when Eldora appeared. She wasn't alone. There were two Musclars on either side of her. One held a knife to the graceful village leader's throat.

"Stop!" the knife wielder ordered.

I obeyed. It felt like the entire world had been flipped upside down. In over a year on Libertine, I had never seen the alien citizens fight. There was no crime that I was aware of. The people on the Free World forged tools, not weapons. None, to my knowledge, had shown any interest in the firearms I kept locked up on the *Condor*. It was a peaceful place, but conflict has a way of showing up when you least expect it.

"Throw down that spear," the Musclar commanded.

"Why don't you lower your knife?" I said.

"I'm giving the orders here," the alien insisted. "Drop it or I'll cut her throat."

"I don't understand," I said, throwing down the spear.

"I wouldn't expect an infidel like you to understand anything," the alien with the knife said. "You are a blind brute and we have tolerated your unbelief long enough."

"Declare your allegiance to the Master of the universe or face the judgement," the other alien said. His squawking words were spoken in a solemn cadence.

"Why?" I asked. "Can't we all live and let live?"

"They believe we are defiling this planet," Eldora said.

"Your disbelief is a bane, a noxious odor to the Starmaker," said the Musclar with the knife to Eldora's throat. "We have claimed this land in his honor. Non-believers must pay the tax or be subject to a believer. This one is our slave now. The others have declared their allegiance. You will do the same or face judgement."

"Take me, not her," I said, spreading my hands wide.

"This is not a negotiation, heathen!" shouted the alien with the knife. "Swear your allegiance now, or face the judgement."

I didn't want to die, but I would have for Eldora. She was a kind person. We had become friends, and while there were times when I struggled with confusing emotions around her, neither of us had sought more than friendship. In fact, I didn't even know if her species even had romantic relationships. Those types of things were hard for me to talk about. What made one person want to be with another person was strange. Eldora and I had a friendly companionship, nothing more. Yet, I didn't want to see her harmed. The Ashi had done that and it was not good. I think I would have let the Musclars kill me if it would have spared Eldora, but then again, I'm not that easy to kill.

Clearing my throat, I spit on the ground and then looked at the Musclars. "That's what I think of your god," I said, and started walking toward them. "You want to make me bow? I say, give it your best shot."

CHAPTER 17

ELDORA EXPECTED TO DIE. I hated seeing the fear on her face. She closed her eyes, expecting to feel the knife plunge into her throat, but I used that opportunity to strike. I was only three long strides from the aliens. I didn't know them well enough to say for certain that they looked nervous. We were close enough to the shore that I was still walking in sand. I let the toe of my boot dig into the loose sand as Eldora closed her eyes. Then I flung my foot up toward the alien holding a knife to her throat. The sand pelted Edora harmlessly, but it hit her attacker's open eyes.

I launched myself forward. As the alien with the knife staggered backward, raising his free hand to his face, I grabbed his wrist and twisted hard. The bones in the Musclar's hand and forearm were delicate. They snapped under the pressure of my attack like dry twigs. The alien screamed in pain and dropped the knife. I followed with a savage punch to the alien's body. It lifted the Musclar off the ground. Then it fell to the dirt, its entire body spasming for air.

Just as quickly as I had attacked the first alien, I swung around Eldora and lashed out at her other attacker. My kick landed just above the Musclar's fetlock near the hoof. The blow knocked one leg into the other, and the alien fell. There was no time to be considerate to the aliens. They had challenged me and threatened my friend. I followed up with a second kick. The top of my foot smashed into the alien's beakish nose. Its head snapped back and blood gushed from the big nostrils as the Musclar lolled on its back, knocked senseless by my kick.

"Are you okay?" I asked, grabbing both of Eldora's arms.

Her large eyes fluttered open. I could see a blood vessel throbbing in her neck. She was trembling with fear.

"I think so," she said, looking down past me at the Musclars.

"They won't hurt you," I said.

"There are more of them."

"Then I'll deal with them too," I said.

Glancing back over my shoulder, I could see the first two aliens who had tried to ambush me from behind. They hadn't moved. That left four to deal with. I took Eldora by her delicate, alien hand and pulled her toward the camp I used. It was set up between the hut where the communication equipment was stored and the *Condor,* which hadn't been flown since Rip left over a year earlier. I had donated the hut that Rip and I had built to the village and slung a hammock inside the shuttle craft instead. It was the most secure place to store my weapons, medical supplies, and tools. There were crates of ammunition and lockers with various rifles and firearms inside. Rip had taken some of the small arms when he left on the slave ship, although I still had the MECH with all of its high-caliber ammunition, missiles, and weapons. It too remained stored in the *Condor,* which had a biometric lock. I slapped my hand on it and opened the rear hatch.

"What are you doing?" Eldora asked. "We can't leave the others."

"The ones who pledged allegiance to the Master of the universe?" I replied.

"They were forced to."

"You didn't?"

"And they declared me a slave," Eldora explained. "The others learned from my mistake."

"They could have stood up for you," I said, pulling a pistol from the locker. It was a simple weapon that fired .9mm bullets. I had three magazines already loaded. One went into the weapon, the other two I tucked into my belt.

"The Musclars were threatening them," she replied, as if that explained everything.

"Well, let's see how they like a taste of their own medicine," I said.

Eldora followed me back out of the *Condor*. I stopped long enough to lock the shuttle craft. Eldora was the only person in the village with access to the ship and the weapons inside. I had made sure she could access it in case of an emergency or if something ever happened to me. But like most of the aliens I had encountered on Libertine, firing a weapon, or even just fighting with someone, was unthinkable to her. Humans had a natural tendency to fight. No one has to teach a preschooler to lash out at their companion when something doesn't go their way. And that hostile response stays with a person throughout their life, even when they choose to deal with anger in a different way. Even the most peace-loving human will fight if they are pushed hard enough.

But that tendency toward violence isn't present in many other races. I had learned that they were like sheep among wolves, which was one of the reasons I hadn't even considered leaving Libertine with Rip and Zaya. How could I turn my back on the innocent people of a world that were endangered because humans had led the overbearing galactic government to them? More to the point, after saving the Musclars from a lifetime of slavery, they had become a threat to the people of the village. I wasn't going to stand by and let them be dominated by the very beings that had been welcomed to the village in the first place.

"I don't understand what you are saying," Eldora said as she followed behind me.

I was walking back toward the huts. The other Musclars had to be there. I didn't know if the remaining, uninjured aliens were hostile, but I was prepared for them with my pistol. It didn't have the stopping power of a hand cannon or even a higher caliber gun. I could have taken my rifle, but that seemed like too much force. It wasn't a combat engagement. Killing the Musclars wasn't my primary goal. Getting them to leave the village was a better option, but I wanted to be prepared in the unlikely event that killing them became necessary.

"It means we are going to threaten them the way they threatened us," I said. "Are they all as hostile as the ones I just fought?"

"Yes... I think... they're keeping everyone together near the communal fire."

"That's what I figured," I told her. "You stay close, but stay behind me."

"Thank you, Hugo," she said in a trembling voice. "They might have killed me."

"You don't have to thank me," I said.

"You put yourself at risk for me," she pointed out.

"I will always protect the people I care about," I told her. "Besides, it's sort of my fault you're in danger... again."

"No one blames you," she said.

"I find that hard to believe."

We slipped around the last hut. It was almost too dark to see. Down the beach, I could make out some villagers moving around the fire that had been kindled from the wood I brought. Every last branch and twig was useful on a world that didn't have abundant foliage. The smell of smoke was drifting through the air. I held the pistol with two hands, close to my chest, ready to point and shoot in the way I had been trained in the Space Marines. If the others saw us approaching, they didn't object. I doubted they could see my pistol and most wouldn't have known what it was if they had seen it.

"You're alive," said Loutar in a loud voice. "Eldora is alive!"

The others were making similar exclamations in their own languages. They gathered around the tall alien. It was a show of respect and care that I had rarely seen in my life. I had certainly never felt it before.

"Where are the Musclars?" I asked Loutar.

"They fled from the village," he said.

I looked to Eldora. "Stay together. I'll be back."

There was fear in her eyes. I didn't know if it was fear for herself, for the village or for me. In that moment, I chose to think it was for me, but there was no way of knowing for certain. As close as I felt to Eldora, and as much as I thought of her as a friend, she was still an alien. We had different emotions, different reactions and different motivations. Perhaps it was my training that drove me out into the darkness that night. Maybe it was because I felt threatened. I had learned early in my life that it was better to face a threat head-on. So, I chased the Musclars into the darkness, stopping only long enough between the huts of the village to let my eyes adjust to the darkness. Then I went hunting.

CHAPTER 18

SOME PEOPLE ARE scared of the dark. For me, it's always been an opportunity. The most fearsome predators hunt in the darkness and I thought of myself as one of them.

It didn't take long to catch sight of the fleeing Musclars. They were moving slowly, timidly down the mountainside away from Lake Tyconda. I went quickly to the edge of the plateau. The lake wasn't at the peak of the mountain, but about halfway up and snugged onto a plateau. The far side of the lake had a thin strip of sandy shoreline before butting up against the rocky cliff that rose several hundred feet straight up. A small stream flowed from the top and streaked down the rock, creating a scenic waterfall.

On the village side of the lake, there was a wide strip of grassy land, flat and rich with good soil. Beyond that, the mountainside angled down sharply, with dark boulders jutting out at odd angles. There were shrubs and a few trees, but it was mostly open ground. I could see the four remaining Musclars creeping down the hill. I could have easily shot them. My gun was natural in my hand, an extension of my own body. Firing it, even in the dark, was second nature. But I wasn't there to slaughter the aliens, even if that was what they deserved. Instead, I watched them until they were far enough down the mountainside that I was confident they wouldn't return.

Back at the village, the four Musclars I had fought were together. Two were injured, the other two just hurt. Their weapons, the spear and knife, had been collected. The rest of the village was watching them suspiciously, as if they were still a threat to contend with.

"Did you..." Eldora asked as I walked back into the village.

"No," I said. "They fled down the mountain. I let them go."

Loutar stepped forward and held out the spear. "This is not a tool I am comfortable with."

I took it and gave the diminutive alien a reassuring nod.

"What do we do now?" another alien asked. It was a strange being that looked more like an animal than a person. I only knew what it said thanks to the language app.

"That's a good question," Eldora replied in the common language. Perhaps if I had spent more time with the villagers, I would have learned it, but instead, I relied on my technology. It crossed my mind that one day I might not have it. I might get stuck with no way to communicate with the people who were part of my life.

"They can't stay," Loutar said. "We can't abide violence against our own."

"I suppose we can send them back to their village in the foothills," Eldora said.

"They'll just come back," I said as compassionately as I knew how.

"What?" asked Gomer, one of the aquatic aliens who had survived the Ashi attack.

"Why do you say that?" Eldora asked.

She sounded frightened and who could blame her? She had no way to defend herself. The idea of a continuing threat was certainly a terrifying thought.

"You said it yourself," I told her. "They claimed this village for their god. They won't give it up just because we gave them a few bruises."

"More than that, I would say," Loutar added.

"You were the one who fought them," Gomer said. "Perhaps if you leave, they will not come back here."

"How can you say that?" Eldora said. "Without Hugo, we would all be no better off than slaves to the Musclars."

"All they desired was adherence to their beliefs," said another alien who was relatively new to the village. Its name was Dobb, and it looked like a hippo or a manatee. Every feature on the alien was bulbous and round.

"Does anyone know what they believe?" I asked.

"It is complicated," Loutar said. "They have many strict laws of behavior. One must be Musclar to truly understand the way of their Master."

"So you would have been second-class citizens at best," I said. "My guess is they will return, probably with more of their kind from Mecula."

"And they will be armed," Eldora said. "They will be expecting a fight."

"So give them one," I said.

"That is not our way," Loutar said. "We are not warriors."

Dobb spoke in a honking voice. "We cannot fight."

"Perhaps, you are mistaken," Eldora said.

"Maybe, but I doubt it," I told her.

"Would you be willing to stay? Your presence here might give the Musclars pause."

"Or it might draw them back here," Dobb said.

"Conflict follows this one," Loutar said. "Forgive me, Hugo. I mean no offense."

"None taken," I said, although his words cut deep. Yet, they were no more offensive than my own thoughts about what my presence had brought to Libertine. The planet deserved peace and all I had brought was the sword. Perhaps it would have been better if I hadn't come. But then, I hadn't made the decision to bring the *Renegade* to the Libertine system. And if I had died in space, the Imperium and their slavers would have still come. There was a war in my own mind about who was to blame and what, if any, help I could give the people who lived on the Free World.

"We shall not decide tonight," Eldora said. "We must secure the Musclars and reconsider everything in the light of a new day."

"Well said," another of the aliens agreed.

"I'll secure the Musclars," I volunteered.

The others didn't like my martial tendencies but they didn't object to me taking charge of the prisoners. After using some restraints from my supplies in the *Condor,* I loaded my rifle, put on the light body armor, and stood watch all night long. In some ways, it felt good to be putting my old skills to use again. I was an average hunter at best. And while exploring had its appeal, there wasn't anything I really hoped to find on the planet. A year of solitude and reflection had proven that I was capable on my own, although it hadn't brought me any more peace than serving with a platoon of Space Marines had.

When the dawn came, I activated the MECH armor. It would be faster to fly where I needed to go, but I was no pilot.

Even flying the MECH was difficult for me. I made sure the mechanized armor suit was synced to the ground radar from the village and the orbital surveillance drones that looked down on the planet. I also engaged those that were keeping tabs on the known hyperspace portals in the system. If someone was going to show up and cause trouble, I wanted to know about it.

Next, I powered up the *Condor's* communication equipment. I needed the signal amplifier to boost the feed from the radar systems to the MECH, even in the valleys between the mountains.

"What are you planning to do?" Eldora asked me.

There was more than a trace a fear in her voice. I imagine she expected to hear me say that I was going to attack the Musclar village and wipe them all out. Most of the aliens on Libertine only had the Galactic Imperium as examples of what soldiers did. The Ashi were militant but also merciless. Any infraction of their laws was grounds for widespread annihilation.

"That depends on what you decide to do with the prisoners," I said.

"They will be banished from the village," Eldora said. "It is not our place to hand out judgement."

"They would have killed you," I said. "Don't you think that deserves more than exile?"

"I would choose peace, if that is in my power," she said. "So, what will you do, Hugo?"

"Make sure they're far enough from the village that I'm not worried that they'll come back any time soon," I said, raising a hand as my comlink chirped an alarm.

"What is that?" Eldora asked.

"Radar is picking something up," I said.

She looked up at the sky. It was a clear, beautiful day on Libertine. Storms did occasionally roll in, but they were usually short-lived and weak. There simply wasn't enough in the atmosphere to build into powerful tempests. And to her relief, there were no invading ships breaking through orbit.

"Where?" she asked.

"Not up," I said. "It's down. A group of people moving up the mountain."

We weren't far from the downhill side. We moved toward it, but didn't have to go far before we saw a group of thirty Musclars moving up our mountain. A larger group, maybe twice as big, was moving through the valley below.

"What are they doing?" Eldora asked.

Of course, she knew the answer to her own question; she was just having trouble believing it.

"Get the villagers," I told her. "Leave everything and flee."

"This is madness," she said.

Not every alien had human characteristics, but in that moment, big tears welled up in Eldora's eyes. She was not built for conflict and the stress of the moment was weighing so heavy on her she could barely stand up under it.

"There's no time for commentary," I told her. "All your people are in danger here. Let the Musclars have it. We'll rebuild somewhere else."

"What will you do?"

"Protect this equipment," I told her. "And the village, if I can. But that might mean people get hurt, Eldora. I can live with that. What I can't live with is letting you get hurt."

"Why do you care?"

"You are my friend," I said. "I don't have many of those. Besides, this is what I do. I've been trained in combat. I have the means to turn this enemy back. It seems like that's what I should do."

Eldora nodded, reaching out with one long, delicate hand. I took hers,and she gave mine a reassuring squeeze.

"Be careful, Hugo," she said. "And thank you. I am glad we are friends."

The Musclars were halfway up the hillside. We both knew there was no time to waste. She hurried back to the village and I suited up in the MECH and went to war.

CHAPTER 19

THE MECH WAS twelve feet tall and heavily armored. It should have thumped as it walked, each metal foot pounding the ground. Instead, it was quiet, the hydraulics and struts absorbing the weight above. Controlling the war suit was a bit like floating. There were no jarring motions for the pilot. It had been designed for a smaller man to control. My shoulders and chest pressed against the padded safety bumpers, but even then, it wasn't uncomfortable.

The MECH also had brilliant stability. Unlike a man, the MECH had gripping toes and a heel spike, which, when extended, could give the MECH purchase on a very steep incline. I moved straight out to the edge of the plateau and looked down the steep hillside to the group of aliens climbing up.

The Musclars were an interesting species. They had the features of goats and birds, a sort of mashup that was unique. They wore baggy clothing but no shoes. Their feet were like a goat's hoofs and gave them agility on the steep incline. They moved uphill almost effortlessly. Many of the invading aliens had spears, which were absolutely useless against me in the MECH. Not only did it have thick plate armor, but I and all of the suit's internal systems were covered with a puncture-resistant, Kevlar median layer and an insulated base that could absorb both kinetic energy and heat discharge. That's not to say that it was invincible, yet the Musclars with their primitive weapons were not a threat to me. The equipment I was protecting, along with the huts on the shoreline and the villagers who occupied them, was a different matter. If I didn't stop the assault, the Musclars could cause irreparable harm.

"Activate the public address system," I said. Much of the MECH's systems and apps were voice-controlled. "Musclar language translation."

An icon appeared on my HUD. The Heads Up Display not only showed me a three hundred and sixty degree view from the MECH's external cameras, but also the suit's computer controls and readouts.

"Targeting app," I said.

The MECH had a variety of weapons that appeared on a list to my right. The computer control tracked my eye movement— each of the weapons lit up as I looked at them. I could engage the machine gun built into the MECH's right forearm and simply mow them down, but I had to consider not only the threat the aliens presented, but how my actions in dealing with them would affect the people of the village I was protecting. If I simply killed the Musclars, it would alienate me from Eldora and her community. They were my only social contacts on the planet. I needed to deal with things in a way they would see as acceptable, not just what was most expedient.

On the HUD, the targeting app showed the enemy at less than a hundred yards from my position.

"Engage PA," I said. "Warning. Warning. I am a military combat platform. You are approaching the village of Lake Tyconda. Turn back. This land and community are under my protection. I repeat, turn back! This land and community are under my protection."

The Musclars hesitated for a moment. I'm sure the MECH was an intimidating sight standing above them. They had to know that I had taken down the slave ship that brought them to Libertine. And yet, they began to chant some kind of litany in their native tongue.

Some people have to learn the hard way. I know, I'm usually one of them. The Musclars seemed to be as well.

"Activate machine gun," I ordered the suit.

A revolving, multibarreled machine gun extended from the MECH's right forearm and spun into action. It was similar to the guns on an attack ship. We had the most ammunition for the machine gun, so while I didn't intend to shoot the approaching aliens, I felt like it was the right weapon to scare them off with. I lowered the gun and fired three quick bursts. The bullets were simple, soft metal alloy slugs. They pounded into the soil on the hillside, kicking up small clods of dirt, grass, and rock.

"This is your last warning," I said. The MECH's computer translated my words into the Musclar language and sent it booming from hidden speakers built into the suit. The sound rolled down the hill like peals of thunder and echoed from across the wide valley. "Do not continue up this mountain or I will open fire on you."

One of the aliens, perhaps their leader, rose up with his spear. He cried out in a loud voice and threw his weapon. It was a good throw, with some power behind it. The spear flew straight toward me, but merely banged against the armored plates and bounced off. The primitive weapon bounced back down the hillside.

"Conflict is futile and will result in either injury or death," I warned them. "Do not continue up the hillside. This land and community are under my protection."

Some of the Musclars saw reason and stopped climbing. They looked unsure of what to do. But the majority of the group continued upward. I didn't want to cause major damage to the aliens, so I selected a different weapon from the MECH's arsenal.

"Lasers," I said. "Lowest possible setting."

The weapons on the MECH weren't designed for non-lethal confrontations. It wasn't a crowd control device, but a combat platform. Small lasers popped out of the sides of the MECH's forearms. I took aim with my right arm and fired a series of blasts. Most of the shots missed. I was aiming at where the Musclar hooves met the ground, but it was a very small target. Aiming too high risked hitting the aliens in a vital area. Four of them were hit with my initial volley. The lasers ripped through their hooves or pasterns. They fell, wailing in pain. Three of them toppled down the hill and crashed into the climbers behind them.

I fired again, expecting the aliens to see the futility of their attack. But they weren't humans. They didn't think the way I did. Something drove the Musclars forward. With a shout of defiance, they charged. I could have continued shooting. Already more than a third of their number was out of the fight, but I didn't relish slaughtering the defenseless aliens. So, I waited. More spears were thrown. None caused damage. I doubted the spear points even scratched the camouflage paint on the MECH.

The first Musclar to reach me was their leader. He had snatched up his spear as he climbed and thrust it hard at me.

The wooden staff snapped in two under the pressure of the strike. The point pounded against a piece of armor on the MECH's thigh, but didn't penetrate or cause any damage. I curled the hand of the MECH into a fist and punched the alien leader. He raised his hands to try and protect his face, but the metal fist broke one forearm and smashed against his head, sending the Musclar leader down the hill. He fell onto his back, slid, then flipped, crashed, rolled and took out two more of the aliens.

In total, eight of the Musclars reached the top of the hill. Three attacked me. I grabbed one's spear, turned it so that the butt of the weapon was facing the aliens, and swatted them with it. They fell quickly, stunned by the blows from the wooden staff.

Five more of the aliens tried to run past me. There was no more time for mercy.

"Target the enemy," I ordered.

Normally, I preferred aiming my weapons. Even those with computer targeting built in weren't as accurate or efficient as a human. But I didn't have time to fight the three aliens attacking me and track down the others. I lifted the MECH's left arm and let the laser go to work. A series of flashes were released, and the aliens were cut down. They died, their wounds smoking from the laser blasts.

I looked around, expecting a second wave of attacks, yet there was none. The survivors were crawling back. Over half were wounded or injured when someone crashed into them. The others were helping those with serious needs to get back down. I didn't expect the group to be a problem again that day. They might never give up the village, but they wouldn't try a direct attack again, any time soon.

In the MECH, I gathered the bodies and laid them in a pile.

I also turned over the Musclars who tried to attack me the day before to those who survived the attack with only minor injuries. Together, they began the long trek back down the mountain.

It was midday before the villagers returned. Their homes and belongings were intact. I wish I could say that was enough for them to accept what I had done to protect them, but the bodies of the slain were too stark a reminder of who I really was.

"They attacked me," I pointed out. "I warned them. I begged them to turn back."

"It is hard to share the cup with one who has spilled so much blood," Loutar said sadly.

"If it were solely up to us, you would always have a place here, Hugo," Eldora said. "But I cannot force the others to accept you. They would leave us and they have nowhere else to go."

I wanted to point out that I had nowhere else to go.

"The Musclars will come back," I told her. "You must be vigilant."

But the warning fell on deaf ears. They simply couldn't conceive of someone who was defeated in a fight, coming back for more. They weren't just adverse to violence; it simply wasn't something they could imagine. They needed protection, although they feared it. If I was going to watch over them, it would have to be from a distance.

I had to use the MECH to move my belongings and the gear from the *Condor*. I would have preferred to move the ship, and it did have a very sophisticated autopiloting program. But the mountains were not the type of terrain to try and land a space-ship in for the very first time. So, I took the solar charging equipment and wind turbines, but left the shuttle.

"At the very least," I told Eldora, "if the Musclars come back, you can hide in the shuttle. There's room for the entire village now that I've removed my gear."

"I hope that we shall never need it," she said.

"I hope so too," I told her.

"Will I see you again, Hugo?"

"Maybe. They say time heals all wounds."

"But you are not wounded," she said.

I knew that wasn't true. I was losing my home. It wasn't the only place that I had lived on Libertine, although the village by the lake was what I considered to be home. And the villagers were the only friends I had. We weren't close and I hadn't been liked by all of them, but I was less liked in other places. In that moment, I could feel a deep wound reopening. It wasn't just the rejection from the villagers but the rejection I had experienced all my life.

"It's just an expression," I told her. "It means that in time, people get past their differences. Maybe someday, I'll be welcome here again."

She nodded. I thought of how unwelcome Rip and I had been when we first arrived there. But Eldora had changed her mind about us. Especially after we had saved her life shortly after the Ashi fighters had destroyed the lakeshore community and murdered most of the villagers. If she had changed, maybe the others could, too. But I also knew that the Musclars wouldn't give up trying to pin them under their religious fanaticism. That was the way of things and people. There were more Musclars than anyone else and unless the others banded together and presented a united front, the Musclars would seize control.

I was proven right a few days later. I was high up on one of the mountains that had a cavern. The outer part of the cavern was wide and surprisingly cool. It remained dry even during the occasional rainstorm, which made it ideal to store the gear I had taken from the Condor. It also had a spectacular view of the surrounding country. I could just make out the edge of the Lake

Tyconda plateau, as well as the foothills and grassy plains. From the edge of the cavern, I could run the radar. From above it, I had access to good, direct sunlight for most of the day. There was a spring nearby and easy access from below, making it an ideal camp. It was from there that I saw the ragtag refugees from Solace.

They were shuffling through the valley below my camp. I used the scope on one of my rifles to make them out. Premier Uggar was easy to recognize. Gathering what little food I had stored up, I went down to check on them. I found eighteen aliens, battered, bruised and weary. They had been banished from their colony high in the mountains.

"The Musclars attacked us," Uggar said with disbelief. "They had weapons."

He said it as if it were unimaginable that someone would create instruments of war. I, of course, had a small arsenal of weapons in the cave on the mountainside.

"I'm sorry to hear that. What did they want?" I asked.

"Besides possession of our homes?" Uggar asked. "They were forcing their religious laws on us. Anyone who refused was either exiled or..."

"Killed?" I asked.

Uggar nodded. He was completely alien, with a body like a slug, and eyes on stalks over his gaping, toothless mouth. And yet, his response to the question was universal.

"How many of you did they murder?"

"Eight. Twelve others were taken as slaves. Everything about them is repugnant. Why come to a free world only to make slaves of the inhabitants?"

I could have reminded him that coming to Libertine wasn't their choice, but I didn't want him thinking about my own role in their presence on the Free World.

"Have you considered fighting back?" I asked.

"How? Why? We would be massacred. Is that what all violent races long for, slaughter and death?"

"No," I told him. "I want peace. But there are times in a man's life when he needs to stand up for what is right. And to fight, especially for those who cannot fight for themselves."

That was a turning point for me. For the first time in my life, I felt like I had a purpose. On Libertine, there were people from across the galaxy. They were all different, but what they had in common was their inability to fight for themselves. Perhaps I was there to fight for them.

I was not a religious person. Even as a Marine in combat operations, seeing people die around me, facing death myself, I had never felt drawn to God. But I had felt that there was something larger than me, larger than even the entire human race. Evil was certainly real. I had seen it manifested in a hundred different ways: as a child abused by his parents, in the care of the state where both staff and other children preyed on the weak, as a Marine sent into violent situations where cult leaders or criminals did whatever they wanted to whoever they could reach, it was widespread and real. And if evil existed, then so must good. I had just never felt a connection to that invisible presence that seemed always to shadow me, but was never revealed fully. But as I thought about what I could do on Libertine and how my skills were useful, I felt a connection. It was like a light coming on in my mind. Suddenly, I felt as though I had been uniquely created, my life up to that moment molded by both my talents and by the situations I had experienced. There was a purpose to it all ... and a purpose for me. I didn't fall on my knees in worship, but I did acknowledge that perhaps there was more to life than I understood. That I could turn to the one who had created me with an openness that I had never experienced before.

"Where are you going?" I asked Uggar

"We must find a new place of refuge," the alien said in his screeching language. "A place where the Musclars will not harm us."

"They will go to all the colonies," I said. "They won't stop until everyone is under their ideal of law."

Uggar and those around him, as alien as they were to me, looked frightened. I understood that they had every right to be afraid. They had experienced violence, perhaps many times in their lives. They had fled to a world that offered little but was free of the violence they feared. But eventually, even that had been snatched away. Their homes, the lives they had worked to build in the colonies on Libertine, were being taken from them - and that wasn't right.

"They tried to take Lake Tyconda," I said. "But I was there, and they failed. You can rest there until you decide what to do next."

"Will you show us the way?" Uggar asked.

"Yes, I will. It isn't far, but it is a steep climb. Rest for now."

"Here?" Uggar asked.

"Yes," I told him. We are safe here, I promise you that."

"And you will ... protect us?" His voice trembled with fear.

"That's what I was sent here to do," I said. "I won't let anyone hurt you now."

CHAPTER 20

THERE WERE no Casians in the group of refugees. I knew there were some in Solace that my former platoon had trained on the *Renegade* to fight. We even built special harnesses and guns that could be strapped onto their wide backs and controlled with battle helmets that were custom-made to fit onto their large, elephantine heads. The Casians had been like the other races on Libertine, non-militant and peace-loving. Yet, they had seen what was possible when just a few humans had defended their world from the Ashi. It had sparked a desire to fight back.

What had happened to them on Libertine was anyone's guess. I knew that in the northern habitable zone, they had been assigned to various colonies and given guard duties against the sand vipers, which were big, serpentine creatures that preyed on the livestock that the *Renegade* had delivered to the people of Libertine. I had only been north once since getting stranded on Libertine and then only to deliver groups of refugees to join the colonies there. I had, however, been in communication with the northern colonies. There were no reports of the Musclars there trying to take control and spread their religious law, but I guessed it was only a matter of time.

What I needed was a Casian with the technical skills to pilot the *Condor*. If I was going to protect the helpless, it couldn't be by hiding them in the hopes that the Musclars never found them. I couldn't simply protect one community or they would eventually find a weakness and exploit it against me. That meant taking the fight to the Musclars and there was no doubt they were spreading their religious law across the continent. They had murdered or enslaved anyone who resisted, which meant there were people in the other colonies besides Lake Tyconda that needed my help. I could not, and would not, tolerate slavery when it was in my power to set those helpless individuals free.

But even with my weapons, the MECH armor, and my combat skills, I still needed help. On the Renegade, most of the Casian volunteers had been drone operators. They looked like six-legged elephants, but they had a knack for technology and learned to fly combat drones in space and in gravity, such as the atmosphere of a planet. If one of the Casians could learn to pilot the *Condor,* we could travel between the colonies much faster and thwart the plans of the Musclars. All I needed to do was find and free a willing candidate. For all I knew, the Casians had joined the Musclars, which would mean a much more difficult task in freeing the colonies.

After letting the group from Solace rest overnight, I led them up the mountain to Lake Tyconda. It was not an easy journey and some of the refugees were injured. I suited up and carried a few of them in the MECH armor, which had no trouble lifting them and navigating up the narrow trails with the additional weight.

Eldora and Loutar met us on the plateau. They didn't look happy, and I wasn't sure if it was because of me or because of the people from Solace. I climbed out of the MECH and joined the group who were discussing the events at the primary colony.

"What has happened?" Eldora asked.

"We were attacked," Uggar proclaimed, his voice loud and distressed. "Thrown out of our homes and banished from our own colony."

"And we were the lucky ones," another member of the motley band of refugees said.

"Some were murdered," said an injured female alien with red skin.

"Others were kept as slaves," Uggar continued. "Anyone who refused to accept their arcane beliefs and primitive laws was attacked."

Eldora looked at me with fear in her big eyes. I stayed silent. My job had been to guide the group. What they did, and how the villagers of the lakeside community responded to them, was not my business. I was not a member of either group, and while that pained me somewhat, I thought in that moment that it was probably for the best.

"We will lend you aid, of course," Loutar said.

"How is it that you were not attacked?" Uggar asked.

"We were," Eldora said. "But Hugo stopped them."

That caused the entire group, including Loutar, to stop and think. They had rejected me because of my willingness to fight. But faced with the reality of what happened at Solace, they couldn't help but think of me in a different light. And I took advantage of the moment to lay out my plan.

"I'm going to Solace," I said. "I will not let slavery take root on Libertine. I need help from one of the Casians."

"One was slain," Uggar said. "The other two have been enslaved."

"Then they won't object to my freeing them."

"You plan to fight the Musclars?" Loutar asked.

"I doubt they will give up without a fight," I said. "It's not my intention to harm anyone, but slavery is an evil that must be stamped out."

"Slavery is a fact of life across the galaxy," one of the other refugees said.

"But it was never supposed to be accepted here," Uggar said. "On the Free Worlds, no species can be owned as property."

"A lot has changed," Loutar said. "Slavers have discovered this world."

"And the Imperium," another refugee said.

"We have not seen them in a year," Eldora said. "This is still a free planet. I am not a warrior, but I support what Hugo is trying to do."

"It might be better if he just stays here," Loutar said. "Let the Musclars have Solace."

"How can you say that?" Uggar suggested. "You would not feel that way if Tyconda had fallen and you had lost everything you cared about in this world."

I held up a hand. "I know how groups like the Musclars think. They won't be satisfied with just Solace. They'll target every colony, including Lake Tyconda. They want everyone to believe what they believe. Those of us who refuse will be eliminated or enslaved."

"You speak as though you have experience with this kind of thing," Eldora said.

"Not personally, although in the history of my people, we faced many groups like the Musclars. They claim that they speak for God, but in reality, they are only looking to enrich themselves. Actions speak louder than words."

"If you attack the Musclars in Solace and fail, they will turn their wrath back on us," Loutar said.

"I can't guarantee you I'll be successful in freeing the primary colony or the people held in bondage there," I told him. "But I can guarantee that the Musclars aren't through with Lake Tyconda. I bought us some time but they will return. And if they're smart, they'll find a way to strike when I can't help you."

"Like when you're off fighting somewhere else," Eldora said.

"That's right. It's why we need to work together," I told her.

"We aren't fighters," Uggar said. "Though I regret that now more than ever."

"I don't need fighters," I said. "But I need communication and transportation. Which is why I need the Casians at Solace. They can learn to pilot the shuttle."

Eldora turned and looked at the *Condor*. She nodded, understanding what I was driving at.

"You can outmaneuver them," she said. "And if they come back here while you're gone, you can return in haste."

"That's right," I said, then turned to Uggar. "I could also use some intelligence."

"You seem smart enough to me," Uggar said, seriously.

"No, I mean, I need information about the colony," I said. "I need to know where the enemy will be, where they could go, what types of weapons they could use against me. I need to know where the Casians are being kept and what other people have been enslaved."

"You should know who has joined the Musclars, too," Loutar pointed out.

"That's right," I agreed.

"If you can free the slaves, will you leave the Musclars in peace?" another of the refugees asked.

"I suppose that depends on what you want. It's your colony, after all. If you're fine leaving it with them, then I won't argue or fight to run them off."

Uggar sagged. "They have taken our homes, our food, the livestock, everything."

"I cannot agree with violence," the refugee named Leks said. She was a small, three-legged alien with colorful fans that spread wide on either side of her neck. Her body was thick, the legs short; her arms were like flippers. "We had so much and they had so little."

"That doesn't justify what they did," Uggar said. "They slaughtered innocent people."

"Are we any better if we do the same to them?"

I listened to them discuss the best course of action. My own feelings were strong on the matter but I pushed them down. If the refugees didn't want me to kill, I wouldn't. At least, I wouldn't seek to kill. But I also knew the Musclars wouldn't give up what they had taken without a fight. Even if they abandoned Solace, it would only be to give them time to regroup and come after everything again. They would never be satisfied and they certainly had no qualms about killing. It would be a weakness on our part to try and deal with them in a non-lethal fashion, yet I didn't see that we had any other choice.

"I suggest we give them the chance to surrender," Uggar said. "If they will agree to leave Solace, we will not hinder them. But if they insist on staying, we cannot guarantee their safety."

"Not if you go in with weapons," Loutar said. "But they have weapons. They have stolen lives and caused much pain. I once thought as you do, Leks, but now I must argue that the Musclars have chosen a life of violence. They cannot complain when it is visited back upon them."

Soon, the decision was made that Uggar should return to Solace with me. He would answer my questions, then go to the Musclars and give them the chance to leave the village. If they would go peacefully, they would be allowed to take up to half the livestock and food stores. However, the personal belongings of the residents and any people they had forced to be their slaves must be returned. I would have preferred to strike them when they least expected it. Giving them the chance to surrender, while noble, would ruin the element of surprise. But if they hoped to stop me with knives and spears, I wasn't worried about their resistance. The hardest thing would be stopping short of slaughtering the aliens, yet I had done it before. At least for now, we would have to put them on their heels. When they regrouped, I was certain they would attempt to seize control again. I could think of countless groups throughout history that had fought and re-fought for the same ground, time and again. It was a fact of war, if not of life, that those who sought to control others would never stop. Eventually, the time for fighting would come and then it would be bloody.

CHAPTER 21

I USED one of the woven hammocks that Loutar made and created a sling for Uggar. The sluggish alien didn't have the anatomy to hold onto the MECH. He certainly couldn't keep pace. I could have simply held him, but the metal armor would have been uncomfortable at best and more likely would have caused the alien harm.

Not that I cared overmuch about Uggar. He had been a rude, difficult colony leader. When Rip and I tried to help them set up their communications gear, our efforts had been met with resistance. Nor had Uggar done the right thing with the cattle and food that were given to them from the *Renegade*. Those supplies had been sent down to the planet in hopes of helping the local population transition from merely surviving to thriving. Yet, Uggar and his leadership council had kept all the supplies for themselves, sharing none with the other colonies. Or, at least, hoarding them until the other colonies came bowing and scraping to beg for assistance.

My interactions with him in the year I had been on Libertine were limited. I did my best to avoid Solace. No one likes to go where they aren't wanted and Uggar had made it clear that I was not wanted in his village. Nor were the Musclar refugees. Rip and I had brought a few to the mountaintop community of Solace, but I had little doubt they were mistreated and marginalized. Still, they had wanted to stay and I hadn't realized then that there was a purpose to their presence in every colony on the planet. In that regard, we had both been wrong. And the snailish alien seemed like a changed person since getting banished from Solace. I did my best not to hold the past against him.

With Uggar in the sling that was attached to the MECH's left arm, we made good time back to my base of operations in the cavern on the mountainside. There, I gathered weapons and supplies, taking the time to completely recharge the MECH's power bank.

"This is your home?" Uggar asked as he slowly scooted his thick body around the cavern.

"For now," I said. "I spend most of my time out hunting or foraging."

"You are a strange species," Uggar remarked.

"Is that so?"

"It is. What do you hope to find out in the wild places all alone?"

"Resources, I suppose. Food, building materials, anything that might make life a little better."

"Why not live in a colony?"

"I prefer being on my own."

"And your companion? Did you run him off or did he leave on his own?"

I didn't really want to talk about Rip. He was my friend,

although his choice to leave had been hard to accept. Not that I blamed him exactly, but I couldn't honestly say I was happy to be left on Libertine all alone. And, of course, he owed me nothing. In fact, I owed him my life. But, it still stung to think that he chose a woman he barely knew over me. It shouldn't have been surprising. I was not the kind of person who made friends easily. Yet, I felt that our time together on Libertine had bonded us together.

"He took the slave ship and left," I said. "I thought you knew that."

"Ah, I think I did hear something of that sort. I'm afraid I've been much too self-centered to have cared what happened to you."

That brought me up short. I turned around and looked at Uggar. The alien had no discernible body language. He stood nearby, still looking at the cavern with the big eyes that were attached to his head via stalks that seemed to sway and move all the time. Other than those eyes, his only other facial feature was a huge mouth. I couldn't tell if he was being sincere. Even his words were hard to judge, given that they had to pass through the language device for me to understand what he was saying.

"And that's changed?" I asked.

"I have seen the error of my ways," he replied. "In the past, Solace was the center of the various colonies in this hemisphere. But over time, we found less and less to talk about. Had I been more concerned about others, I might have been warned about the Musclars. Instead, we were caught completely by surprise with their attack."

"They attacked Solace?"

"They invaded us. There were more than fifty of them and most were armed. We were completely unprepared for it. They gathered our citizens and demanded that their people be put in charge. It was outrageous, but what could we do? And then they insisted that we accept their religion. Those of us who didn't were punished."

"I'm sorry that happened," I told him. "I guess I've been petty about our differences as well. I should have known the Musclars were going to occupy Solace and come to warn you."

"You are helping us now," Uggar said. "Which is more than I have the right to ask of you. Know that it will not go unrewarded."

I wasn't seeking a reward but it did feel good to know that my help wasn't being overlooked either. We gathered what we needed, activated the MECH and continued on toward Solace.

The mountains that formed the center of the southern polar region were not stark, craggy peaks. They were gently sloping in many places, with plateaus and wide ridges. While there wasn't an abundance of trees, the hillsides were green with grass and dotted with shrubs. Ribbons of flowing water meandered down from the high peaks. The temperatures were cooler at the higher elevations.

Solace was the first and primary colony in the southern hemisphere. When Libertine was first discovered, it was kept a secret from the Galactic Imperium. The first colonists were engineers and terraforming workers that set up dozens of refineries that utilized the planet's vast stores of fossil fuel to pump carbon dioxide into the atmosphere. The process on a large world like Libertine was slow, but the planet already had a thin ozone layer and some liquid water on the surface.

Libertine was a hot world, just a little too close to the system star. A thicker atmosphere would deflect much of the solar radiation and allow for a more temperate global temperature. The added carbon dioxide in the air was also necessary to foster the growth of flora, which in turn released oxygen into the air. It was a beneficial cycle that would, over time, make more and more of the planet habitable for a large variety of lifeforms.

But the upkeep on the refineries was dangerous and difficult. Added to that was the infrequent traffic from outside the system. Keeping the Free Worlds secret limited access to the things that were needed to keep the terraforming situation from succeeding, including supplies for repairs and fresh workers. Over time, as the number of available and willing workers dwindled, more and more of the terraforming stations had fallen into disrepair, which stalled the growth of the habitable land. Most of the planet was still a hot desert, covered in seas of sand.

As we climbed our way up the winding trails that led to Solace, I could see out past the foothills and grasslands to the great, gray desert beyond. It was beautiful and foreboding, as if the planet was a scale that tipped back and forth. One minute, the habitable land grew; the next, it retracted. One couldn't help but realize that it wouldn't take much for the climate to change and destroy every living thing on the planet.

"Are you happy living here?" I asked. "Do you ever think about going somewhere else?"

"I was one of the first colonists," Uggar said. "I was very young when I was brought to this world. I cannot imagine living in another place."

"What world are you from?"

"Larkis IV is where my kind originated. We spread among several planets before being hunted almost to extinction by the Ashi."

"They hunted you?" I asked, not understanding the appeal. Uggar wasn't fast or stealthy. He wasn't dangerous, that I could tell at any rate. And then suddenly it dawned on me. "They ate your kind?"

"We are considered a delicacy," Uggar said. "Although it is not the compliment you might think."

I didn't think it was a compliment at all. Humans were at the top of the food chain on Earth. And the very idea of being slaughtered for food seemed abhorrent to me.

"I'm sorry," I told him.

"For what?"

"For what happened to your people," I confessed. Not that I was to blame, but I still felt bad about it. "That's terrible."

"I am one of the lucky ones. One day, I will lay a clutch of eggs that will increase my kind in the galaxy."

That stirred up many questions, but I kept them to myself. I didn't think that talking to Uggar about how his kind reproduced was polite conversation. And I certainly didn't want him to start grilling me about how humans mated.

We reached the ridge where Solace was located late in the afternoon. There were trees, but not many. Certainly not enough to approach the village without being seen. So, we waited until the sun went down, then set out again through the darkness. The MECH had excellent low-light amplification. The sky was clear overhead and thousands of stars shone bright. It was more than enough ambient light to give me a good view.

"This is far enough," Uggar said.

I had the MECH in stealth mode. It moved slower, but dampened the sound of its servos so that it was nearly silent. We were less than a hundred feet from the edge of the colony, which was laid out in straight lines with a wide town square in the center. There were clear lines of sight straight through the colony. I could see that a bonfire was burning in the town square, which was an extravagant use of combustible materials. The villagers of Lake Tyconda would not have approved.

"You sure?" I asked Uggar as I set his sling down.

The snail-shaped alien wiggled forward. "This is my colony, my responsibility," he said bravely. "If I can't bring them around with reason, I'll leave it to you to do the convincing."

I couldn't smell the meat roasting on the huge fire, but my suit picked up the scent and alerted me. With the MECH's digital zoom, I could focus on the aliens in the center of the town. Some were dancing in celebration, others were huddled together looking fearful.

"They are feasting," I said.

"That's not surprising," Uggar said. "They must have torn down a structure to build a fire that big."

I couldn't help but wonder what they had to celebrate. Was it simply the abundance of food? Or their victory in taking the primary colony? Time would tell. I lowered the MECH into a squatting position and waited. The armored suit had a variety of features for reconnaissance and surveillance. I activated the long-range microphone, which utilized a parabolic dish to help pick up and amplify sound waves. It was built into the right shoulder of the MECH's long arms. The unit unfolded quietly as Uggar advanced through the empty street toward the center of the colony.

The surveillance equipment immediately picked up a chanting song being sung by the Musclars. To me, it sounded strangely like birds singing just before dawn. The language app translated the alien voices. They were declaring that their god had given them victory over every enemy. I was going to have to dissuade them from that notion.

Uggar reached the square undetected. I felt a wave of sympathy for the strange alien. He had been full of pride and avarice when we first met. I thought he was a self-important bureaucrat. But we had gotten to know one another better on our journey into the mountains. I still didn't know a lot about Uggar, but his concern for Solace and the people who called it home was real.

"Please, please," he shouted. "I must have everyone's attention."

One of the Musclars moved quickly toward him, followed by a group with spears.

"You were warned not to come back here, Uggar."

"This is my home," the banished Premier declared. "It is not your home."

"It belongs to god now, and I suppose we can find a more permanent way to deal with you."

The Musclars with weapons moved toward Uggar.

"Wait, I am here to warn you," Uggar shouted. The other Musclars, dozens of them, were moving closer to hear what he was saying. I could see some of the townspeople moving closer, too. "You must return Solace to us and go back to your own village," Uggar said. "We have been remiss in our duties to help you. So we will share the livestock with you, but you must return all property to its rightful owners and make restitution for those you killed. We can have peace and cooperation. There is no need for violence."

"Our god gives us strength," the leader of the Musclars said, "so we can take from infidels and heathen. Everything here is now consecrated to the Bearer of Souls. We have made sacrifices to him here. Solace is forever ours and you have trespassed on sacred ground. Take him!"

"You don't understand," Uggar said. "If you won't cooperate, others will come and force you out."

They mob grabbed Uggar. There was no doubt in my mind that he was about to be the next sacrifice to the Musclar god. They began to drag him toward their bonfire. The townspeople cried in distress, while the Musclars shouted for Uggar's death. I stood up in the MECH. The armor was taller than most of the structures in the colony, which were made of prefabricated panels that locked together. They were strong and flexible, built to withstand storms and even earthquakes, but not an attack. I moved swiftly through the darkness. Diplomacy had failed and it was time for a show of force.

CHAPTER 22

"ACTIVATE FLAME THROWER," I ordered.

The MECH's voice controls caused a small nozzle to extend from the top of its metal hand. A small flame flickered to life in front of the nozzle. I had made a promise to refugees from Solace and the villagers of Lake Tyconda that I wouldn't kill the Musclars indiscriminately. Instead, I needed to reveal myself in a way that conveyed my martial prowess and convinced them that fighting me was a losing proposition. Injuring the aliens and damaging the colony was also to be avoided. That didn't leave me many options, but I had to do something.

"Extend all blades and spikes."

I had a long, double-edged blade that was spring-loaded into the left forearm of the MECH, which I had used to good effect in close-quarter fighting with the Ashi. But the suit also had defensive blades and spikes that could extend from sections between plates of armor that would make getting close to the MECH a dangerous prospect. Razor-sharp metal extended from the elbows and shoulders of the armor. Pointed spikes covered the legs of the fighting platform, along the back, too.

"Engage public address system," I ordered. "Full volume. Activate the warning siren."

A wailing sound pumped from the MECH's speakers. The siren rose and fell in pitch. The sudden, unexpected auditory assault caused everyone to react. The Musclars leading Uggar toward the bonfire hesitated, ducking as if an attack were imminent. Several of the townspeople fled in abject terror. I added to the siren by sending a jet of fire straight up into the air. I was still thirty feet from the edge of the square, but suddenly illuminated by the jet of flame.

"Release Uggar and throw down your weapons!" I ordered; the translation of my words screeching from the MECH's public address system.

"There is the abomination!" the leader of the Musclars shouted. "Attack!"

It seemed like a foolhardy decision. I knew the aliens had no chance of stopping me with their crude spears. Just getting close enough to use them would be dangerous with my defensive systems engaged. But then, from somewhere beyond the town square, guns blazed. I'll admit I was caught completely off guard. Bullets from belt-fed machine guns filled the air. Every fifth round was a tracer. The bullet was filled with glowing phosphorus so that the shooters could hone their aim. I saw the barrage, much of it too high or wide to hit me. And for a split second, I hesitated. That hesitation was costly. Bullets smashed into the MECH's armor and ricocheted. Alarms went off, and flashing lights meant to warn me of danger lit up the HUD. Not that I needed to be warned. I spun around and dove behind a home. But the gunners were relentless. Bullets ripped through the structure.

"Stealth mode," I ordered.

The spikes and blades retracted, as did the flame thrower. I had to move quickly as the home I had hidden behind collapsed. Years of combat training kicked in. I started crawling forward on the MECH's knees and elbows. It was a difficult maneuver, and debris from the barrage of weapons was raining down around me. It was dark, my vision dimmed by the brightness of the bonfire. But I knew I couldn't stay where I was. The shooters weren't slowing down. Their relentless fire had followed me behind another building, which was being blown apart.

Rolling onto the MECH's knees, I engaged the jet pack. The armored platform shot into the air like a rocket. I was pressed down hard into my seat by the gravitational force. For a few seconds, I couldn't breathe, and then the upward progress slowed. I was well above the colony. To my left and right, the ridge fell away. It would have been simple to angle into one of those two directions and flee to safety. But I wasn't the type to run away from a fight.

"Flares," I said, launching a burning red device that shot upward and then filled the ridge with light.

I was falling by that point, but activated the boosters in the MECH's hands and feet to slow my descent. The gunners, there were four of them, were using the weapons designed for the Casians. Two were mounted on the alien pachyderms that were being pushed out into the streets. Even from several hundred feet up, I could see that the Casians were being forced against their will. The other two gunners were using weapons on stands. They were positioned on top of two different structures. They were trying to maneuver the weapons into a posture that would bring them to bear, but the twin rotating barrels of the machine cannons weren't designed to shoot straight up.

"Activate laser blaster," I said, relying on the voice controls.

There was a lot going on. Flying, or controlling my fall, wasn't easy. It took almost all my concentration to stay upright and focused. One wrong move and I could go tumbling down with no time to pull out of the fall. And that didn't account for the various system warnings flashing on the HUD. The MECH was made to withstand enemy fire, but I hadn't escaped unscathed. Several of the defensive blades and spikes had been broken off. Some couldn't retract at all. The flamethrower fuel line was compromised. The MECH was slowly filling with flammable gas, which, beyond the obvious danger, would soon suffocate me if I didn't open the armor up.

"Engage targeting assist."

It would have been easy to simply blast away at the gunners, but I was trying to stay true to my word. I set the computer to target the cannons, not the shooters operating them. The MECH had descended to less than a hundred feet above one of the guns. The other was yanking his weapon around to get a shot. I beat him to the punch. My laser was probably the least powerful weapon on the MECH, but it hit the firing block on one of the cannons, melting the metal and setting off the bullet in the chamber. Only the bullet couldn't shoot out of the compromised barrel, and instead blew apart. Bits of metal shot out in all directions, ripping into the gunner's flesh.

At fifty feet, I turned my laser straight down, but the Gunner below me was smart to realize the danger he was in. He leaped off the top of the building and landed gracefully before racing away into the shadows between the buildings.

My landing wasn't so graceful. In fact, I went right through the roof and into the structure with a crash. There were still enemies to deal with, but my head was starting to feel light. I was off balance and my thinking felt sluggish. So, with the MECH surrounded by debris from the crash, I hit the eject button. The suit opened up, and I climbed out. The air on top of the mountain was thinner than that in the MECH, and by the time I got out of the armor, I was breathing heavy.

The MECH was still powered up. I closed the armor and pressed a button that opened a narrow compartment on the back of the MECH's left thigh. Inside was my rifle. Most Marine Commandos preferred their own weapons rather than the standard-issue Marine rifle. I had used many types of guns throughout my career, but for this mission, I had chosen a rifle that would fit in the MECH's leg compartment. It was a Sterner M88, a classic weapon that was both rugged and reliable. It fired old-fashioned .223 rounds. They were pointed, soft-alloy bullets, simple and effective, yet deadly. I pulled back the charging handle and let it snap back into place. There were eighty-eight rounds in the extended magazine. The stock was a simple two-piece with a spring shock absorber inside. The shoulder piece folded up and locked into place. There were two pistol grips. I had personally upgraded the barrel to titanium with a shroud that had narrow slits, and added a suppressor to keep the recoil to a minimum. It wasn't my favorite weapon, but I knew it and trusted it. Among all the weapons I kept from my time on the *Renegade*, it was the one I used the most while hunting and exploring on Libertine.

My head cleared pretty quickly. The air was thin and dusty inside the structure, but it wasn't tainted by the flammable gas from the MECH. I went to the door, which was already hanging open. Outside, a group of Musclars was approaching. They were cautious and I didn't blame them. They might have seen me crash in the MECH, but they knew the big fighting platform was deadly. I raised the rifle into the air and fired an extended burst on full automatic. The chugging report was enough to make them duck and run for cover.

I stepped back inside, opened a panel under the MECH's right side, just above the hip. There were buttons inside that controlled the fighting platform's basic functions. One opened the MECH so that a person could get inside. Another powered the entire unit up, including its weapons capabilities. There was an auto defense mode and a sentry mode; both of those were Autonomous Operating features. But what I was interested in was the air cycling mode. It took several minutes, but the suit could vent the flammable gas and fill its oxygen tanks through filters built under the MECH's back plates. I started the air cycling function and then hurried back to the door.

The light from the flare overhead was flickering. The shadows seemed to move as if they had a life of their own. I ran out and ducked down between two more structures. Within seconds, the first team of Musclars, leading an enslaved Casian, appeared. One had a long pole with a chain at one end that was looped over the pachyderm's head. Casians were big, six-legged creatures with a prehensile trunk and long, delicate tails. Their bodies were wide and powerful, their skin thick, while they were highly intelligent beings with a knack for operating machines. My platoon on the *Renegade* had designed the twin, rotating barrel machine cannons that could fit on their backs and were controlled via special headsets. The Musclars had enslaved the Casians in Solace and were forcing them to use the military tech against me.

The other Musclar had a prod. It was shorter than a spear and had two small blades on a Y-shaped tip. I could see blood flowing down the back legs of the Casian. My fury exploded and I charged them. Normally, I would have just shot the Musclars, but instead, I ran toward them. The alien with the chain tried to get the Casian to turn and shoot, but the big alien wasn't cooperating even when the other Musclar stabbed him repeatedly in the backside with the prod.

I smashed into the alien with the chain. It was a straightforward shoulder block, but the alien barely weighed half as much as me and my momentum sent him flying toward the Casian. He hit the big pachyderm in the side and dropped to the ground. My focus was on the alien with the prod and I didn't see the Casian stomping on his captor, but I heard the bones snapping under the big alien's feet.

The Musclar with the prod brought his short weapon to bear, and thrust it at me. I batted it aside with my rifle, then rammed my knee into the Musclar's midsection. The alien doubled over in pain, dropping his prod. I snatched up the prod and stabbed it into his shoulder. The alien squealed in pain, but I wasn't finished.

"How do you like it!" I snarled, stabbing him again in the thigh.

The Musclar dropped down on the muddy street. I wanted to keep stabbing him, but another group of aliens was rounding the corner ahead of me. I kicked the alien in the face, snapping his head back and knocking him unconscious.

Eight Musclars lowered their spears and charged straight at me from just thirty feet away. I had no time to run and no way to avoid their charge. They weren't as big or strong as I was, but without armor, I had no way to stop their spears from ripping through my flesh, save one. The weapon was at my hip. I dropped the prod, raised the rifle, and felt a thrill of power as my finger found the trigger. Killing intelligent beings isn't fun. It haunts everyone I know who ever did it, whether it was in combat or self-defense. The taking of a life is a burden to the human soul, but there are times in a person's life when they have no other choice. I wasn't thrilled with the power to take life, but I

won't lie and say that the power to stop my foe wasn't intox-
icating.

It took just three pounds of pressure to pull the trigger. The
M88 was in fully automatic firing mode. At the last second, I
pushed the barrel down and pulled the trigger. The gun
responded instantly, unleashing a volley that swept across the
line of my attackers. But aiming low, my bullets hit their hooves
and lower legs. It was complete carnage. Flesh, bone and hooves
flew in all directions. The Musclars fell face down in the mud,
all of them screaming in agony. Their spears were dropped and
their entire attention was turned to their ruined legs. They
would probably never walk again. They might, in all likelihood,
bleed to death from the wounds. Although, at least they had a
chance to live.

I turned back to the Casian. It had stomped its captor into
jelly and raised his trunk, bugling in defiance. Reaching out, I
pulled the chain from his head, but that was all I could do before
more bullets tore into the building beside us.

"Get down!" I shouted.

Perhaps covering the Casian's head with my body was a
foolish thing to do. I felt a surge of heat as bullets flew over us.
The pachyderm knelt down, going to its knees and then onto its
side. I tried to protect him and the bullets missed us, but the
debris from the houses on either side of the street pelted into us,
sometimes puncturing into my skin.

When the barrage of deadly bullets subsided, I rolled to my
knees, twisting around and bringing my rifle to my shoulder.
Once again, two Musclars were forcing the Casian to fight us. I
fired a quick burst. The alien with the leash was cut nearly in
two as my bullets punched through his narrow body. His
companion, seeing that I was still alive, dove behind the enslaved
pachyderm. That was a mistake.

With six legs, the Casians were formidable creatures. The enslaved alien balanced on four legs and kicked out with its back legs. They hit the Musclar in the chest and knocked him into the side of a house so hard he was killed instantly.

"Are you okay?" I asked the Casian beside me.

Of course, he couldn't understand me. I saw bloody wounds on his flesh, but they looked minor. My own back and legs burned with cuts and bruises. I could feel splinters digging into my skin and the muscles beneath, but there was no time for medical assistance. That would have to wait. I could have gone back into the structure where the MECH had crashed. I could have destroyed Solace and everyone in the colony. But at the time, I was too angry to think things through. I took off running toward the square with just my rifle in hand.

The Musclars were not complete fools. They were cruel, honorless beings who took advantage of the innocents around them. It was impossible to tell how many were left, but they were crowded into three groups. Around them, or at least between me and the Musclars, they held the innocent residents of Solace, including Uggar. Many of the locals were bleeding and looked as though they had been abused.

I pulled the language device from my pocket and activated the device as I clipped it to my shirt collar.

"Stop right where you are," the leader of the group ordered. "I demand that you leave this place. In the name of the Keeper, you must leave us!"

"I am not subject to your beliefs," I said, trying to remain calm, but failing. "Let these people go."

"We are the true heirs and righteous stewards of this colony. It has been declared for the Bearer of Souls. It is you who trespass, infidel."

"This is Solace, a free colony, on a free planet," I said. "You were given safe haven here after *I* rescued you from slavers."

"It was the divine who brought us to this planet. It is his will that we claim it in his name."

I knew there was no use in arguing with the religious fanatics. And thankfully, as my index finger inched closer to the trigger of my M88, it was Uggar who took up my side in the conversation.

"There are only two choices left," Uggar said. "Surrender or slaughter. Release us and take your people from our colony, and we can all live in peace."

"Peace is for the afterlife," the Musclar said. "Slay me, intruder, and I shall be swept away to glories you cannot img—"

I had already switched the M88 to single fire. The leader of the Musclars was growing bold and had moved out from behind the female Glosser he was hiding behind. My shot hit him in the forehead and blew the back of his skull out in a fountain of gore. Thankfully, the light from the flare overhead was dimming. But the report from my shot was loud enough to shock the crowd.

"Let them go!" I shouted. "And throw down your weapons."

Not all of the Musclars obeyed but some did. Most of the colonists dropped to the ground. They weren't injured, but the stress of the situation and the abuse from the Musclars had robbed them of strength. Three of the religious fanatics held onto their spears. Two rushed at me, but I shot them in quick succession. The bullets punched through their chests and took them down before they were close enough to bring their weapons to bear. The third was lingering in the deeper shadows. He threw his spear. It arced over the defeated Musclars and their captives from Solace. I saw it in the flickering light from the bonfire. There was no time to think or plan. My body didn't need it. Years of muscle memory kicked in and I dropped forward, rolling over one shoulder and coming up to my knees with the rifle held ready to fire as the spear dropped into the ground behind me with a thud.

"The next time any one of you tries to kill me, I'll slaughter the entire group of Musclars," I said.

"Heed the warning!" Uggar shouted. "I beg you."

"Move!" I shouted. "Walk to the fire and sit down."

Most of the Musclars obeyed. They weren't fighters. I had no doubt they were happy to join in the abuse of the captives, but they weren't brave or strong. Watching them walk, their shoulders slumped, their arms wrapped around their narrow bodies as if they were cold, showed all the classic signs of defeat.

"Uggar, see to your people," I said. "Have someone gather the spears and knives."

"Yes, I agree," Uggar said.

There were stragglers, of course. Some of them stared at me with hatred in their eyes. I couldn't blame them for that. I had spoiled their party. Not to mention killing several of the Musclars, but that had been their own fault. We gave them the chance to surrender. And I had done my best not to kill until it became absolutely necessary. But I wasn't going to risk my life to save the Musclars. They had caused too much havoc already.

"Keep moving," I told the stragglers with a wave of my rifle.

They obeyed, but it was clear they were biding their time. I stood guard over them. In the distance, the wails of the injured Musclars echoed. It was an eerie sound.

"What should we do now?" Uggar asked as he came shuffling up beside me.

"Can't let them go in the dark," I said. "They will use it to sneak back into the colony and slaughter your people."

It was clear that Uggar simply couldn't fathom so much wanton violence.

"We have their weapons," he pointed out.

"In a fight, anything is a weapon. A rock, a stick, their teeth, anything can be used to hurt you."

To their credit, the colonists helped the injured. The Casians carried those with shattered, bleeding hooves and broken legs from the fight in the street back to the square. Others bandaged their bleeding limbs. I refused to let the uninjured Musclars help. They had proven themselves to be conniving and I wasn't about to give them an opportunity to do more harm. It wasn't merely because I feared what they might do to me or the colonists. I was actually more concerned about having to hurt more of the Musclars. My promise to the villagers at Lake Tyconda was ringing in my ears, although I didn't think I could hold back if the aliens rose up against me again. In my mind, sparing them was a mistake. They would simply bide their time, plotting their revenge. I didn't like the idea of looking over my shoulder for the rest of my life, yet I didn't want to be a killer. Perhaps I already was, but I didn't want to indulge my violent tendencies.

The Musclars weren't the only beings who needed medical assistance. Many of the locals had been hurt, too. A search was made of the colony. Every structure checked until we were certain that there were no more Musclars unaccounted for. What surprised me was the number of colonists who came out of hiding. They more than doubled the number of their oppressors and it was clear there were rifts between certain groups of the local residents. Uggar didn't have to explain to me that some of the colonists had readily agreed to the Musclars' demands.

"It will take time to mend relationships," he said.

"People died," I pointed out. "It's going to be hard for the survivors who lost love ones to be okay with the colonists who joined the Musclars."

"I agree," Uggar said. "But we must try."

It was a long night. Maybe I had gotten used to the civilian life. I was certainly not in the habit of staying up all night. As my adrenaline faded, so did my energy level. However, I stayed on watch over the Musclars and lit a few oil lamps to give me light to see by when the bonfire died down.

In the morning light, an accounting took place. There was a lot of damage from the machine gunners and the fight in the streets. Seven Musclars had been killed by me, one by Thelo, the Casian who had stomped his captor to death. There were nearly that many with severe injuries. In the colony, it was clear that the Musclars had been wasteful with resources. A third of the cattle had been slaughtered. Property had been thrown out of several of the structures without care. The colonists who had been enslaved were treated worse than animals. They showed signs of being whipped, beaten, cut and abused. It was clear to me that Solace would never be the same again.

My own wounds were minor. I had cuts and bruises on my back. A few larger splinters had to be removed. I was seen to by the same Glosser who had been a slave to the leader of the Musclars. Her name was Acey and she was a willowy alien with a long, curved neck that resembled a swan. She also had four arms and a very delicate touch. She removed the splinters from my back and applied bandages from my own first aid kit that I recovered from the MECH.

Getting the fighting platform out of the structure it had crashed in was no easy matter. I basically demolished the building, getting the MECH free. But I also discovered the armored fighting suit was useful in building things up, not just blowing them up. The MECH could lift thousands of pounds and move heavy objects easily.

While I helped clean up the colony, including moving the

bodies of the dead - some Musclars, others were colonists left to rot on the outskirts of the village - Uggar gathered a council and decided what to do with the Musclars.

"They cannot stay," Uggar told me. "But we cannot simply kill helpless beings."

"Not sure they're helpless," I said.

"At this point in time, they are helpless," Uggar replied. "We have decided to give them some livestock and send them back to their village."

"They will come back," I said.

"Maybe, but they won't forget what you did here any time soon," Uggar said. "They have agreed to stay in the foothills."

"And you believe them?"

"Peace requires that we believe them; it has always been this way," Uggar said. "What would your people do, slaughter them?"

"Maybe," I said. "Don't get me wrong, we don't practice genocide, but if you aren't going to keep a guard over them or defensive systems here in Solace, you will be vulnerable. They believe they have a right to this colony. You know that."

"I do," Uggar said. "And I know we have no right to ask for your help, Hugo. You have already done far more than could be expected of someone we treated so poorly, but if you will help us, we will build defenses and learn to look after ourselves."

I thought that was the first sensible thing I had heard from the Premier of Solace. It was progress and there was nothing wrong with that. Maybe, if they were careful, they really could live in peace.

"Of course, I'll help," I told him.

The Musclars were allowed to make litters for their injured. Others were sent ahead with over a dozen of the animals that had been gifted to the colony by the Captain of the *Renegade*.

They were simple animals, herbivores that bred easily and could be harvested for protein-rich food. I oversaw the exodus of the Musclars. It took them two days to reach their village in the foothills. Spending days inside the MECH was possible, but not ideal. I was exhausted, and the MECH was nearly out of power as I climbed back up into the mountains. My plan was to get some rest at the cavern after I had notified the refugees from Solace that it was safe to return. However, the reception I got at Lake Tyconda was not at all what I expected.

CHAPTER 23

"NEWS of your accomplishments have reached us," Loutar said as I climbed out of the MECH. "Welcome back."

He was just one of a group that had come from the village to meet me. Eldora was there, and several others, including Leks from the group of refugees.

"It's safe for your colonists to return to Solace," I told Leks.

"Thank you," the avian alien said, her colorful neck flaps twitching.

"You were the hero," Eldora said. "Uggar is reporting that you saved many lives."

"I guess things were worse in Solara than we thought," I said.

Loutar had moved around me to inspect the MECH. "You were injured in the fighting?"

He was pointing to some of the damaged spots on the fighting armor.

"Minor wounds," I replied.

"It seems we have been saved by your sacrifice," Leks said with a bow. "Thank you."

"It was..." I honestly didn't know what to say.

"Uggar filled us in," Eldora said. "It seems that the communication equipment you established here was needed. We are grateful to you, Hugo."

My first instinct was to say I was just doing my job or my duty, but those cliches weren't true. I had no obligation to help anyone on Libertine. In fact, it could be argued that I had incentive not to help.

"I'm glad things are getting worked out," I said. "There's still a lot of damage to the colony."

"Structures can be rebuilt, but lives often cannot," Loutar said.

"The Musclars were violent? That is what we were told," Eldora said.

"They used the guns that were in the colony to try and stop me," I said. "But they weren't trained."

"Guns!" Loutar said. "They have no shame."

"Some of the refugees are returning," Eldora said. "Some wish to stay. We have welcomed them into our community. And, after reconsideration, we are all in agreement that you should be part of Lake Tyconda as well."

I don't think anything anyone could have said to me would have been more surprising. The shock was clear on my face.

"Are you well, Hugo?" Leks asked.

"Yes, I'm fine," I stammered. "You want me here?"

"We do," Loutar said. "I am ashamed to admit that I was against you at first. I did not understand your ways. Perhaps I was naive."

"We all owe you a debt of gratitude," Eldora said. "You have done nothing since you arrived but try to help us. It is unfortunate that much has changed on Libertine since your arrival, but that is not your fault. It was inevitable that the

Imperium would find us. We are grateful for your protection, Hugo."

"I'm happy to do it," I said.

"Will you join us then?" Loutar asked.

My life was full of disappointments. Since childhood, I had been rejected. Even in the Space Marines, I was often ostracized. And my experience up to that point on Libertine had been different. No one had wanted me around. I couldn't blame them, and I honestly thought that solitude was what I wanted as well. But having lived pretty much on my own, save for periodic visits to Lake Tyconda since Rip left, I had come to learn that I didn't thrive on solitude the way I thought. For years, I had been searching for a place to belong. Yet, suddenly, it felt like everything I wanted was being given to me. My eyes stung with tears and I could hardly bring myself to speak.

I nodded. "Yes," I managed to say as I fought to hold back the tears.

"Excellent," Eldora said. "Lake Tyconda is your home. You are ours, Hugo, and we are yours."

It wasn't a formal ceremony. I wasn't being given anything other than the right to live among the villagers at the lakeside community, but it felt like a major shift in my life. I had a home. I had neighbors. It was more than just an emotional moment for me. It seemed like the broken pieces of my life were suddenly fitting together.

That night we celebrated. It wasn't a wild party, but rather a warm, inclusive time. The population of the village had doubled and there was a lot of work to be done. But as we gathered around the small fire, shared food, drink and stories, I felt at home for maybe the first time in my entire life.

That night, I slept in a hammock outside. It was warm enough and the sky was beautiful. I could see thousands of stars above me ... although not the danger that was approaching Libertine.

The next day, I took the MECH back to my cavern and began gathering my things. That's when the attack alert sounded from the radar equipment I had set up. I should have been warned when the enemy entered the system. I should have been aware when the Ashi ships made orbit. But I had been so focused on the threat posed by the Musclars that when I activated the MECH, I failed to sync the surveillance equipment with the armor's computer system. In fact, when the alarm first sounded, I was inside the cavern gathering my belongings and didn't hear it until I came back up to the surface.

The sound was not a welcome one. I had several guns tucked under one arm and a metal box full of bullets in the other. I dropped it all and raced over to where I had the equipment placed and my guts turned to ice water.

Threat Detected! Impact Imminent. Take immediate shelter.

I looked up. There were three bombs dropping through the thin atmosphere. I couldn't tell what I was seeing. Dark clouds of smoke billowed from the bombs. The friction from the direct entry was causing flames and smoke as the projectiles raced toward the surface of the planet.

My first instinct was to rush back to Lake Tyconda, but there wasn't enough time. Even if the MECH was fully charged and I could fly around to the wide plateau, I couldn't save the people there. It was an awful realization. My only hope of survival lay in the caverns I had called my home. And even that was marginal. Maybe I could survive underground. I had no idea who was attacking or what bombs they were dropping.

For a moment, I was frozen as I wrestled with the terrible truth. Eldora was going to die. Lake Tyconda was about to be destroyed. Solace, too, and Uggar, and all the colonists there. They were exposed, perhaps even targeted by the orbital bombers. The Musclars in Mecula down on the foothills were no better off.

Despite the fact that it felt like I was ripping my own heart out of my chest with my bare hands, I sprinted to the MECH. It powered on quickly, but also warned me that it had only twenty percent power, and certain systems like flight controls were disabled. I ignored the warning and snatched up the solar charging device. It was big and weighed several hundred pounds when fully assembled. That was no problem for the MECH. I carried it quickly down into the cavern, then raced back to the surface.

The bombs were closer. I could see and hear the keening whistle of the devices falling. I gathered the weapons and ammunition I had been in the process of carrying out of the shelter, then returned. The first bomb hit while I was making my way down into a lower chamber. The entire mountain rocked with the impact. There was nothing left for me to do but get as low as I could with as much of the vital equipment as I could move.

I felt and heard the second impact a few seconds later. It rumbled like thunder and the mountain shook so hard that I heard rocks falling as parts of the cavern collapsed. The cave system was complex. It ran deep into the mountains and I hadn't bothered to explore it. Most of what I did was in the large cavern just inside the valley. There had never been a need to go deeper, although I had checked several of the lower caverns, which were smaller and dark. I didn't want some nasty predator to come crawling up from the dark and thinking I was its next meal.

There were deeper caverns and passages that branched off in many directions. I knew a person could easily get lost in deep caves that were like labyrinths with no light and no way to know what direction a person was moving. But I moved my weapons and the solar charging equipment down into the cave until I ran into a passage that had collapsed. Of course, my fear was that the entire cave structure would crash down, burying me alive. When the third bomb crashed down, the blinding light of the explosion even reached into the depths of the cavern.

I was afraid the mountain was crumbling. Dust filled the passage I was in and blinded me. All around, I heard the cacophony of rocks shattering and breaking apart. Fear choked me even though the MECH suit protected my body and filtered the dust from the air I was breathing.

The shaking and rumbling didn't subside quickly. I felt danger all around me, but by some stroke of good fortune, the narrow passage I was in didn't collapse. The weapons and solar equipment were safe. I was safe, at least for the time being. My pragmatic mind held together long enough for me to plug the MECH into the power bank that was still holding charge from hours spent in the bright, Libertine sunshine. With the suit's power recharging, I let my emotions tumble down into the dark abyss of despair. I shut the MECH's power to minimal, leaned my face into the padding that was meant to keep me alive in a fight and wept for all I had lost.

CHAPTER 24

I HONESTLY CAN'T REMEMBER the last time I cried. I hadn't shed a tear when my platoon mates were killed in combat. Usually, there was no time to grieve in a fight. There was always a release of emotions after an engagement, but I usually smothered my feelings with some type of sleep aid and then worked myself to exhaustion the following day in the nearest gym.

Typical, I suppose, although that was my way of dealing with things. In my experience, weakness of any kind was exploited by the people around me. I had to put on a strong persona and never let people know how bad they hurt me. But I was devastated by the attack on Libertine. There was no doubt that all the people I had met and come to know in Lake Tyconda, Solace and the other colonies were all dead. In fact, I was probably trapped inside the cavern with no hope of escape, but my own well-being was the last thing on my mind. I thought of Eldora, the compassionate alien who watched over the people of the village by the lake. She had befriended me, consoled me and eventually even won over the beings around her so that I was accepted into the village. That one night with them had been the highlight of my life. It was better than graduating from boot camp or completing the Special Operations Tactical training that allowed me to be a special forces commando in the Space Marines. It was better than the commendations from my superiors. I was an alien among aliens, yet they had felt more like family to me than any group of humans ever had.

I thought of Loutar, the diminutive alien who was so talented and so principled, yet he had changed his mind about me. He had realized that I wasn't an enemy or that my martial skills didn't make me a monster. Had any person I ever met shown such self-awareness and the ability to change? I didn't think so.

Despite our differences, I felt the pain of losing Uggar. Together, the pair of us had worked hard and risked our lives to save Solace. Yet, it had all been for nought. The enemy had come and the cowards hadn't risked fighting us face to face. They hovered safe in orbit above the free world and doomed every innocent person living on Libertine.

My grief turned to fatigue and I didn't fight it. The MECH wasn't comfortable enough to sleep in for long, but with my emotions so raw and my head pressed against the cushions, I let oblivion take me and prayed that I would never wake up. Of course, I did wake up. When I did, the world seemed quiet and still around me. Much of the dust had cleared and when I powered on the MECH's lights, I could see the chamber I was in. Not much damage had occurred there, but the tunnel that led down deeper into the mountain had completely collapsed.

The big armored fighting platform was charged up to sixty-five percent power after my emotional nap. And while I still felt raw, bitter and angry, I was also curious. Moving forward, toward the big cavern that led out to the valley, I discovered that the passage was compromised, but not completely impass-able. It was, however, too narrow for the MECH. I left the exterior lights on and the MECH facing the narrow connecting tunnel, then climbed out of the armored fighting mechanism.

"Thanks, big guy," I said as I stood before the MECH. "Thanks for taking care of me. That was pretty hairy, huh?"

Of course, the MECH didn't respond. I wasn't losing my mind. But strangely enough, I did feel a sense of appreciation and kinship with the armored fighting platform. It felt like we were in deep trouble, but we were in it together.

There was just enough space in the compromised corridor for me to squeeze through. I had to crawl and squirm, but I wiggled my way between the fallen blocks of stone. I even passed a vein of something that glittered white and gold in the rock face. It made me think of Rip, and I wondered what he was doing while I slithered through narrow, unyielding gaps in the fallen rocks.

When I reached the other side, I could tell I was in the big cavern, but it was hard to see. The opening had completely collapsed. There was no light other than a few weak spots among the rocks. I still had gear in the big cavern, weapons, medical supplies, and food, mostly. I had a few blankets made by the villagers at Lake Tyconda as well. Just the sight of them made me want to explode. If there had been an Ashi in the cave, I would have fought him with my bare hands at that moment. It didn't matter that they were twice as tall as me or exponentially stronger than I was.

I moved slowly over to the stones that littered the cavern, leading to what had once been the wide entrance. I guessed it might be possible to get out, but I would have to remove some of the stones. Most were much too big, but if I climbed up the pile, there might be enough loose stones near the top that I could wiggle out.

But it wasn't like walking to a doorway. I could barely see anything at all, and the floor of the cavern was cracked and uneven. In my supplies, I had some glow sticks. They were simple devices, each one filled with an easily breakable canister inside, along with two types of chemicals. When the inner canister was broken, the chemical inside it mixed with that outside the canister. The result was a glowing reaction that cast light all around and lasted for hours. I found some and broke one. It glowed to life and allowed me to see as I made my way through the debris field near the cavern opening.

I started up one section, but the stones were moving under my weight and I feared that I might cause more stones to fall if I kept going. Getting crushed to death was not my goal. After restarting the climb twice, I was finally able to reach one of the narrow slits that light was seeping through. There, I moved some stones about the size of my head. An opening was made, not large enough to exit through, but big enough that I could see outside. What I saw shocked me.

CHAPTER 25

DEVASTATION ISN'T a strong enough word to describe the scene. It was a gray hellscape. It looked like I had been transported to the moon in some strange, demented dimension. I expected to see monsters lumbering across the plains.

The cavern was halfway up the mountainside. But much of the surrounding mountains were gone. The soil had been scraped away, like icing on a piece of cake. Under that, the rock had been ground down to dust in places. The foothills were leveled, the grassy plains a dull, dusty expanse as far as I could see. Ash was falling like snow, only in gray, powdery clumps.

A few miles away, I could see the impact crater. In fact, it was impossible not to see it. The crater was a massive, bowl-shaped indentation into the ground that sank down hundreds of feet. There was only one thing I knew of that made that kind of crater, a kinetic bomb. Jar heads on SDF Fleet ships called them *Rods of the Gods*. Humans used tall cylinders of tungsten steel. They got hot as gravity pulled them down from orbit, but no propellant was used, and no warheads were necessary. They fell,

rushing toward the ground, heating up to incredible temperatures, and then exploding on impact with the force of a major
nuclear bomb. They were supposed to be clean weapons due to
the fact that they released no radiation. But testing showed that
they filled the air and surrounding landscape with heavy metals
and created unstable molecules that led to problems in the environment.

It was soul-crushing to look over and realize the plateau
where Lake Tyconda had been was completely gone. It had
been hit with the blast wave, with part of the mountain crumbling, the lake boiling away to nothing and the village vaporized, including all the residents who lived there in peace. It
made me angry the more I thought about it. The villagers and
colonists on Libertine were no threat to the Imperium. They
weren't violent. They hadn't begun a rebellion. They were
simple people living quiet lives. Their only crime was not
wanting to be subject to the Imperium's tyrannical oversight
and abuse. If ever there had been any doubt about the Ashi and
the Galactic Empire being evil, they had proved it beyond all
doubt on Libertine.

I crawled back down the pile of rocks and used my glow stick
to clear a path to my stash of belongings. That path led back to
the passage where I had to wiggle through to reach the MECH,
but I did reach it. Once I was settled back inside the fighting
platform, I went to work moving the stones. It was slow work,
but not strenuous. The MECH did the heavy lifting. My job
was choosing the order of the stones and how best to take hold of
them. Eventually, I cleared enough of the stones that the
MECH could pass through into the larger, main cavern. There
was enough loose stone in the cavern that a person could easily
build a home with it. Perhaps one day I would use them to make
a monument to the people of Lake Tyconda. It wouldn't do for

the people who had taken me in and accepted me as one of their own to be forgotten.

Once I finished with the connecting tunnel, I plugged the MECH back into the charging bank. There was enough stored energy to recharge the MECH to full power one more time. After that, we would need to harness solar energy, but that wouldn't be an easy task with so much dust and ash in the air.

I spent another hour moving small stones on the pile that led outside the cavern. It was probably a good thing that the entrance had collapsed. As long as I could dig out a stable opening, the cavern would be much more difficult to find. Not that there were any living creatures on Libertine to worry about. I wondered if the Ashi had bombarded the deserts as well as the habitable zones in the north and south polar regions. There was no way to know until I got out of the cave.

My communication and radar equipment had been completely destroyed. The only way to communicate with the northern colonies was to travel to the other side of the planet. I didn't think the MECH could fly that far. I really didn't know what I was going to do, but I couldn't just sit around and hope for rescue. That would never come. No one knew I was there. Even if they had known, one look at the mountains and they would assume I had been vaporized like everyone else.

That meant it was up to me to find a way to survive. I just hoped the Ashi hadn't bombed the planet into a completely uninhabitable wasteland.

After an hour of moving rocks, I was too tired to continue. I spread out the blankets that had been woven by the residents of Lake Tyconda and made myself a bed on the hard stone floor. Within seconds, I was asleep.

When I woke up hours later, I was shivering. The cavern had always been about ten degrees cooler than outside. It was a natural, geothermal process. Air from higher altitude was pulled into cracks and crevices that led down the caverns. The air cooled as it passed through the stone and was sucked back out of the big cavern. It had been inviting when I first found the cavern, but it was much colder than I expected it to get.

Fortunately, the MECH was fully charged by that time and so I got back into the armored mechanism, which had climate controls for the pilot. Warmed up and ready to work, I got started moving stones. To my surprise, it didn't take long for a small hole to open up as I moved some of the larger rocks. A few hours of steady work got me a passage large enough to move the MECH through.

It was dawn of the following day, but still very gloomy out. I decided to explore a little before moving the solar equipment. It wouldn't be much use without direct sunlight, and the sky was still thick with clouds. It felt better to be out of the cavern. My little valley was stripped bare of vegetation and left a dusty, barren place, although it hadn't been hit as hard as the Lake Tyconda plateau. My spring had turned into a stream. It gurgled and flowed out of the rock, running down the wrinkle in the mountainside.

"Alright, let's start with an environmental scan," I said, activating the application on the MECH's computer system. The armored fighting platform had built-in sensors that could measure everything from weather to atmospheric content. The report popped up on my HUD.

"Are you kidding me?" I said out loud.

The air was still breathable with plenty of oxygen and nitrogen, even though the quality registered as hazardous due to the dust still floating around. What really shocked me, though, was the temperature. As long as I had been on Libertine, the temperature remained steady in the low nineties during the day, and rarely dropped past eighty-five degrees Fahrenheit at night. But in the dawn after the attack, the temperature was reading fifty-two degrees, with the barometric pressure dropping.

Almost as if to illustrate the readings of the scan, a gust of wind made the dust around me kick up and swirl. I was no meteorologist, but I knew enough to understand what was happening. The warm surface air was rising and colder air was falling beneath it. The faster the air moved, the stronger the winds blew. But that wasn't what gave me pause. The real danger was all the dust in the air. As it swirled and flew, it inevitably bumped and rubbed together, creating static electricity to build up in the air. That strong electrical energy would eventually need to be released. A storm was coming. Something powerful, something wild. Yet, all I could do about it was to go back into my cave and hope that it didn't last too long.

CHAPTER 26

THE TEMPERATURE CONTINUED TO FALL ... and soon
after I returned to the cavern, the sky lit up with flashes of lightning. At first, the electrical discharges were horizontal, just
flashes of light and peals of thunder hidden by the thick clouds.
Then the rain came. Not a rain shower, but a torrential down-
pour and the lightning followed.

I made sure my gear was high and dry. I even moved the
solar charging bank so that if the water ran into the cavern, it
wouldn't ruin the electrical equipment. The water flowed down
the mountain in rushing streams that wore away the dust and
powdery ash from the bombardment. From the opening of my
cavern, I watched brown river rise. I could no longer see the far
side of my small valley, much less the crater where the foothills
had once met the grassy plains. It was too far away and the rain
was coming down too hard. The daylight was nearly extinguished by the dust, clouds and falling rain. Even so, that only
made the lightning more dramatic.

It rained hard all day. I heard, but couldn't see, sections of the mountain crumbling from erosion. The entire landscape was being altered and I was amazed at the power of nature unleashed.

During the year I had spent on Libertine it rained periodically, although it was a soft, soaking rain, warm and in many ways refreshing. It was the only respite from the heat most of the time. There seemed to be little in the way of wind on the planet. Perhaps that was different in other parts of the desert world, but at the southern pole, it was a very calm, almost stagnant weather pattern.

The bombardment had changed that dramatically. Flash flooding was spilling across the mountains, filling the valleys. Outside my cavern, a river had formed. It was slowly rising toward my refuge. As night fell, I expected the waters to breach the opening in just a few hours if the rain didn't stop. So I went back into the cave and built a bulwark out of stones. There wasn't much dirt to pack between them, and certainly no clay. It was impossible to make a waterproof barrier, but I could slow the flow.

With my cave as water-tight as I could make it, I slung my hammock between the arms of the MECH and wrapped myself in the blankets. It was so cold as night came on, that the rain had turned into half-frozen slush and when I got up to check on things around midnight, I found a glowing world of snow. It was a blizzard, the wind howling and snow falling in thick clusters. Just outside the cavern, the river still raged. It was loud, the water gushing just beside the big stones I had piled up in the hopes of keeping it out of the cavern. Somehow, the night was bright despite the storm. The snow reflected the starlight that filtered through the clouds. It was still dark outside, but I could see more than I expected: the dark, swirling surface of the river, the shadowy crags of the mountain peaks, the open expanse covered in snow.

The hot, desert world was cooling rapidly and changing before my eyes. Inside the cavern, it was warmer, but not comfortable. My body had gotten used to the hot weather on Libertine. I guessed the temperature had fallen close to freezing. All I could do was put on all the clothing I had, including my boots, wrap myself in the blankets and try to sleep.

The next morning, I was met by a completely different world from the one I experienced the day before. The storm continued, the wind whipping hard through the mountain passes. Snow swirled, both from the sky and as it was kicked up by the wind. I could see more, though. There were drifts building up, thick banks of snow filling the nooks and crannies of the mountains. Below my refuge, the world had turned bright white. Snow lay in a blanket across the plains. The impact crater had changed, too. Water from the flash floods had emptied into the massive, bowl-shaped impression. I was shocked by the beauty of it.

The only positive thing I could say that morning was that the river hadn't yet breached my cavern. But it hadn't diminished either. Nor had the weather calmed. But the cold had turned the rain to snow and the snow was soothing to my nature, a more gentle substance. I worked through the morning setting the charging station up on a solid foundation of large stones. It was nearly as tall as the MECH when I finished. There was no solar power to be harnessed, but the charging station also worked with wind turbines. I had two. They were small, tri-blade turbines. It didn't take me long to get them set up just outside the cavern. The cables were draped high and covered with a rubber coating so that the water from the snow didn't short them out. Soon, I had a steady supply of power coming in, which I knew I would need to keep the MECH fully charged and to help me warm up my dark home.

The cave was a big space but with snow blanketing the mountain, there was almost no air flowing through it. That allowed me to convert the medical robot to a simple radiator. It took in power and expelled that heat into the cave. It never got warm enough to be completely comfortable, but it was warm enough that I didn't worry about freezing. That night, I slept better and on the third morning since the bombs fell, I made a plan. The snow was continuing to fall; the wind continued to blow. As the snow built up on the mountainsides, it was becoming more difficult to move through. I knew I couldn't stay in the cave forever. In fact, I had exactly four days worth of food left. It was prepackaged, highly processed food in hermetically sealed pouches. The label said it would remain edible for a decade. After eating fresh protein and vegetables harvested from the land over the last year, the MREs were disgusting. Yet, I understood that food was fuel. My body needed it to survive and there was a very limited amount of it in the mountain cave. That meant I needed to find another source of fuel for my body and that required leaving my refuge. The snow was going to limit what I could do. It might eventually build up so much that it would be impossible to do anything.

I loaded what I considered to be my essentials into an ammunition crate. They were designed to be moisture resistant, although there were no guarantees that I wouldn't open it and discover all my gear was soaked. But that was a chance I had to take. The MECH would get me down the mountain. From there, I could head toward the desert. Perhaps it would be warmer there. Perhaps the violent storms hadn't upended the environment completely, like they were doing in the mountains. Of course, that all hinged on the Ashi's bombardment of the planet. If the Galactic Imperium had bombed the entire world with their kinetic weapons, I was doomed. But there was only one way to find out.

Back inside the MECH, I picked up the crate of gear and tucked it under one big mechanical arm. I was careful getting out of the cavern. It was dark, the doc-bot shut off, the wind turbines tucked back inside, so that nothing indicated that I had been there. Looking back at the entrance from the outside, I felt a pang of regret. The cavern had saved my life and been my shelter. I couldn't help but wonder if I would ever see it again.

The river was still so close to the entrance to the cavern that I had to be careful not to fall into the icy waters. The mountainsides were no longer the gentle slopes that were easily traversable. They were steep, rocky cliffs that were covered in ice and snow. Climbing down was possible in the MECH, but I knew there was a better way.

Combat operations, especially those on the ground, always took time. The MECH had enough power to be operational for days unless the flight capabilities were used. I had never pushed the fighting platform to its limit. I needed all that power to ensure I found a way to survive on the devastated planet. But the fastest way to use up the MECH's power was to fly. Still, I knew it was also the most efficient way to travel any real distance through the blizzard conditions.

Flying was still difficult. It was easier for me to point the MECH in the direction I wanted to go and let the jetpack shoot me in that direction. I pointed the big platform north and activated the thruster.

"Fifty percent power, engage," I said.

The jet pack ignited like a rocket and I went arcing away from the mountain.

"Disengage jetpack," I ordered. "Extend all flaps."

I was still shooting over the landscape. Below me was the crater. Water was still pouring in and I gauged that it was nearly three-quarters filled. Half of the water had frozen. There was a crescent of dark, liquid water, surrounded by snow-covered ice.

The MECH had boosters on both feet and each hand, but one arm was holding my supplies, which meant I would have to slow my fall with just the three boosters. The MECH was at the apex of its trajectory. For a moment, I felt weightless as I stopped moving up, but hadn't yet started falling back down. For that moment, I had slipped out of gravity's relentless pull. I tried to savor the feeling, to stay in that moment that both thrilled me and gave me a sense of false peace. But all too soon, I felt my body pulling upward against the safety harnesses. The MECH was falling, not straight down, but in a forward-moving descent. I managed to swing the legs forward so that I was falling in a mostly upright position.

"Activate boosters," I ordered.

The MECH's voice controls were essential to controlling the big, armored device. My arms were in sleeves that controlled the MECH's arms. Likewise, my feet were on pedals to control the MECH's legs. My hands had a variety of triggers and joysticks that operated the weapons. The mechanism had sensors that caused the MECH to mimic my body movements. If I turned, it turned. If I bent, it bent. There were optical controls for parts of the unit's computer input, but ultimately voice commands were needed. I didn't mind. Space Marines were trained to vocalize their actions. It was part of functioning as a unit in the chaos of battle. So, utilizing the MECH's systems via voice commands was second nature.

With steady bursts by my feet, I was able to keep the MECH aloft. It was a lot like jumping from one invisible block to another. I raced forward in a bounding motion and slowly made my descent back toward the ground.

The HUD that I looked through was capable of displaying a wide range of information. I had flown more than ten miles in just under a minute. I was still four hundred feet above the ground, and moving forward at a speed of six hundred miles per hour. It was both thrilling and frightening at the same time. But the most important display on my HUD was the MECH's power supply, which was at ninety-nine percent. I had hardly taxed the sophisticated mechanism's energy, which was reassuring. My hope was to find something that would allow me to keep living long enough to either escape Libertine, or take revenge on the beings who had destroyed it, before I passed the fifty percent mark in the MECH's power bank. If there was nothing but desolation to the north, I wanted to go back and die inside my cave. Or perhaps climb up onto what was left of the plateau where Lake Tyconda had been and die inside the MECH, leaving the iron warrior as a monument for whoever might find it in the future.

I couldn't help but think about Lawash. It was the first planet I had set foot on when the S.D.F. *Jericho* left the Sol system. Lawash had been bombed just like Libertine, only it was a total planetary bombardment. The Ashi's orbital weapons had poisoned the air and water with heavy metals. The planet had taken on a lunar quality to the surface, but there were the beginnings of flora starting to show, and some structures had survived after hundreds of years. I remembered well the vine-covered pyramid. Master Sergeant Steel had recovered the Arodoni Power Supply in the maze of tunnels under the huge structure. Perhaps, a group of Space Marines might find the MECH one day and retrieve my logs. Then people would know what happened on Libertine, and what had happened to innocent people living in the villages and colonies that were slaughtered by the Imperium.

As I passed the two-hundred-foot mark in my descent, I had to use all my concentration to slow the MECH for a landing. I fired the boosters in short bursts and slowed both my descent and forward motion until I could touch down on the snowy plain. I actually pulled it off and managed to keep the MECH upright. It was my best landing ever in the heavy armor, but there was no one around to witness it.

I had traveled nearly sixty miles. The desert should have been in sight, but all I could see was a world covered in snow.

CHAPTER 27

I PUT the MECH into a steady run. My progress was much slower, but moving the MECH on the ground used far less energy than flying. The snow was deep, up to the knee level on the MECH, which would have been waist high to me without the armor. Moving through it unassisted would have been slow and exhausting, not to mention wet. But the MECH was unfazed. It plowed through the snow easily, chewing up mile after mile on the flat plain.

Below me, the ground was hard. I suspected that rain had fallen on the arid ground, as the grassy plains turned to desert. The suddenly saturated soil was then frozen. The weather app on the HUD showed that it was still below freezing. It was an abrupt climate change for the hot planet. Still, I knew the farther north I traveled, the warmer it would be.

Hour after hour passed. I kept the MECH moving even when my stomach growled for food. Rationing the MREs seemed like the only sensible thing to do until I found a new source of sustenance. My body needed to start conserving calories, so I ignored my hunger and kept moving.

I can't say for sure how it happened. Perhaps the Ashi had spotted me from orbit. I wasn't a very big target, although a thermal scan or an electromagnetic survey would have easily picked me up. I tend to think the gun ship just came across my trail in the snow. I hadn't seen the Ashi patrolling over the mountains, but perhaps they weren't going that far south. Why should they when they knew the explosive power of their bombs would annihilate every living thing for miles in every direction of each detonation? Not to mention the fact that the suddenly shift in the environment would send survivors moving north. But in time, I would learn that the ship that attacked me that morning wasn't the only vessel searching the planet for survivors.

A politician might argue that since I was in the MECH that the Ashi were justified in attacking me. I wasn't just a survivor, I was a combatant after all. Yet the best warriors get to know their enemies. It isn't enough to be able to guess what your foe was going to do; if you really wanted to defeat them, you had to know why they were doing it. The Ashi didn't attack me because I was in the MECH armor. They were looking to exterminate every living person on Libertine. They were sending a message to the other Free Worlds. Resistance to the Galactic Imperium was the same as rebellion. It would never be tolerated. Those who did would be exterminated.

So they tried to exterminate me, only they didn't know who they were picking a fight with.

The MECH had short-range radar. It picked up the enemy ship as it closed in on me from behind. I kept moving in the same direction, running north over the frozen landscape and made no indication that I was aware of their presence. There was no need to do anything different on my part. The MECH could reach up and swat down the gunship without much assistance from me.

"Prepare surface-to-air missiles," I said, opening a panel on the back of the MECH via voice command. "Heat-seeking warhead one, fire!"

Those words were the sum total of my efforts. The suit dialed up the right weapon from the arsenal, set the missile's detection tech to seek out a heat source, and then lit it off. The missile, which was as long as my arm from shoulder to wrist, shot straight up out of the MECH, then turned and raced back toward the Ashi gunship. If the pilot of that vessel recognized the danger, they did little to avoid it. Even though I was still moving forward, I monitored the attack through a combination of radar and the MECH's rear-facing cameras. The gunship slipped to the side as the missile raced toward it. At first, the Ashi vessel seemed to have succeeded. The missile raced past it, but then it turned. The pilot tried to gain altitude, but he couldn't outrun the missile or shake it free. The rocket-propelled warhead rammed into the rear of the gunship and exploded. That's when I turned.

Black smoke was billowing from the craft. I couldn't see the damage, it was too far away and not oriented toward me. But the ship began to fall. I could tell by the way it moved that someone was trying to steer it, to control the inevitable crash. The vessel came down hard, smacking into the ground and churning up a channel of snow as it plowed forward until its momentum was arrested.

The explosion had been loud. The crash was louder still and made the ground under the MECH's feet tremble. But afterward, all was quiet again. Only the wind made any sound on the vast, empty plain. At least until the survivors of the crash made their way out of the craft and then the real fun began.

I had yet to really use the MECH in what I considered hard combat. While I was keenly aware that I was miles from my base, with no back-up and limited ammunition, I was also brimming with fury over what the Ashi had done to Libertine. The innocents they killed were my friends ... it was payback time.

The hatch on the gunship was pinned from the frame bending when it crash-landed. There wasn't a full unit of warriors on the gunship. It was meant to chase down enemies and dispatch them from the air. I could see two large laser cannons on the sides of the cockpit. I can't say for sure what made them hesitate to fire on me; perhaps their orders were to get close enough to identify the MECH before blasting away at me. I didn't bother asking. I could hear the crew pounding on the hatch to get it open. Smoke was wafting from the back end where my missile had completely destroyed their engines. The crew would either break free or die. So I waited.

"Activate machine gun," I said, causing the rotating cannon to pop up on my right forearm. "Open short-range mini-missile bay."

Slots on the front of the MECH's shoulder slide down, revealing twelve small missiles in each bay. Would I have enjoyed going toe to toe with the Ashi and deploying the spring-loaded blade on my left arm? Undoubtedly, but I was too worked up and ready for maximum carnage. When the hatch burst open, the ship seemed to vomit the big green aliens. They were huge bipeds with powerful muscles on their massive skeletal frames. We had learned to fight them on Casasil. The Ashi had bone plates around their vital organs in their chest, but their stomach was vulnerable. I unleashed hell and let the machine gun chug away at the aliens. Blood and tissue flew in a gory spray against the side of the ship. There were six Ashi in the group. Two wore headsets that revealed they were the pilots.

The other four carried the Ashi laser rifle, a bulky, unwieldy weapon. I didn't know the exact specs on the guns, but I gathered the weapons from the dead aliens anyway. With my limited resources, I needed all the gear I could lay my hands on.

A quickly look inside the ship showed that it was small for the Ashi, who at full height were even taller than the MECH. There was room for four warriors and two pilots. The rest of the ship was filled with large power blocks to run the engines and laser cannons. The engine bay was on fire, filling the interior of the ship with smoke. I went around the vessel and used the MECH's big hands to shovel snow onto the damaged equipment. The snow sputtered and hissed as it landed on hot metal, which began to pop and crack from the sudden change in temperature. I didn't care. I wasn't planning to use the ship for anything but distraction and cover. In the wide open frozen plains, there was no good place to fight from. The only option was the enemy ship, yet it had the upside of attracting more of the enemy, which was exactly what I wanted.

I can't say that dying was what I wanted. But it certainly would have been a welcome end to my pain. The loss of my friends was like an open wound. It ached every moment of the day. On the other hand, of course, what I really wanted was revenge. I wanted to fill the world with the bodies and blood of my enemies. So, I extinguished the fire in what was left of the engine bay, then went inside the passenger cabin to wait for the Ashi to come to me.

That's when I discovered that humanity had something in common with the Ashi ... and it opened up a world of possibilities that I hadn't thought possible.

CHAPTER 28

I HAD ONLY BEEN in the enemy ship a few seconds when a message popped up on my HUD.

Control Network Discovered. Would you like to join?

"Yes," I ordered.

It was flabbergasting to think that the Ashi computer technology and humanity's were similar. Of course, the MECH had been built by the Arodoni computer and onboard production plant found on the *Renegade*. But however it worked, the CPU of the MECH could sync with the gun ship's computer system, which was still active despite the crash.

A list of warnings flashed red on my HUD. The gunship was suffering catastrophic failure of all major systems. The warnings weren't in a language I could read, but the iconography was enough to give me the gist of what was happening.

"Shut down power to the engines," I ordered.

Immediately, two of the blinking warnings disappeared.

Another icon was what I thought might be life support systems on the ship. I had no need for that either.

"Shut down life support and flight control systems."

The rest of the warnings vanished. My eyes flicked down to the Ashi ship's interface icon in the lower right-hand corner of my HUD. As my eyes focused on it, the icon expanded, and then a new set of alien readings came to life before my eyes. The ship's computer was still powered up, as were the weapons. The left laser cannon was offline. I knew that because the icon had a jagged line over it. But the other cannon seemed to be functional and the HUD showed the ship had over seventy percent of its stored power still available.

I looked over at the communication icon. It looked like a series of sound waves. When I stared at it, a list of ships with small images of them appeared. Two were the standard military ships, a third, very squat ship was listed below the others and then a much longer list of gunships. I counted nineteen of the gunships, which I guessed were searching the planet for survivors just like the one I had shot down.

"Activate radar," I said.

Another icon came to life on the HUD. That should give me enough warning if another gunship came snooping around. I knew it was inevitable. There were probably orders being issued at that very moment for the closest ships to investigate what happened to the ship I had brought down. That's what I wanted, but my plan was to show the Ashi what I had in store for them.

I left the interior of the gunship. It was convenient that the Ashi were themselves so large. The MECH was wider than an Ashi warrior, but only by a couple of feet, which made it possible for me to take cover inside the Ashi ship easily enough. Outside the crashed gunship, I went to the bodies of the warriors I had killed. Their middles were torn to pieces by my machine gun fire, but their heads were undamaged. I extended the blade of the double-edged dagger from the MECH's left forearm. It sprang out and I used it to saw the heads off the six Ashi. It was gruesome work, but no less than the savages deserved. I had heard bits and pieces of intel about the Ashi. The alien Artifact called GIGI claimed that the Ashi were all about courage and valor. Yet their ships had bombed Libertine from the safety of orbit. I couldn't think of much that was less valorous than hurling massive kinetic bombs at civilians from space.

I picked up the severed heads and tossed them on top of the ship. The Ashi were no doubt looking down at me from space. For all I knew, they might just drop another kinetic bomb on my position, but before they did, they would see what I was capable of. Whether the Ashi admitted it or not, I knew they would be afraid.

Soon, the radar began to beep a warning. I was already back inside the cabin of the gunship by that time. Having left my grisly warning on the hull of the ship, I turned my attention to their weapons. The laser rifles were similar enough to weapons that humans made, only much larger. I knew a large bore on a laser meant a greater release of power, but comparatively less distance. I shot one of the bodies of the Ashi at close range. The result was a massive hole in the thick body of the alien. It had burned through flesh, muscle, and even the thick bone plate that covered their internal organs. I propped another of the headless corpses up and walked out thirty feet. From that distance, the laser blast was potent. It knocked the corpse down and left a nasty wound across its chest, the size of a dinner plate, but it didn't burn through the bone or reach the organs. In my mind, the lasers were like shotguns, only they had squarish frames, a massive grip and no trigger guard. Nor did they use curved triggers, that a person could hook their finger around. Even if the gun hadn't been twice the size of a standard-issue Marine laser rifle, it was still strangely different. The trigger was a plunger, yet it worked essentially the same way as a human weapon.

I couldn't read the power meter on top of the Ashi rifles. But they were all operational. I set them up just inside the ship. If things got hot, I could always snatch one up and utilize it to save the MECH's limited ammunition.

The approaching vessel was another gunship. It was coming in from the north. I stayed out of sight and waited to see what it would do. The ship circled overhead. I heard a barking growl via the ship's computer system. It did me no good to tap into their communication system. I could activate my language app and read what they were saying on my HUD, but I didn't want my field of vision compromised by words. Besides, it was obvious what they had to say. Their people weren't just dead, they were butchered, perhaps even desecrated. So, I waited and before long, my patience was rewarded.

The ship circled low, then landed. I moved to the hatch of the vessel I was in, kneeling in the MECH armor just inside the shadows. The Ashi gunships weren't heavily armored. I could see the pilots inside the cockpit. They looked like brutes or uncouth barbarians from an era lost in the annals of history. But it was obvious they were sophisticated beings with both strength and intelligence. The hatch opened on the side of the ship and four warriors came out. They were soldiers. I recognized the teamwork and efficiency of their movements. But they had no armor. They wore only short kilts with wide leather belts. They carried the bulky laser rifles and a knife in a sheath that hung from their belt. I knew from personal experience that they were fast, powerful warriors. Their weapons didn't frighten me as much as the aliens themselves and I didn't want them to spread out before I attacked.

Everything happened fast. I saw the enemy, recognizing their background, then launching my attack within just a couple of seconds. The pilots of the gunship were fast, too. Even before I fired at the troopers, the pilots were revving the engines on their vessel to take flight again. Only I wasn't going to let that happen.

One strafing barrage from the cannon on the MECH's right forearm ripped through the four warriors. I hit them before they could spread out and I knew right where to aim. They might have survived if I had aimed for their center mass. But their guts were where they were weakest, and the depleted uranium-tipped rounds from the MECH's rotating barrel machine gun tore huge holes right through them before peppering into the side of the gunship. It still managed to lift off, although it made the fatal error of turning away from me, which exposed the engine exhaust. I didn't need the powerful ground-to-air missiles to take it down.

"Launch mini-missile," I ordered.

The compartment on the MECH's shoulder was already open. The mini-missiles didn't have the sophisticated tracking software. They were simple point-and-shoot weapons, yet they packed a powerful punch. The missile streaked across the open space and right into the gunship's exhaust port. There was an explosion, but it wasn't powerful enough to rip the ship apart. Instead, flames shot out of the exhaust and into the engines, cracking and destroying the essential components within. The ship didn't go down right away and I'll admit I was concerned that I hadn't done enough. It continued flying, rising up through the air for nearly fifteen seconds after my rocket hit it. I was considering firing a more potent weapon at the gunship, but then a dark stream of smoke began to pour out of the back of the ship. I smiled, knowing what was coming.

The Ashi pilots had made a fatal mistake. They had been right to try and get as far away from me as possible. Perhaps if I hadn't fired my rocket at them, they would have swung around and lit the ship I was sheltering in with laser fire. But, knowing they were under attack, they ran away. Only, instead of staying low, the gunship climbed for altitude. That was what cost them their lives. I watched as the ship rose up, stalled, then dropped like a stone. She went nose down from several hundred feet in the air. There was no follow-up explosion, but I knew it wasn't needed. The ship had smashed down on the Ashi pilots and killed them both.

I also knew the next gunship wouldn't make the same mistake. The pilots had enough time to radio in and alert their superiors to the fact that I was hiding in the crashed ship. The next vessel to reach me would shoot first and ask questions later. But I was ready for that, too.

The MECH was a combat platform, which included camouflaging technology. The weather was playing in my favor. The ground was covered with snow and more of it filled the air. I stepped out of the Ashi gunship and activated my boosters. They weren't really made for propelling the MECH into the air, but they got me off the ground so that I didn't leave tracks in the snow. Using the hover feature, I moved about a hundred yards from the ship I had been in, and then settled.

"Engage active cloaking," I said.

Of course, I couldn't tell that anything had changed. But the MECH's outer shell suddenly shifted to white. If a person were really looking for me, they could probably spot the MECH. The camo wasn't perfect. Yet, as long as I wasn't moving and all around me the world was white, I had a pretty good chance of blending in.

The second ship circled at nearly a thousand feet overhead. I knew the alien pilots could see the bodies I had left, including those with severed heads. The snow was starting to form a barrier over the first Ashi I had killed. Their bodies were no longer warm enough to melt the falling snow. But there was plenty of blood splashed all around them. And the second group was still very distinct.

The ship was in range of my surface-to-air missiles, but I was waiting, biding my time. Eventually, the Ashi would stop sending their ineffective gunships after me and launch a heavy strike. I wanted to take down as many of the gunships in my next attack as possible. Nor did I have to wait long. The MECH's radar picked up a pair of gunships moving toward my position at speed.

"Targeting app," I said, bringing the computer system to the forefront of my HUD. The gunships were already labeled on the targeting system as Echo three, four, and five. "Engage heat detection."

The word **Heat Seeking** appeared on my HUD. I used my eyes to highlight three of my five remaining surface-to-air missiles. They would be fired in quick succession, but each one tasked with hunting down a different Ashi vessel.

The gunships came in fast and low. They opened up with their laser cannons, sending up huge plumes of steam as the heat from the weapons impacted the ground and the first airship. The lasers must have reached the power or fuel because the gunship exploded in a spectacular ball of flame. Bits of hot metal and polymer flew in all directions. Some of it almost reached me, but fell short. The gunships, focused entirely on the crashed vessel, flew right over my position without slowing down.

"Fire!" I ordered.

Shooting the missiles was a bit like launching fireworks. There was satisfaction in the jolt as the weapon was flung upward by the spring-loaded mechanism. Then its own booster engaged, causing the missile to streak off toward its target. And that, of course, was followed by a moment of heightened antici-pation while I waited for the detonation.

Two of the missiles streaked off toward the gunners, and the third raced straight up. I left my camouflaging system on, but started moving. Without cover, the enemy could pinpoint my location. I had nothing to hide behind, and wasn't going to give them a stationary target to shoot at.

The first missile reached the gunship and took out its engines. It was only about a hundred feet in the air, and while it couldn't fly, it did deploy all its flaps in an effort to slow down its descent. The ship managed to keep its nose up as it dropped and slid across the snow.

The second pilot was wily. He turned sharply into the path his companion had been just a moment before. The missile chasing him wasn't smart enough to tell the difference between the heat of the gunship's exhaust and the explosion of the other ship. It flashed through the flames and lost its connection to the target.

High above me, the ship that had been monitoring the fight turned up and climbed for even greater altitude. The missile followed. The chase lasted only a few seconds. I was surprised the gunships had no defensive systems. All human fighter vessels and small troop carriers had chaff and decoys, as well as signal scramblers. The Ashi gunships were built for a different kind of warfare. They used lasers, which had their place, but didn't have the explosive power and kinetic energy of a projectile weapon.

The third gunship exploded high overhead. I could only deduce that it had pushed its engines for maximum speed and the result had been catastrophic when the missile caught it.

Of the three ships, only one was still intact. It had turned sharply, while the missile seeking it shot out and away, the tiny inboard sensor trying to reacquire its target. I kept moving. The MECH's camouflage would make me harder to see, but I couldn't remain invisible while I was moving. Every instinct was telling me to move as fast as I could. The MECH ran, its metal feet thumping hard onto the snow, packing it down and kicking it up, seemingly at the same time.

An alarm sounded. Laser fire pelted the ground behind me. The last gunship was trying to take me out, but I could see the missile hot on its trail. Perhaps the pilots hadn't seen it. Or maybe they just didn't care. I had to respect their resolve, but I didn't have to let them kill me.

"Activate jetpack," I ordered. "Thirty percent."

Just as the lasers were closing in, the jetpack sent me shooting upward, high into the air. The gunship was flying low, and suddenly, I was above it. The pilot tried to correct course, but the missile found it first. The entire back end of the ship exploded. I was looking down, my arms and legs outstretched to control my descent. Smoke and debris billowed from the back of the ship, which quickly went down. It hit the ground and bounced back up. Two Ashi fell out of the gaping hole in the rear of the ship. They dropped and rolled behind the ship, whose momentum kept it moving.

I had no time to watch them. The ground was rushing up at me. Firing the boosters, I slowed my descent to a safe speed and hit the ground running. The MECH struts bore the brunt of the impact, but I felt them bottom out for a moment. The entire device shook, although nothing broke. I had the MECH running at top speed, straight for the first gunship to go down. The passengers and pilots had survived. I saw four warriors climbing out of the ship, their weapons already pointed in my general direction.

Usually, in a gunfight, whoever fires first wins. But the Ashi didn't have a bead on me. In fact, I didn't think they knew I was there at all, just that something dangerous could be out there. They fired blind, just blasting away. Maybe it made them feel better to think they were fighting back. But they weren't aiming at me. Most of their laser fire was well off the mark.

I returned fire, using my machine gun. It spun fast, spewing thirty rounds a second. Two of the warriors went down from my barrage, but the other two were spread out just far enough that they could dive for cover. One made it, one didn't. He dove the wrong way and flew headfirst into my gunfire. His head exploded from multiple impacts. Blood sprayed across the snow in a vivid blue color.

The fourth warrior was smart and fast. He hit the ground, rolled and came up firing. He didn't have to guess where I was any longer. And he had a decent base as he was on his knees instead of his feet. Perhaps he might have killed me if things were different, if I wasn't in the MECH. Then again, I would have been a smaller target and maybe he would have missed. I can't say. All I know is that his first shot hit me center of mass. Unfortunately for him, that was the most armored portion of the MECH. His laser blast hit and did nothing. I just kept running.

His second shot went between the MECH's legs. His third, fired just before the bullets from my return fire ripped through his guts, severed his spine and killed him instantly, hit the MECH's left knee. It was the perfect shot at the perfect instance. The knee was flexed and the armor protective plates opened for just a split second. The laser found its way in and turned the metal joint into molten slag. The MECH went down ... and me with it. We fell, rolling forward. Alarms sounded as the rotating barrel of my machine gun hit the frozen soil and bent the mounts. It wouldn't turn and I was afraid to fire it. As I pushed myself back into an upright position, I looked toward the ship. The pilots inside were near panic. The crash must have ruined their safety harnesses, supposing the Ashi believed in that sort of thing. They were looking up, straight up, and I didn't need to be told why. The Ashi in orbit had launched another kinetic bomb and it was heading straight for us.

CHAPTER 29

I REALLY HAD no plan other than to kill as many Ashi as possible. I didn't care if I died in the process, but I wasn't going to make it easy for them.

"Engage Jetpack!" I shouted. "Full power!"

It felt like I had been punched hard in the stomach. The MECH shot into the air. Not straight up, I was leaning forward slightly, although I rocketed through the air so fast that the gravitational forces nearly caused me to pass out. Sparks floated at the edge of my vision and, for a few seconds, I wasn't able to draw a breath into my lungs. But once my body adjusted, I forced air in. It wasn't easy but I did it. Then my eyes focused on the warning flashing across the HUD.

Vacate Blast Radius Immediately 8/40 kilometers.

The bomb was still falling and, when it hit, it would send out a shock wave that would crush the MECH with me inside it. I had to get away from the blast radius before that happened. But my mind was muddy, as if thinking clearly was as difficult as drawing breathing under the weight of the increased gravitational force.

"Engage... auto... pilot," I wheezed.

Autopilot engaged.

I felt the MECH's trajectory shift. I was no longer flying in the same direction I had started in. My blurry eyes looked at the flight readout on my Heads Up Display.

Altitude 9,210 feet

Speed 609 mph

Direction North-northeast

As the MECH leveled out, I realized that I wasn't in control of the arms and legs any longer. The jetpack was still blasting away at full power, which was a concern, but not as much as the blast radius from the bomb behind me. It was easier to breathe and I panted a little as my head began to clear.

The flash of the kinetic bomb caused the MECH's cameras to go blank for a moment. The HUD's main feed, which was a composite of the various cameras mounted in the head of the MECH and which had sensors to detect my motion, went dark. The readouts however were still visible and the light from the flash flooded the slit in the chest armor. It was so bright I had to squeeze my eyes tightly shut and I instinctively turned my head to the side.

As the light faded, I opened my eyes again. The first thing I saw was a new message on the HUD.

You have successfully reached minimum safe distance.

"Radar," I said, thinking there might be other bombs dropping. The kinetic warheads were just big, dense objects. They didn't produce electromagnetic energy, which could be picked up by scanners. But they still reflected an echo from radar that would show them moving through the air.

There were no other bombs, but there were other gunships. Several showed up on my radar, in fact. They had probably been sent to deal with me before it became evident that I was more than a match for them.

An idea suddenly came to mind. It was incredibly dangerous and probably stupid. But it was also audacious and right up my alley. First, I had to run a diagnostic on my suit.

"Shut down the jetpack," I ordered, retaking control of the MECH. "Disengage autopilot."

The propulsion stopped hurtling me through the air, but of course, I was still airborne. My altitude showed that I had climbed up over eleven thousand feet before shutting down the jetpack.

"Shut down radar," I said. "Mask my electromagnetic signature."

I brought up the MECH's current diagnostics

Power 59%

Life support 100%

Armor 77%

Functionality 60%

She was still airtight, and there was plenty of breathable air in the system, but the MECH's knee was shot. It would need a major repair, perhaps even a joint replacement. There was no time for that, even if I was able to figure out how to do it. I didn't have the tools or spare parts, so that meant I was limited in what the MECH was able to do.

I still had weapons, though. Not everything in the arsenal, but enough to do some major damage. There were six of the powerful, air-to-air missiles. They were the most potent weapons on the fighting platform and could be used in atmo or space. The machine gun was ruined. Actually, it was the mounting brackets that shifted it from its place in the MECH's forearm to the upright firing position that were broken. They were too bent to function and wouldn't let the air-cooled, rotating barrels spin properly. I was also down several ground-to-air and mini missiles on top of all that; the flamethrower and several of the armor plates were damaged. The HUD's readout confirmed all that. While it wasn't ideal, especially given what I was thinking of doing, I still felt confident that I could cause some major havoc. If only my luck could hold out a little longer!

Most smart Marines will tell you that before beginning any combat operation, it is imperative to know the exit strategy. I didn't have one, but I didn't mind that too much. I would be happy to kick the bucket as long as I could take out as many of the big, green bastards as I could, before I died.

The video feeds came back on, and I could look around as if I were the MECH. At ten thousand feet up, I could see a long way across the surface of the planet. Somehow, I had outrun the storms. There were still clouds above me, although much thinner. Below, I saw plenty of dull browns mixed with white patches of snow. That told me the Ashi hadn't bombarded the entire planet. Libertine was damaged but she wasn't dead. In fact, the ash and dust kicked into the atmosphere by the Ashi warheads, along with the copious amounts of CO_2 from the smoke, would only enhance the terraforming of the world. The surface had cooled considerably and not just on the poles. There was even more water on the surface of the world than before, as moisture was pulled out of the atmosphere in the form of rain and snow.

The Ashi had succeeded in wiping out the colonies, but that didn't mean Libertine couldn't survive. She could, and would, I was confident of that. More people would come, start over, rebuild. I still felt the awful ache of grief over the people of Lake Tyconda and Solace, even Mecula, yet I knew their legacy would live on. The Ashi had done a terrible thing, but I was going to make sure they paid a very high price for it.

I wish I could say I was successful in my first attempt at catching one of the gunships. Using my boosters, I came in slow over the top of the nearest one. But coordinating an inflight connection was harder than I thought. I went flashing in front of the gunship, which then tried to turn and shoot at me. I had to drop back and use a half dozen mini-missiles to disable their engines. There was no use in following them down as the ship began descending for an emergency landing. My goal was to stay up and catch a gunship before it made its way back up into orbit.

My power banks dropped below fifty percent after using the jetpack to climb back up above ten thousand feet. To my surprise, the next gunship was much lower. Not that I should have been surprised. They were fast attack vessels with lasers meant for much closer distances. They probably liked to work at around an altitude of five hundred feet or less. I considered making the dive, but there was a third ship not far away. I changed course for the third vessel and prayed that I might somehow find success.

The third Ashi gunship was making its way upward. It was cruising north and climbing. I took my time maneuvering toward it. With a little luck, I flew in from behind and just a couple thousand feet above it. Then, trying to be patient and consuming even more power, I waited for it to come up to me. As it gained altitude, I moved closer. Eventually, we met at a little over eighty-five hundred feet in the air. The gunship had a pair of large rings built into the frame that stuck out on either side of the vessel's roof. I caught one, clamping one hard with the MECH's hand, then pulling myself down onto the upper fuselage and stretching the MECH's one good leg across to the other ring. After clamping on with one leg and one foot, I felt pretty secure, while I left my left arm free and activated my laser cannon. It would use more of the MECH's precious power, but I was resigned to the fact that this would be my final mission in the armored suit. I could have left it on the mountains, a frozen monument to the people of Lake Tyconda. Instead, I decided to use it one last time; let the dead Ashi be a monument to the innocents that had died for no reason other than their desire to live free.

The Ashi gunship continued to climb, but it was a slow slog. Eventually, we broke free of the planet's gravity and drifted up into orbit. I felt a shift in the ship's engines. There was no sound in the hard vacuum of space, but I felt the vibrations as certain ports closed and other vents opened. Like many hybrid vessels, the gunship wasn't built for long-range flights through space. It had thrusters, probably utilizing compressed air, to move it in zero gravity. It turned and, ahead of us, I could see three Ashi ships. Two were war vessels, big ships with laser cannons and thick armor. The third was a strange, pot-bellied vessel, which I knew was the bomber.

My stomach seemed to flip inside me after a few moments, until I realized the gunship had been latched onto with an artificial gravity beam. We sped up, although it was harder to judge movement in space when there was no way to feel the motion. I relied on my HUD. Even though I had powered down most of my systems so that I wouldn't stand out on scanners, I had been able to sync the MECH's computer system with that of the gunship. I was careful not to do anything that would reveal my presence, but I did monitor the ship's speed and location. The bigger ships projected some type of energy between them that allowed the smaller ships to triangulate their distance from the larger vessels, and their speed to them, as well as relative to the planet and even the system star. I sat still and laid the MECH as close to the hull as she would go to avoid detection. The time for revealing myself would come, but not while I was clinging to the enemy ship and stuck in a gravity beam.

CHAPTER 30

THE ASHI WERE in no hurry. The gunship was slowly pulled toward the attack ship. I used the time to contemplate my life. The odds were good that I would be dead soon and, if so, I wondered if it had really meant anything. Was there meaning to life? I was no philosopher, but I contemplated my existence as I stared out into the cosmos. There was a time, not too long ago, when most of humanity believed we were alone in the universe. I knew that wasn't true. There were thousands of inhabited worlds just in our galaxy alone. In some ways, that made me feel small and insignificant, yet I also felt as though I was part of something grand.

My accomplishments weren't measured in personal relationships. I never had much success with those. I could count the number of people I felt that actually cared about me on one hand. All of them were recent additions. Master Sergeant Remmy Steel and Staff Sergeant Laila McPherson from my last deployment. They had cared enough to get to know me. They recognized my strengths and weaknesses, pushed past the walls I had set up to keep people at bay and built a platoon that actually cared about the people beyond the weapons and mission parameters.

Albert "Rip" Van Winkle had sacrificed his future to save my life. Our time together on Libertine had forged a bond that I would never forget. As I floated toward the enemy ship, I wondered what Rip was doing out in the galaxy.

Then there was Eldora. My relationship with her had been strange and wonderful. She was an alien, and yet, she accepted me. With her, I felt more comfortable than I ever had with a human being. That's maybe odd to say, but absolutely true. Of all the people I missed in my life, she was at the top of the list. That was partly because I felt that I had let her down. Not that I could have saved her from the Ashi bombardment. The best I could have done was to give her the MECH and let her race for safety, but then she would have been left alone to face the Ashi. If she didn't starve to death or get killed just trying to escape the blast zone, she would have been hunted down and murdered.

Eldora's memory was both sweet and bitter. It brought me joy, but also pain, and focused my rage against the Ashi into a red-hot laser that was going to cost the aliens dearly.

I pressed the MECH down onto the roof of the gunship as it was slowly brought into a cavernous hangar inside the Ashi ship. It was, from what I could see, a vessel built for utility. Pipes, vents, bundles of electrical wiring, and various mechanical components were visible in the ceiling of the hangar, which I guessed filled the entire lower portion of the alien ship. But I was more interested in what was on the deck. There were dozens of Ashi, big, beefy aliens with green skin, wide jaws and small, narrow eyes. They spoke in rough barks and growls. From where I lay, it seemed that most of the aliens present were technicians. There were two other gunships on the wide deck. I saw the aliens moving hoses and pipes to those ships. The Ashi moved in and out of them with a variety of tools. I didn't see a lot of weapons and that was a good thing.

"Prep mini missiles," I said, utilizing the MECH's voice controls. "Activate the laser cannon."

The barrel of the laser cannon dropped down from the bottom side of the MECH's left forearm. It was time to get busy.

"Fire missiles," I said.

The targeting system had already designated where each of the mini missiles would go. All I had to do was sit up and turn the MECH's large body. At the same time, I began to fire my laser, starting with the warriors who had just disembarked from the gunship I had rode in on.

Sudden carnage erupted around me. The mini-missiles shot out and exploded into the other gunships. Fuel vapors ignited and sent waves of flame flashing around the hangar. The laser blasts from my cannon scorched down through the skulls of the warriors who dropped dead before they could even react to the assault. Yet, it wasn't my work that did the most damage. The explosions or fire must have triggered some type of automatic response by the ship itself. The upper decks were sealed and the artificial gravity shield protecting the hangar bay was shut off. Suddenly, the hard vacuum of outer space sucked everything on the deck that wasn't bolted down out of the ship, including me.

Fortunately, I was in a hermetically sealed battle armor with both heat and oxygen. The Ashi were not as lucky. Those who weren't killed by the mini missile attack I had launched or the laser barrage from the MECH cannon were flash frozen in less than a second. I can't say they died that quickly, but they certainly couldn't last long with no air to breathe. All three gunships were jettisoned, too. I found myself floating in a cloud of space junk. It was not what I had planned, but battles never go according to the script. In combat, things are messy. People die, resources are used up or destroyed, the unexpected always seems to happen and the best-laid plans get turned upside down with no warning. A successful commando has to be able to improvise on the fly, especially in a combat zone with no communication with one's superiors.

I had always enjoyed solo missions the most. I feared letting my team down more than dying, but I had trouble staying within the bounds of an assignment. It was better to just fight and let me do what came naturally, which was why, as I drifted away from the Ashi ship, I activated the powerful air-to-air missiles.

"Target the engines," I said, ordering the tactical system to focus the missile computers onto the parts of the alien ships I wanted them to hit. "Fire."

Four missiles were launched in quick succession. They flew up over my head, then their boosters kicked in, propelling them through space at thousands of miles per hour. They went shooting out of the debris field in three directions. One arced up and over, then plowed straight into the exhaust port of the bomber. It exploded, setting off a chain reaction. Red-hot bits of metal ignited the flammable gas used to fuel the ship. That explosion then set off some of the bombs inside the vessel. It blew apart into a million pieces and sent a shock wave flying through space.

At the same time, two more missiles flew across to the Ashi warship that I hadn't been inside of. One missile impacted the cowling of the exhaust. It did damage, but not enough to shut down the ship. The other followed the first, finding a crack in the hull that had been caused by the first missile and flying inside the ship, where it exploded and sent a jet of gas and debris shooting out of the spacecraft. To my delight, all the running lights on the Ashi ship went out. It was an indication that the ship had lost power. Better yet, when it was hit by the shockwave from the bomber, it began to drift down toward the planet. With no way to arrest its motion, the big ship was caught in the planet's gravity. It was only a matter of time before it would be yanked down and ripped apart as it entered Libertine's atmosphere.

I would have called that a lucky shot, but I wasn't actually aiming the missiles. I launched them and let their onboard guidance system do the job of finding the right target.

From the MECH, which had video feeds from cameras that covered all directions, not just in front and behind the fighting platform, but above and below it too, I saw the carnage. I also knew the danger. The blast wave was going to scatter the debris I was hiding in. A collision in space could destroy the MECH or, at the very least, compromise the armor and expose me to hard vacuum. I didn't relish getting sucked through a tiny crack in the MECH, so I fired my boosters.

With no gravity or friction, the boosters were more than enough to propel me through space. I followed the fourth missile, which was actually the first to find a target. It had shot straight back into the hangar and exploded against a bulkhead that covered the ship's complicated electrical network. Think of it as the brain of the ship. All the systems, from artificial gravity to engines - and even life support - were routed through the ship's electrical system. The missile ripped open the bulkhead and did catastrophic damage to the delicate components within the compartment.

I flew into the hangar just as the shockwave from the bomber hit. The ship was tossed like a toy in a bathtub. I managed to lock onto the deck with the MECH and just held on. Of course, there was no sense of motion, but one second I was floating through the hangar and the next second the floor rushed up toward me.

Holding on, I watched the large opening and saw the debris sailing away into deep space. To my chagrin, I also saw escape pods launching from the other warship. The crew was escaping, but at least they would be trapped on Libertine until help came. And the planet was not a hospitable place after being pummeled with orbital bombs by the Ashi. They would reap what they had sown. I couldn't help but feel like that was justice for all the innocents who had died on the planet already.

CHAPTER 31

SPACE IS A DANGEROUS PLACE. It's one of the many reasons that every human spaceship is designed with back-ups and emergency systems in case something goes wrong. So, it was no surprise when red emergency lights came on in the darkened hangar. I looked around and found an airlock for emergency entry into the ship's upper levels. Of course, I couldn't read the signage inside the alien vessel, although the MECH's computer was equipped with translation software. When I looked at the alien script, the translation appeared on my HUD.

There was no gravity in the hangar, which was fine with me. The MECH's ruined knee made it nearly impossible to walk, but in zero-gravity, I could float. The boosters were even able to propel me, so that while I might not be as agile as someone not in a large mechanized fighting suit, I could actually move quite easily.

"Booster at one percent," I said. "Activate close quarters defensive weapons."

A fan-shaped series of short gun barrels rose up and over my shoulders. They were larger bore and loaded with shells that were filled with soft metal pellets. They weren't effective beyond fifteen feet, but were perfect for close quarters, especially when confronted with multiple adversaries.

With a little effort, I flew across the hangar toward the emergency airlock. It had a manual release, which I operated with the MECH's powerful hands. It was a simple lever, but in zero gravity would have been hard to work up and down. I locked the MECH's feet to the deck, using electromagnets, and pumped the handle until the airlock was open wide enough to get inside.

It was impossible to know how many Ashi had been killed, but they had lost two capital ships. That had to be painful, especially since they were dealing with just one man. You could argue that I was more than just a man in the MECH fighting armor. I had greater capabilities, including flight and a larger arsenal, too. Still, I had survived the bombardment by sheer luck and was able to enact my revenge due to years of military training.

I was also aware of the Ashi disdain for life. It was evident in how they treated their enemies, but even more so in how they treated their own kind. I had seen the wounded left to die with no help from their comrades. In fact, I wasn't even sure if the Ashi had a concept of friendship and community. There were a lot of the big, green-skinned aliens. However, from what I had heard, all they did was fight. Other beings governed the galactic Imperium. It was a question for sociologists, not me. All I knew was they didn't care if their own kind lived or died. It was one of the reasons they had simply vacated the hangar when I attacked. On a human ship, it might be better to clear the deck in an emergency, yet the humans working in the area always came before the equipment. The Ashi should have been given warning and time to flee to safe spaces before the gravity was shut off and everything was sucked into outer space.

From the airlock, a ladder led into another chamber on the upper deck. For all I knew, ten thousand aliens were waiting for me there. But I had come to kill the Ashi, and as long as they lived, my job wasn't over.

I propelled the MECH upward with a pull on the ladder. With no gravity, there was no need to climb anything. A light push was all it took to send the heavy fighting platform floating upward. In the next chamber, I worked the handle to open the door just enough to see if I was walking into a trap. What I found was nothing short of remarkable.

There were two Ashi in a large room. I recognized it as an engineering space, although what the big, dangerous machines did was a mystery. Nor was it the equipment what I found to be remarkable. What really scrambled my brain were the slaves being used to clean and service the machines. Perhaps I shouldn't have been surprised that the Ashi were using slaves or that there was a variety of aliens carrying out their demands. In fact, one of the slaves not only left me dumbfounded, she damned near got me killed.

As I slowly cranked open the door, I saw a human woman. She wore dirty coveralls, and her hair was tied back into a messy braid. There was grease and oil on her face. It looked as though she hadn't washed in days. But there was no mistaking who it was or the fact that she recognized me, too.

One of the guards, I learned later they were called overseers, turned toward me. He had a short whip in one massive hand and what looked like an electric cattle prod in the other. If all things had been equal, he could have killed me. He recognized me as a threat and flew into action, while I was still shocked by the sight of Zaya. She had flown off in the slave ship with Rip over a year ago, yet there she was, floating between two big machines in zero gravity. It dumbfounded me to realize that she was on this Ashi warship.

But while I stared at Zaya, the overseer swung the electric prod straight at the MECH's head. I saw the attack coming, but it was too late to stop it. I instinctively raised one hand, which raised the MECH's hand. The prod pounded into the MECH so hard it bent, although it did no damage. Instead, it prompted me to action.

With my other hand, I blasted the alien using the MECH's laser. At close range, it burned straight through him and into one of the machines. Smoke began to billow from the hole in the equipment, while the Ashi overseer dropped to the deck. I immediately swung the laser mounted on the MECH's left arm toward the other Ashi overseer who was trying to flee. They had both been steady, their boots clamped to the floor, probably with magnets like my own. But when he jumped, he was launched through the air toward another hatch. Nothing on the alien ship was small, except for the slaves who were less than half the height of the big Ashi overseers. The alien flew over a pair of terrified slaves who were contorting their bodies in an attempt to get out of the way. I didn't know if they were more afraid of my laser or the overseer. Either way, I fired at him. The beam of highly focused light hit him in the rear while he was bent forward, reaching for the hatch controls. It burned up through his body, scorching through tissue, bone and vital organs. A second later, when he reached the hatch, his lifeless fingers did nothing to open the heavy doorway. Instead, his head crashed into the metal with the entire mass of his body pushing him forward. As he bounced back, there were blobs of alien blood bubbling up from a cut across his head.

"What are you doing here?" Zaya asked in awe.

"Killing them," I snapped. "Why are you here? What happened to Rip?"

That was the vital question, and my words seemed to hit her, like a physical blow. Her eyes turned hard and I remembered the obstinate slave who resented me for freeing her.

"I'm a slave," she snapped. "We're trying to get the engines back online."

"Well, don't," I said, engaging the booster in my free hand to send me sailing across the wide room toward the hatch.

"Where are you going?"

"To find more Ashi."

"You'll find more," she said. "There's only about a thousand of them on this ship, you idiot."

"Good," I said. "I didn't come here because I was looking to hide."

"You were on Libertine," she said.

"That's right."

"Nothing good ever happens in this system."

"That's what the Ashi are going to think. I already took down two of their ships. This one's next. If you want to survive, I suggest you find an escape pod and get off this tub."

"We can't," Zaya snapped. "We're slaves. We can't work the controls."

"You don't know how?"

"It's biometric," she said. "Only the Ashi can launch an escape pod."

"What kind of reader?" I asked.

"It's a hand plate," she said.

I activated my magnetics and landed beside the dead overseer.

"Extend dagger," I ordered.

The double-edged weapon was spring-loaded. It shot from

the end of the MECH's forearm just above the metal hand. One chop severed the overseer's hand halfway up his thickly muscled forearm. It floated toward Zaya with blood extruding in small, spherical blobs that floated through the air.

"There you go," I said. "Problem solved."

"And what do we do on Libertine? We'll probably die down there!"

"Everyone who stays on this ship is going to die for sure," I told her. "The choice is up to you. What's through that door?"

"Slave quarters, then the galley," she told me. "Above that is a thousand Ashi who want you dead."

"They're welcome to try," I said, turning back to the hatch.

The emergency power had restored the lights and the hatch controls were active again. I pressed a button with the MECH's big finger and the metal doorway slid aside. I stepped into what had to be the saddest compartment on a space vessel I had ever seen. It was dark. There were no lights in the long compartment other than a few emergency lights over the doorway at either end. On both sides were small compartments. They looked like dog kennels. There were rough hewn openings in the front. Otherwise, they were completely enclosed. It was hot in the chamber, the temperature reading on my HUD went up fifteen degrees. I could see troughs to either side of the walkway. Some had water drifting up out of them; others seemed to have contained bodily waste. It made my mind spin to think of the unsanitary conditions. The filth was drifting through the large chamber, and there was no way to avoid it. Some of the hovels had what appeared to be straw drifting around just inside the openings. A few looked to have flea-infested blankets wadded inside. That was the extent of the slaves' meager possessions on the Ashi warship.

I made the MECH push itself forward and went sailing

through. The blobs of water and filth hit the armored suit and splashed. I was spared the smell, but was soon covered in alien excrement. When I reached the next compartment, I expected things to improve. They did not.

Zaya had been right. The next compartment was, in fact, the galley for the ship. It was essentially a huge butchering center. The Ashi had hundreds of fattened animals on board. Each day, dozens were slaughtered and prepared for the huge aliens to feast on. But the lack of gravity had turned the galley into a madhouse. Half-butchered carcasses drifted among large globs of floating animal blood. There were knives, saws, bones and animal hides gliding around the room. The aliens themselves had taken hold of their work tables and were waiting patiently for the artificial gravity to be restored. I took full advantage.

From the opening to the galley, I opened fire with the laser cannon. Some of the aliens tried to avoid my deadly barrage. They soon lost their footing and were drifting hopelessly with the animals they had recently slaughtered. I used the electro-magnets in the feet of the MECH to keep me anchored, but I didn't remain in one place. That was a recipe for disaster. In combat, mobility is everything. So, I charged forward into the galley, blasting away. Shots that missed, and some that went clean through the enemy, sizzled into the appliances along the wall of the galley behind the Ashi, preparing the food. Shelves of supplies were torn open, the contents adding to the mass of debris that was floating through the air.

A huge water tank was punctured. The liquid came pumping out, but not in liquid form exactly. It came flowing out in large, seemingly gelatinous streams. As they waved and pulsed, the serpentine blobs broke into smaller bits. They merged when they crashed together and seemed to explode when they touched any solid object.

It was chaos. I charged through it, shooting at anything I thought might be alive. When I reached the next compartment, I barely managed to step through it before a squad of Ashi warriors came rushing down an angled platform. I was in another section of the ship's engineering facilities. There were huge metal tanks connected to one or another by pipes with large valves in between. I didn't have to read the translations of the labels painted onto the tanks. It was clear that they held fuels and that the liquids were highly flammable. I stepped between two of them as the Ashi warriors hurried down the ramp. They weren't looking for me. I suppose it was the release of the escape pods that got their attention.

I waited for them to get close. They moved in stiff formation, marching with their magnet boots almost as if they were moving through deep snow. None of them had laser weapons, but they were all armed with large curved knives or clubs. I waited until they were just a few paces away before stepping out. For one split second, their eyes widened with surprise ... and then I began shooting.

The lasers cut down the Ashi warriors, who, for whatever reason, didn't try to get away. Instead, they charged at me. However, I was in no danger. The laser mowed them down as if they were a patch of tall weeds. Their magnetic boots held them to the floor. The blast wounds cauterized and didn't bleed, but a greasy, black smoke wafted up from where I shot them. It was pure slaughter, and while I relished it, the killing didn't ease my pain. I wanted to kill the Ashi for what they done on Libertine, although no matter how many ships I disabled or warriors I killed, it didn't satisfy me. I pushed through the bodies, knocking them aside like bowling pins. When they were pushed, their magnetic boots came off the metal deck and the bodies went spinning through the air in a macabre display.

Up the ramp were more enemy soldiers. I charged up it, using the zero gravity and the MECH's boosters to guide me. I found myself in a huge chamber. It was part barracks and part training facility. Zaya hadn't been lying about the number of warriors. There were easily several hundred of them. The chamber had a high ceiling and I let myself gain altitude before opening up with the laser. Some Ashi died, others realized the danger and rushed to get their own weapons. I caught them pulling open compartments where their big laser rifles were stored on racks. With a new target to shoot at, I blasted away. Dozens of aliens died. I did my best to shoot those closest to the guns, however others sacrificed themselves to buy a little more time for their comrades. It was wholesale slaughter, but it didn't last long.

Because I was focused on the aliens trying to arm up, I didn't have time to thin the crowds beneath me. It didn't take long for the Ashi to form a chain of sorts. They climbed up one another to reach the feet of the MECH. Within seconds, I was pulled down. Fists pummeled the armor, but did no damage. Likewise, clubs were useless. The Ashi preferred big, curved knife blades. Some stabbed into the armor, but couldn't puncture the thick Kevlar layer. I waited as long as I could, then activated the crowd repelling weapons on the shoulders of the MECH. There were a dozen barrels on each shoulder. They went off simultaneously, creating a booming report that echoed through the ship. The pellets ripped through flesh and splintered bone. The air was filled with a gory haze. I used the cover to slip back down the ramp into the engineering section of the ship.

Sometimes in battle, timing is everything. No sooner had I slipped back down to the lower deck than the newly armed warriors began firing. Their bunks were ripped to pieces and many of their own comrades were gunned down by friendly fire.

There was pandemonium above me and I had to admit that Zaya was right. There were too many warriors to fight head-on. I needed a new strategy.

I found it all around me. The tanks of liquid fuel were thick-walled, yet made of soft metal, probably so that they could flex under the pressure of artificial gravity. I extended my double-edged fighting dagger and rammed it into the nearest of the tanks. The fuel came pouring out in long slivers that floated in the air. I stabbed my blade into another tank and then it was time to run.

I used my boosters and raced back through the galley and the slave quarters. It was part flying and partly physical maneuvering. There were a lot of obstacles in my way, but I knew it was only a matter of time before the liquid fuel snaked its way up to the main level where the Ashi warriors were shooting it out with a phantom. All it would take would be one laser hitting the fuel, or even hitting metal close to the fuel. The heat would ignite it and the flames would carry back down to the canisters, which would explode and rip the ship apart.

I went past the engineering section and into a maintenance corridor. There were large round doors that had been sealed off. I hurried down the section, looking for a way out of the ship. I found it near the end of the long maintenance corridor.

Zaya was there, opening one of the last escape pods. She was alone and near her were several crates of goods. Where she had gotten them wasn't clear but each one was labeled. My computer translated the Ashi script, and I read *Protein* on two of the crates, *Tools* on another, and the fourth box said *Electrical Components*.

She saw me coming and the disappointment was obvious on her dirty face.

"You're still alive?"

"And you're busy stealing," I said.

"I'm saving," she said. "You're the one who said you were going to destroy the ship."

"True," I said. "We should hurry."

"You don't need this," Zaya said, flinging away the hand of the overseer that I had severed for her. "Not with that fancy suit you're wearing."

"I need a ride back to the surface," I told her. "And answers."

She pushed in the first crate.

"I don't think there's room."

"We'll make do," I snapped. "Move!"

She was used to obeying orders. We pushed the crates into one of the empty seats and strapped them down. There were six seats in the pods, all of them Ashi-sized, which meant that a human was too small to fit into the restraints. I sat next to Zaya, and put one of the MECH's arms in front of her, pinning her into the seat.

"What's that for?"

"To keep you safe," I said, hitting the launch button with the MECH's other hand.

There was a loud blast of compressed air. The escape pods were considered vital tech and so had emergency power. There were no windows in the pod, and no way to know what was happening outside of it. Except I had the MECH, which in space had no difficulty connecting to the orbital satellites the *Renegade* had launched while in the system. On my HUD, I got a video feed from the nearest of them. There were more escape pods launching, but within seconds of getting visuals, the Ashi warship exploded. In truth, only half of the ship was destroyed, and thankfully, it was the opposite end of the vessel from where we were cruising toward Libertine. The other half flipped over, and I could see the open decks and debris. No one could have survived the explosion. While there were dozens of escape pods still making their way toward the planet, I could see no other Ashi vessels in space.

The mission that I had come up with was a success. And yet, for all the lives I had taken and all the equipment I had destroyed, I still felt that none of it really made up for the people who had died on Libertine. Maybe it was because revenge was never truly satisfying. I might be able to say I avenged the death of the innocent civilians on the Free World but that didn't bring them back. Nor did it make their absence in my life any less painful.

I closed my eyes for a moment and just breathed. Libertine was pulling me back. I knew the force of attraction was gravity, and yet, it felt like fate had a hand in bringing me back to where my journey began. I thought about the first time I had come to Libertine. It had seemed like a raw, yet open world, full of possibilities. The second time I entered her atmosphere it had been as a refugee who was thankful for the chance to still be alive. That had only happened because of my friend Rip, whose memory made me open my eyes and turn to Zaya. She was staring straight ahead, her hands on the thick metal arm of the MECH.

"I think it's time for some answers," I said. "Start talking and don't lie to me. What happened to Rip?"

CHAPTER 32

"HOW SHOULD I KNOW?" she snapped.

Part of me felt sorry for her. Zaya was a slave. Taken from her home when she was a child, sold as a slave in outer space, and surrounded her entire life by aliens. It was enough to drive anyone insane, but Zaya wasn't crazy; she was spiteful and rude.

"He left with you," I said.

"So, he ditched you and then he ditched me," she said.

"Somehow I doubt that," I said.

"How else would I end up on an Ashi warship?"

I could tell she was lying. There was just the slightest hint of shame on her dirty face. Mostly, she seemed angry and frustrated, but there was shame, too.

"I know Rip pretty well. He was smitten with you."

"He was a dope," she said.

"A dope who loved you."

"I don't know what you're talking about."

Of course, she was lying. I had seen them together. They were on Libertine for a full week before they left on the slave ship. Every day, they hurried off together—a few times, I watched from a distance on the Lake Tyconda plateau. With binoculars, I could see them holding hands or walking with their arms around one another. It was clear they were more than friends.

At night, they would return to camp and I saw the looks between them. Of course, Rip was conscious of the fact that he had won the girl. There had never been much doubt in my mind about who would gain her affections. I would have liked to have been the one she connected with, but I simply had no experience in romantic relationships. It was a one-sided contest from the start.

And I could tell by the way Rip talked about her that he was infatuated with her. He glossed over her prickly attitude and saw only the good qualities in Zaya. She had been born on Earth and had a history of terrifying night visits by alien grays. Most of those episodes had been wiped from her memory, yet they eventually came back to her. Each time the secretive aliens visited her, they grew bolder, until eventually they carried her away.

For a while, she was kept with other humans who had been abducted. They were taught the common language that was used by various species across the galaxy and then eventually sold as slaves. But not before she had been exposed to a wide variety of medical experiments. When she was taken aboard the slave ship, she managed to rise in rank among the slaves because of her initiative and mechanical aptitude. Then, according to Zaya, I ruined it all by disabling the slave ship and killing her masters.

Rip should have known he couldn't trust her. But they had grown very close. Rip thought he was giving her back the life she wanted. It never occurred to him that she had no desire to be back among her own kind.

"You did something to him," I said.

"That's a lie," she insisted.

We were bumping through Libertine's newly thickened atmosphere by that point. The seat harnesses held me fast, but only the MECH's arm was keeping Zaya from bouncing around inside the escape pod.

"You might as well tell me the truth."

"Why should I tell you anything?" she snapped. "You've caused me nothing but trouble."

"I've saved you from a life of servitude twice," I replied. "You should be thanking me."

"I carved out a life for myself that wasn't half bad. You ruined that."

"You saying you'd rather be a slave?"

"I had a home, status and enough value that I was allowed privileges. I had seen a hundred worlds with the slavers. I had done more than probably any other human being."

"You abducted innocents and sold them into slavery," I said. "That's repugnant."

"That's the way things work in the galaxy. You start out as a slave and, if you're lucky, you become part of the trade."

"So when you saw your chance to get the ship and take off together, you sold Rip on the idea."

"That wasn't hard," she said. "He hated this world."

Her words were true and they stung. I knew I wasn't worth staying for, not to Rip. He had saved my life, but then he was stuck on Libertine. I never knew the real reason he didn't want to go back to Earth, yet he wasn't happy on Libertine. While I understood why he wanted to leave, it still hurt that he didn't want to stay.

"And after the two of you left, then what happened?"

"He bamboozled me," she said, feigning outrage. "I thought

he liked me, but we weren't on Highloft Station a day before he abandoned me and took the ship."

"He just left you behind?"

"That's right. I had nothing, no way to survive."

"And how did you end up a slave again?"

"That's what happens when you have debts you can't pay."

"What debts?"

"We refueled the ship, smart guy. Rip said he could pay. I didn't know how and he didn't bother telling me. Then he goes and leaves me with the bill. The admin group sold me to pay for his fuel. You happy now?"

"Good story," I said, "but unconvincing. Rip was a Marine. He was a man of honor."

"That's what you think."

"I know it. He sacrificed his future to save me. That's not the kind of guy who skips out on a girl that he cares about ."

"He never cared about me. No one ever cared about me."

"That's not true and we both know it," I said as the chutes on the escape pod deployed. The unit must have had some kind of inertial damping technology because I could barely feel the pull of gravity as we slowed.

"You, on the other hand," I said, "seem like the kind of person who would do anything to get ahead."

"I'm a realist and there's no law against ambition. Even for slaves."

After that, she clammed up. I could have tortured her for the truth, but I could pretty well put it together. Either she left him behind to deal with her debts after refueling the slave ship, or, and this seemed to fit the circumstances better in my mind, she had turned Rip over to the Ashi. Perhaps she thought she would be rewarded. Instead, the Galactic officials impounded her ship and sold her to the nearest slaver. It was a horrible thing to think about a person, yet nothing about Zaya was soft and fuzzy. The poor woman was all grit and steel. I would have admired it if she hadn't sold out my closest friend.

I was the first one out of the pod, and once again, I was shocked at what I found. Libertine had changed.

"Wow, this is different," Zaya said.

She had come out behind me. I turned, saw her tangled, frizzy braid sway in the breeze. On my HUD, the temperature read seventy-two degrees Fahrenheit. I knew we were too far from the polar regions for the temperature to be so cool. The sun was out. There were thick, fluffy clouds in the sky. But it was the landscape that was the biggest change. It was still barren, but the soil was packed down hard and there were rivers and streams flowing.

"This was all sand," I said.

"Where's it all gone?"

"Packed down by heavy, heavy rains, I think," I told her while simultaneously running a scan on the MECH's sensors. "The soil is still silica, but it's different somehow."

The answer hit me a few moments later. For soil to be changed it has to have organic matter, otherwise it is just sand. There was no organic matter in the deserts or, at least, not enough to change the content of the soil. But there was a lot of organic matter from the polar regions that had been blasted into the sky. The rain must have washed it down and mixed it with the sand.

"And that?" Zaya asked, pointing to something standing out in the landscape to the north of us.

"I'm not sure," I said. "I think it might be a terraforming platform."

We gathered the crates from the escape pod. There were also some survival supplies on board, but we could only carry so much. I did the heavy lifting in the MECH, however with one leg damaged, it was slow going. We walked toward the terraforming platform. It was a large structure separated into four sections on top of a square scaffolding supported by big pylons that were buried deep.

We had to circle around to find the ladder that led up to the platform, which was nearly twenty feet above the ground. My guess was it hadn't been so high before the bombardment rains. I knew in the mountains, the rain had been torrential. It seemed as though it had been here as well. The flow of water and sand had changed the landscape dramatically.

"This is wild," Zaya said. "What happened to the people here?"

I climbed up onto the decking still in the MECH, but then shut down the unit. It had just barely a quarter of its operating power left. I climbed down and looked at the MECH. There were scorch marks and dings on the metal plating. It was worn, but it had served me well.

"Hugo?"

I looked over at Zaya. She was standing near a strange dome-shaped module and looking in through a dirty window.

"What is it?"

"It's a house," she said. "I mean, it's like a real house."

I walked over to her and gazed inside. There was a small kitchen and strange-looking furniture. Against the far wall was a nook with a bed.

"This must be where the workers lived while they were on station," I said.

"What do you think happened to them?"

I shrugged. "Some got hurt, but most just finished their time on station and moved on to other jobs. I'm pretty sure the locals manned the terraforming stations in exchange for homesteads in the polar regions where it wasn't so hot."

"And they just quit?"

"That's what I heard," I told her. "They just lost interest."

We went around to the door. It was closed and held in place with several simple locking mechanisms. They were easy to unfasten, and we went inside. The interior was dusty, but otherwise unchanged. There wasn't much moisture until the bombardment a few days earlier, and so no mold or mildew had set in.

"This is wonderful," Zaya said as she went around opening the windows. "I can't believe it."

I couldn't believe the change in her. The prickliness was gone. In fact, she sounded almost likable.

"It's a suitable domicile," I said as I slid open a panel that led to a bathroom. "They must have had running water."

"And electric," she said, pointing to several lamps on side tables. "It's different, for sure, but it reminds me of home."

I nodded. It had some nostalgic qualities. I was used to barracks ... and over the last year, I had spent my share of nights out in the open, sleeping in a hammock. In all those nights, it had never been as cool and comfortable as it was at the station we found ourselves in.

There were four separate dome-shaped apartments, and in the middle of them was a larger one without beds: just a large kitchen and some recreational devices, along with a pretty decent-looking communications array.

"If we could get that going, we could sync up with the satellites," I said.

"What good would that do?" Zaya asked.

But it was a genuine question, not a snide insult masquerading as a question.

"For one thing, we would know if more ships entered the system," I said. "There are weather satellites, too. Plus, if there are any survivors in the north, we could possibly make contact. At the very least, we could figure out where we are now."

She nodded and we moved on to explore the rest of the rig. There was a drilling section and a refining plant. Both of those were straightforward and showed some signs of wear and tear from the blowing sands. But it was the fourth section of the station, which we discovered was called HLT-87, that was the most important. It was a workshop filled with tools, supplies, parts and equipment for repairing the drill and refinery. We even found generators that ran off the fossil fuels that were being collected by the drilling well and refined at the adjoining plant.

"Look," Zaya said, filled with excitement. She was pointing to a schematic of the platform. I couldn't read it, but maybe she could. "I think they have a well," she continued. "Hugo, we could live in this place. Not just survive, but really live."

"Okay," I said, not quite sharing in her enthusiasm, yet still feeling as if luck had finally broken my way on Libertine.

I don't say that because I was with a woman. Nor did I mean to imply that there was any sort of relationship with Zaya. She was there with me and we had shelter. It was much better than a cave and more secure than a tiki hut on the beach. I had gone from losing everything to finding a place ... and perhaps even a future on Libertine.

We spent the rest of the day turning things on. First, the generators. They had to be primed and some of the fuel lines that ran to tanks in the refinery had to be replaced. Fortunately, there were a lot of replacement parts in the workshop. Tools, too, which made the meager crate of supplies that Zaya had stolen from the warship seem insignificant.

Once the generators were back on, we got the well powered

up and pumping. Next were the lights on the station itself, although I didn't want them on. Despite the good fortune we had found, there were still dangers on Libertine. Sooner or later, the Ashi survivors would discover us and we didn't need to use the station's exterior lighting that would undoubtedly draw them in.

That evening, Zaya enjoyed her first hot shower in decades. There wasn't clothing on HLT-87, but there were bolts of cloth and tools for sewing. It seemed to me there were a lot of supplies intended for when the climate changed on Libertine. But the terraforming process had taken longer than expected and was eventually shut down. The workers simply left the rig the way they had found it, including all the supplies stored in lockers inside the workshop.

We didn't have bedding, however the beds in the apartments were soft. We cut some fabric to act as blankets and, after a good scrubbing, I slept pretty well. The next morning, I set out to repair the MECH. Zaya was able to adapt the charging port and utilize the generators to refill the MECH's power bank. I was able to take the knee joint apart. There were no spare parts for a MECH, but Zaya utilized what we had and fabricated a new one. She was like a child in a toy store and also a genius inventor, at the same time. No problem confounded her. They were opportunities for her to use the tools and supplies, which thrilled her in a way I hadn't thought possible.

With the power up, I got the satellites synced to the communication equipment in the primary pod. I was able to bring up video feeds of the space around Libertine. There was plenty of evidence of the battle. Several larger chunks of the warship and bomber were still in orbit, as was the dead vessel that was slowly descending into the planet's atmosphere. But there were no other vessels in the system. We were all alone. That might have bothered me if Zaya's personality hadn't changed so completely. She talked to me and listened when I talked. Sure, it was mostly about the station, which she had not only fallen in love with, but was already laying claim to. It had become her little kingdom and nothing pleased her more than exploring it.

The second night, with the MECH fully charged and repaired, I knew I needed to return to the cave in the mountains.

"Why?" Zaya asked me when I told her about my plan.

"I have supplies there."

"We have everything we need right here," she pointed out.

"Not everything," I reminded her. "We need food."

We were living off the crate of protein. It was unflavored, but mixed with water, it contained vitamins and minerals that fueled our bodies. I thought it was like drinking oat milk, but with even less taste, but Zaya didn't seem to mind. There was enough to last the two of us about three months.

"If you say so," she replied.

"There are weapons there, too."

"You already have the MECH."

"But it needs reloads on nearly everything."

"It just seems sudden," she said. "We just got here."

"I know," I admitted. "But I can get more food, and the weapons will allow us to hunt."

I didn't tell her there was a chance that no game existed on the planet. I didn't want her to worry and it would be devastating for her to discover that, after finding a home, that we would starve to death in it.

"And you'll come back?"

"Of course, I will," I said. "The mountains are only three hundred miles south of here. I can fly there, get what we need, and come back."

"If you don't crash and die. Rip said you weren't any good at flying in that thing."

Rip was still a major sore spot. I hadn't pressed for more answers, but her voice quavered a little every time she said his name.

"I'm getting better," I told her. "Look, I'll be in radio contact almost the entire time."

It shocked me that she didn't want to be alone. But something about the terraforming rig had changed Zaya. It was as if something she thought she had lost forever was her's again. She didn't want to be alone. She wanted to share it with someone, even if I was the only other person on the entire planet.

"Go then," she said. "Just make sure you come back, no matter what."

"I will," I promised, even though I had no idea how hard it would be to keep that promise.

CHAPTER 33

FLYING, it seemed, wasn't so difficult if one got high enough. There was actually a freedom to it. Of course, had I crashed or if the suit ran out of power before I reached my destination, that would have been bad. Zaya would have been left all alone, which, after a couple of long days together, was not something I wanted. It seemed like all I needed to connect with a person was to be stranded on an alien world together with no other humans.

As I made my way south in the partially repaired MECH, I had time to think about things. I was once more contemplating life or, at least, my life. It felt good to be alive was the one certainty I could settle on. I still grieved what was lost, from Rip to the people of Lake Tyconda, but I could also see a future. Perhaps it was hot, running water and soap that made the difference, but I was enjoying the new climate and accommodations at HLT-87.

As I flew over what had formerly been the borderland between the desert and the grasslands, I saw signs of life. There was still snow on the ground, and in it tracks made by wildlife that had survived the bombing and the sudden upheaval of the weather. I was too high up to make out what they were. In fact, if it weren't for the MECH's scanning, I would have missed the tracks altogether. I had the system running visual and radar scans. My fear was running into Ashi survivors, yet what I found was evidence of Libertine survival. The HUD showed a tinted view because of the dazzling brightness of the snow and overlaid on top of the vid feed were geographic features that were lost on me at two thousand feet above the ground. But with the MECH's technology, I could zoom in and examine minute features up close; like the tracks in the snow, which were highlighted by a yellow line at the normal viewing distance.

To my consternation, the mountains looked completely different from when I had lived there. I had mapping software, although the MECH's signals didn't reach into space and there weren't enough satellites to form a perfect GPS map. So, I looked for the crater, thinking that would mark my particular mountains and allow me to navigate to the cave. It was the first mistake of several I made that day.

It's funny how things change in our memory. I can vividly remember that three bombs were dropped on the day of the bombardment. I heard the first two and then saw evidence of the third. Yet, when I traveled back to the mountains, I forgot about the other bombs. So, when I came upon a crater, I assumed it was the one near my cave. Only it wasn't. The Ashi had targeted both sides of the mountain chain, as well as the primary colony near the center. With the terrain changed by the shockwave from the blast, then covered with snow, it didn't surprise me that nothing looked the same. I spent almost half the day searching for my cavern in the wrong place before it occurred to me that there was probably more than one crater. I took to the air again, painfully aware that the MECH was down to half its total power.

It was early afternoon when I finally reached the cave. Finding it wasn't easy. The entrance was nearly filled with snow. Had the storms continued, it might have been lost to me. But eventually I found it. The river outside the cavern entrance was still running high. The water in the crater had overflowed and formed new rivers that were pushing north through what had been wide grassy plains. There was no grass left, not that I could have seen it under the snow. The temperature had risen a little, but not much. It hovered right at the freezing mark, and the wind was still blowing the frozen ice crystals into massive drifts in certain parts of the mountain.

I climbed up through the snow and into the cave. My gear was still there, and more importantly, the ammunition for the MECH. I needed to hurry if I was going to rearm the combat platform and fly back to HLT-87 before dark. Hurrying was my second mistake. I should have looked around more. I should have seen the scat from the animal that had taken refuge in the cave. I should have noticed that something had been sniffing around my gear, or at least, I might have seen some hair from the beast.

During the year before, as I hunted in the mountains, I had seen signs of large predators, but I hadn't actually seen them. Once, at night, I thought I saw one. But it was just a shadow in the gloom. I couldn't make out the beast's features.

Once I got to the cave, I immediately powered down the MECH. I had used more power than expected, by flying. The snow was deep enough that I opted to fly as I searched the mountains for my cavern, even though it consumed energy much faster than climbing through the snow would have. Still, if not for the armored suit's flight capabilities, I would probably still have been searching for the cavern in the wrong place.

I opened up the MECH and climbed down. There were still crates of ammunition for the fighting platform. Cases of missiles and boxes of belt-fed ammo for the rotating machine gun. That particular weapon was still broken, but Zaya was confident it could be fixed. I was busy inserting the big air-to-air missiles into the back of the MECH when the attack came. I never even heard the animal moving in the darkness of the cave.

One second, I was perched on the side of the MECH, having just pushed down a missile into the launch frame. It snapped into place with a satisfying ~Click!~ then I heard a snarl, and at almost the same time, something hit me. I fell off the side of the MECH. I was at least ten feet up on the frame of the MECH. Loading in the missiles wasn't easy and had to be loaded from the top down, which meant climbing up to the MECH's shoulder. I fell hard on my side and immediately recognized the fiery sensation in my hip and leg as coming from lacerations, but there was no time for indulging my pain. My survival instincts kicked in just as the predator, who had jumped up toward me - swiping me with one paw and then falling back - rebounded on top of me. In that split second, my hand had found a rock on the cave floor. It was more of a rock shard, a shattered chunk of stone. As the heavy beast landed on my chest, I felt its hot, fetid breath on my face, just as I smashed the rock into the side of the creature's head.

The strangest part of the entire attack was that I never quite saw the beast. It was dark in the cave, with only a little bit of light filtering in from the opening nearby. I saw four legs, felt dense, prickly fur, and the weight of the creature. It jerked away from me when I hit it, squealing with pain. The jagged edge of the stone had torn open a gash along the side of its head. It was big like a tiger, yet it squealed like a pig. I sat upright, and it came at me again, swiping at me with one paw. The creature had long claws extended, one of which caught me on the chin. It ripped a chunk of bearded flesh from my face and I screamed in pain. I also threw the rock at the predator. It hit the beast somewhere tender and sent it bounding back into the darkness.

I staggered to my feet. My heart was pounding in my chest, and blood was dripping from my chin. It was also soaking the side of my pants, which had been torn to shreds along my left side. My right leg, hip, and shoulder were also hurting from the fall. Nevertheless, I had been hurt before. I had been hurt during special combat training. The goal of which was to teach Marines that they could keep going despite their physical condition. I had been wounded in combat on several occasions. It was never a pleasant experience, but once again, my training kicked in. Despite my wounds in the cave, I hobbled over to where I kept my rifles. They were all loaded and ready for action. I grabbed the first one I could reach, the Sterner M88 Classic. It had a flashlight clamped onto the mount over the barrel. I snapped it on and swung the bright beam around the cavern. There was no animal to be found. I guessed it had retreated back into the cave. Part of me wanted to follow, but instead, I utilized the recharging stations and set up a couple of lights. They weren't made to illuminate a large space and there were still plenty of shadows for a predator to hide in. But after making a search of the main cavern, I sat down on a stone and sprayed antiseptic into the wounds on my leg and chin. Bandages came next. It was quick, sloppy work. I just needed to stop the bleeding so I could continue my mission of rearming the MECH. I found my gun belt and slung it around my hips. I normally didn't wear it in the MECH, where my big frame left little extra room, but the predator in the cave had given me reason to keep my weapons close to hand. I had a Jagger HC in a thigh holster and a K-Bar combat knife in a sheath on the opposite side. The belt helped hold a pad of gauze onto my hip and the pistol holster did the same on my upper thigh. I cinched them down tight to help stanch the bleeding and it actually felt a little better with the belt on.

The wounds slowed me down. The cuts weren't too deep, but they hurt just the same. I was also worried that some alien bacteria might poison my blood. It was impossible not to think of Lieutenant Colt, who had succumbed to a parasite of some sort that had driven him mad. I didn't want that and would have to warn Zaya to keep a check on my behavior as the wounds healed.

I got the MECH loaded with the last of the missiles, and then more rounds for the MECH machine gun, and shoulder-mounted weapons. I loaded my other rifles into the big crate the missiles had come out of. Next, I put in all the food I had left in the cavern. The rest of the space was filled with ammunition and batteries for the rifles, and stuffed in the blankets from Lake Tyconda before snapping the lid down.

Every inch of me hurt and I was all too happy to climb back into the MECH and close it back up. The cavern was probably filled with the scent of my blood. The predator would be back and I wanted to be gone ... or at least protected, when it did.

I set up the wind turbines outside the cave to recharge the power bank, and also to help mark the cavern. In the MECH's navigation app, I marked the location, but without GPS, it wasn't as certain as I would have liked. Finally, I picked up the heavy crate, cradling it in the MECH's powerful arms. I had no idea how much the weight and drag would drain the MECH's power on the flight back to the terraforming platform. That was my third - and nearly fatal - mistake.

The sun was almost down when the rig came into view. I had to look past the MECH's warning that was flashing on the HUD to see it. I was down to less than five percent power in the big platform. Landing without using the boosters on the MECH's hands was much more difficult than I had imagined. Plus, the weight was all wrong with the heavy crate held high against the MECH's chest. Somehow, I managed it, landing just a few hundred yards from the platform.

"Zaya, are you there?" I asked via my comlink.

"Where else would I be?"

I was relieved to hear her voice. After the day I had experienced, it wasn't hard to imagine danger around every corner.

"I'm running low on power."

"No surprise there. You took your sweet time getting back."

"It took me longer to find the cavern than I expected."

Perhaps I should have told her about my run-in with the predator and my wounds, but something stopped me. Maybe it was pride or some intuition that she would use the information against me in an argument. At any rate, I left that news for later.

"Do you need help?"

"Negative. I'll get the MECH back to the workshop and charging. Then meet you after."

"Copy that."

I couldn't tell from her voice if she was pleased or not. With Zaya, or maybe it was just me, but I never could tell what other people hoped for if they didn't explicitly spell it out. Did she want to see me? Was she relieved that I was still alive? Was it just the thought of being all alone that bothered her or was my safety really a concern for her? I had no idea. There was nothing between us other than companionship. She was attractive in a rugged sort of way and I'll admit that I liked being with her. Yet, if that was even a remote possibility, it seemed to me to be a million miles away.

I carried my crate of ammunition, weapons and food back to the workshop. Nothing seemed amiss. I got the MECH powered down just before it ran out of energy. Then I connected the charging cables and began that process. Satisfied that my gear was in order, I took some MREs from the crate, along with the blankets from Lake Tyconda. They were simple, unadorned blankets made from plant fibers, but they were warm, and I thought I might gift one to Zaya. Perhaps she would appreciate an addition to the home she was making in the rig's dome apartment.

The big primary dome was dark and I didn't bother going in. Nor did I think that anything was amiss. I would have liked to spend the evening with Zaya, but it wasn't necessary. I certainly needed a shower and the chance to do a proper job looking after my wounds. Still, I wanted to see her, if only to give her a food pouch and the blanket. MREs are nothing a person would crave, although after days of eating nothing but bland protein mixed with water, the meal pouches seemed like a gourmet dinner.

I went to her apartment first. The door was open, but the interior was dark, and finally I realized that something was wrong. I dropped the blankets, and my hand went immediately to my pistol, but at the same instant, a huge green warrior charged through the door.

The only thing that saved me was the Ashi warrior's size. It had to slow down and contort its body to get through the doorway. The dome was made of steel and strong polymers that the huge brute couldn't just smash through. That gave me just enough time to jerk the pistol free. I was bringing it up as the alien's massive hand hit my opposite shoulder. I pulled the trigger as I was spun around.

Jagger's are called hand cannons for a reason. They are simple, close-quarter weapons. They fired thick shells of tiny circular blades called buzzers through a smooth bore of only eight inches in length. Needless to say, they're only effective for ten or fifteen feet, depending on the target. My shot was low and off target, but the buzzers spread out and ripped a chunk of flesh from the alien's thigh.

We both fell onto the metal deck. It hurt, yet by that time my adrenaline was so high I didn't feel a thing. Unfortunately, I wasn't able to hang onto the pistol. It went bouncing across the deck.

I heard Zaya scream inside her darkened apartment and something inside me went crazy. Rage filled me, and turned my vision red. There was just enough light from the setting sun to see the big alien nearby. He was old enough to have some gray in the thick hair bundle that grew from the top of his skull and was tied in place by what appeared to be a leather band. He had one hand on the flesh wound. There was blood seeping down his leg and welling up between his thick fingers. I could see pointed claws at the end of each digit.

He wore nothing but a thick kilt and a wide belt. From that belt, he pulled a big, curving knife. To me, it was as long as a sword. I rolled away from the alien. My own combat knife wasn't big enough to fight the alien with, so I snatched up a metal pipe that was propped against the doorway to another of the apartments.

"You want a piece of me?" I screamed. "Come and get it!"

The Ashi warrior was back on his feet. He leaned forward and roared, bearing his pointed teeth and long tusks. I thrust the end of the pipe straight at his face. In that moment, he surely expected to cow me with his roar. What he didn't expect was for his seemingly puny opponent to attack him. I was half his size and not nearly as strong, but that didn't mean I had no strength. I was as much a warrior as any of the Ashi. So, I took the fight to the big, green alien.

The end of the pipe hit the Ashi warrior in his eye. The blow wasn't hard enough to maim, but it had struck in a tender place. The alien reared back, raising his sword arm to protect his face. I had to take full advantage of the momentary shock the alien was stuck in. So, I swung the pipe over my head with a two-handed grip, shifting into a baseball swing that connected across the knuckles of the alien's hand that was protecting its wounded thigh. Another roar of pain, perhaps the pipe had shattered bone, I couldn't be sure.

The Ashi warrior tried to take a step back and faltered, but he did manage to swing his sword at me. I grasped the pipe at each end, holding it across my body to block the swipe of the alien blade. The pipe held, but I was flung off my feet.

As I struggled to my knees, the alien lumbered toward me. He was limping badly. Blood was gushing from his open wound. In the MECH, I could have gone toe to toe with the Ashi warrior. But I had burned through the MECH's power and all I had to fight with were my own wits.

My opponent sensed my weakness. I had landed some lucky blows but hadn't yet caused enough damage to debilitate the alien. Speed and agility were my only advantages, but even that was hindered by the predator attack in the cave. There was a moment of pure terror as the huge brute bore down on me. I had to wait to draw him in before I sprang my attack. In addition, the understanding that I would probably die was like a warning siren that someone was holding up against the side of my head.

I saw the alien roar, but didn't hear it. I felt the deck shudder with each of the Ashi's lumbering steps. It raised the sword. I pretended as though I was going to try and block it again, but just as he started his down stroke, I dove forward. The alien's legs were wide enough and tall enough that I could dart between them. I hit the metal deck on my bruised shoulder, ignoring the pain as I tucked and rolled back to my feet just behind my foe.

The alien started to turn just as I did, only I was putting all my strength and momentum into a strike with the pipe that landed on his thigh wound. The metal hit wet flesh with an awful sound and the jarring vibration stung my hands and wrists.

But it was the alien who staggered backward, roaring in pain. We were close to the edge of the platform by then. The metal deck had a short safety railing that only came up to my hip. It caught the Ashi warrior in mid-calf, tripping him. The alien's arms flailed and the curved knife flew from his grasp as the Ashi warrior fell.

I sprinted back toward where the Jagger HC lay, snatching it up before returning to the railing. But the alien had rolled under the rig and out of sight. It would have been better to finish the big, green warrior before returning to Zaya's apartment, albeit there was no time to waste. I rushed through her door and could smell the alien. It was a huge brute, squatting down over Zaya and pinning her to the floor with one knee. The warrior had a laser rifle. It was big, too big for the enclosed space, and the alien was too slow. It tried to target me, but I dropped to the floor and brought my pistol up in one singular motion. His rifle was nearly pointed toward me when I fired my gun. The Jagger HC is a revolver with six shells. The buzzers ripped through the flesh on the side of the alien's face, including its eye. Blood sprayed.

The alien fired at me, but missed. The laser light was blinding up close. I felt the heat as the beam sizzled through the air. It went out the open doorway and hit a beam that was part of the well. Sparks flew and I fired again. I was half blinded, but the alien was so big he was hard to miss. My second shot shattered one tusk and ripped his fleshy jaw to ribbons.

It didn't drop the laser rifle, but its primary hand was on the trigger. When it instinctively reached up to touch its ruined face with that hand, it couldn't fire at me. It also leaned back against the apartment wall, inadvertently lifting its knee off of Zaya. I didn't have to tell her to run, but years in the Space Marines had left their mark on me.

"Move! Move! Move!" I screamed at her.

She scrambled forward, first on her hands and knees, and then getting her feet under her. I knew that I couldn't kill the aliens with my pistol. It had enough bite to hurt them, but it wouldn't stop them for long. I lowered the barrel and fired one last shot at the alien's wide boot. The garment stopped nearly half of the thin, spinning blades, but some cut through and sliced open the flesh inside. I hoped that slowed him down enough to give us an edge.

I raced back outside and easily caught up with Zaya. She was moving stiffly and struggling to breathe.

"I think... it cracked... my ribs," she wheezed.

"Get to the workshop," I ordered.

It was too dark to see clearly. I almost didn't see the first alien climbing up the side of the rig. He was nothing but a shadow against the landscape, although the moon was starting to rise, and I saw a glint of light coming from blood on the exposed jawbone. Fortunately for us, that alien didn't have a rifle, just the long curved knife. I fired my last two shots at the alien. He was too far away for the Jagger to have much effect, but he dropped back down into the darkness.

Zaya and I raced into the workshop. She collapsed beside the tool bench. I hurried over to my crate and threw it open. My weapon of choice was right on top, an Ambrose Hill XOR. It was a rugged machine gun with a grenade launcher under the barrel. Most Marines didn't prefer it because of the weight, but I found the sturdy weapon to be a perfect fit. In combat, it was a force to be reckoned with. The machine gun fired Shock Wave kinetic rounds. They were thick bullets with explosive charges inside. When the bullets hit, the explosive pushed them deep and fragmented the metal casing for maximum damage. The magazine held forty rounds, plus the grenade revolver held eight thermobaric impact rounds. I could have used it to destroy the entire terraforming rig, but my goal was to save it.

"Stay here," I told her. "Stay out of sight."

"Yeah," she wheezed.

Just before I ran out into the night, I saw her crawl under the tool bench.

The temperature was dropping. My ragged breath was sending plumes of condensation around my head. My first target was the alien in Zaya's apartment. It came crawling out and I fired quickly, bringing the weapon to my shoulder but shooting without really aiming. I had spent hundreds of hours firing thousands of rounds from that rifle. It was like an extension of my body and aiming it was second nature.

The kinetic round hit the Ashi warrior in his forehead, punched through his skull, and turned his brain to soup. He died instantly, falling onto his face, and blood and bone gushed from the hole in his head.

I felt relief, as if the odds had evened, but then another flash of light lit the rig. It was like a flash of lightning, but it was a laser bolt. It passed close enough behind me that I heard it sizzle. I dropped down and moved to the corner of the nearby refinery. The last thing I wanted was to draw fire toward the workshop where Zaya was hiding.

The moon was half full and the sky was clear. Thousands of stars and the planet's single moon cast a silvery light over the rig. It reminded me of nights by Lake Tyconda, first as an outsider, and then, on my last visit, as a member of the vibrant little community. But the barren ground beyond the rig was dark. I felt exposed. There were more alien warriors moving toward us in the dark.

My rifle was custom-fit with a variety of high-end attachments, including a night vision scope. The Ambrose Hill XOR wasn't a long-range rifle, but she could accurately hit targets a hundred yards out. I activated the scope's night vision. I quickly counted eight more warriors, all armed with laser rifles.

They couldn't see me, but I knew the minute I fired at them my muzzle flash would give my location away. Nor did I want an extended firefight. The laser fire from their rifles would damage the buildings on the rig. If they hit the tanks of refined oils, it could cause an explosion that would destroy the entire structure.

The machine gun fired using explosive gas propellant, but the grenades fire using only compressed air. I didn't want to waste the grenades, but it wouldn't do us any good to save the ammo if we were killed. Reaching up to the scope on top of the rifle, I toggled the range finder to get a reading on how far out the aliens were. They had no cover. All around the rig was open ground. There were some geographic features a mile or so away, including a river and some large boulders. But the Ashi were coming straight across open ground, what my superiors in the Space Marines would have called killing ground or no man's land.

They were sixty feet from the edge of the platform. I raised the rifle to give the grenades maximum distance, then fired three in quick succession. The aliens surely heard the shots, but didn't see anything. I raised my rifle back to my shoulder and took a quick glance through the night vision scope. They were spread out in a line. It was good combat discipline, but I knew the explosive power of the thermobaric grenades was enough to take them all down.

I looked away from the scope just as the first grenade hit. It exploded in a fireball that spread out. The flames seemed to grow in the still night air. The light from them lit up the line of aliens. Two had been caught in the blast, another was moving away from it as the second grenade hit, then the third. It was a good attack. I knew that if the Ashi had the variety of weapons and equipment that humanity had developed for warfare, they would be a much more dangerous foe. But their size, ferocity and overwhelming power had been enough to lead to their supremacy in the galaxy. This had caused a stagnation in their weapons research and development.

Seven of the eight alien warriors were killed by the grenades. The last seemed to panic. It was not what I expected from the alien. I could have gunned him down, but when he dropped his rifle and ran away, I hesitated. Watching him through my night vision scope blinded me to what was coming from the other side of the rig. The wounded alien had climbed back up again and was sneaking toward me. He would have succeeded in killing me had not his immense weight made the metal decking creak. I looked up, saw the alien lunge for me and just managed to duck under his blade. I rolled to my back and tried to shoot him, yet the alien was wary of my weapon. He grabbed the barrel. The gun went off, the bullet tore through the palm of his hand, but he didn't let go. Instead, he jerked the rifle out of my hands and flung it over his shoulder.

I scrambled back, cursing my bad luck. I should have found a secondary weapon, but in the rush to stop the aliens, I hadn't taken the time. My foe still had his long, curved knife. He swung it at my head. It was an arrogant tactic. In the Corps, I had been drilled over and over again to take a body shot over a head shot. It might not be as spectacular, but it was much more effective. So, since the alien slashed at my head, I managed to duck under the blow. In a stroke of good fortune, his blade chopped into the corner of the building that housed the refinery. It stuck fast. The alien was forced to tug on the weapon.

There was only one course of action for me. I could run, but that would just delay the inevitable. And I wasn't the type to run from a fight. Instead, I screamed with rage and jumped onto the alien's back. My free hand caught his hair, which had fallen loose and dangled down his back. I held on to it for dear life and, with the other hand, drew my K-bar. Just as the alien freed his own weapon, I stabbed my knife into the alien's armpit. The blade sank down to the guard and I heard the big Ashi grunt in pain.

In a human, the armpit was a weak point. A blade stabbed under the arm allowed access to the chest cavity and the vital organs within. I didn't know enough about Ashi anatomy to know if the same weakness would hold true. Instead, I stabbed my blade up and into the shoulder joint. Then I worked it back and forth, partly to inflict pain, but mostly just in an effort to hold on. I had one hand tangled in the alien's hair, the other holding onto my combat knife that was stabbed into the underside of his shoulder joint. Then, with a sickening pop, the Ashi's shoulder popped out of the socket. The huge alien screamed in agony and flung himself backward. I had the presence of mind to let go of him and jump clear.

The dislocated arm hung limp and had dropped his knife. It was the size of a sword to me, and heavy. The handle was too big around for my hand to wrap around it, but I could hold it with two hands. I lifted the curved blade. The moonlight reflected off the weapon, and I saw terror in the alien's tiny eyes. He couldn't believe he was about to be slain by the human who was half his size.

"This is for Eldora!" I bellowed as I chopped down with the huge knife. It glanced off his upper chest and hacked into the

Ashi's narrow throat. It wasn't a clean cut and I didn't try to pull it free. The alien slapped one hand against his short neck. At the same time, I sawed the weapon back and forth. His windpipe was severed, and so were the arteries feeding blood to his brain. Within a minute, the big brute was dead.

I limped over to where my rifle lay. I picked it up, checked the weapon and then scanned all around that side of the rig for more aliens. There were none. I took my time searching. There were no other aliens in sight. Even the one who had fled was gone. I reloaded my Jagger, retrieved my K-bar and searched every structure on the platform. I even checked under the rig. Zaya and I were alone. The threat was over ... for the moment at any rate.

When I returned to the workshop, I found Zaya curled in a ball under the tool bench, crying.

"Hey," I said. "It's okay now."

I reached out with one hand. She looked at it. Her face was streaked with tears. I had turned on a small work light so she could see me.

"It's just me," I said. "The aliens are gone."

"Are you sure?"

"Positive."

She came out, slowly at first, her eyes wide with fear and pain. Then she clung to me, weeping. I was still holding my rifle, but I wrapped my free arm around her. I couldn't squeeze without hurting her. But I stayed still, one arm protectively around her shoulders, while she pressed her face against my neck and cried.

Eventually, we went back to my apartment. Her's still had an alien corpse in the doorway. I put Zaya into my bed and covered her with the blankets from Lake Tyconda. She cried herself to sleep while I sat beside her, weapon in hand. At one point, I tried to put it down, but she stopped me.

"No, keep it," she said.

"Okay," I replied.

She squeezed my free hand, tucking it under her chin. I thought that was probably how she looked as a little child. It was a terrible thing to be taken from one's home and forced to rely on no one else. I made up my mind right then and there that I would watch over her for as long as she wanted me. That seemed to me like a good way to spend a life.

A few hours later, dawn filled the sky with crimson light. From where I sat next to Zaya, I could see the sun rising. There was just the slightest bit of green starting to show on the dark ground—the first sprouts of new grass. I felt humbled and amazed. Libertine was coming back to life. The bombardment, that had killed so many, had sped up the terraforming process exponentially. That didn't mean it was perfect. But life was returning to the planet and I was part of that.

Out there, somewhere, beyond the horizon, there were more Ashi warriors. They no doubt sought revenge just as I had. They would find us here and come to kill us. That much was certain. I had no illusions about it. The enemy would come again and, as often as they did, I would kill them. That was my future ... and I was just fine with that.

AUTHOR'S NOTE

Thank you so much for joining me on this adventure with Hugo. I can't say, but I have loved his character from the start. Maybe because he's misunderstood by his platoonmates on the *Jericho*. Or maybe it's because he changes with a little help from Master Sergeant Steel. My original plan had been for Remmy to sacrifice himself for the ship. But as I wrote that portion of *Independence* I realized that Hugo would do it for him. And then of course, I couldn't let Hugo die. Nor did I feel like that was the end of his story.

There's more to come. Hugo and Zaya's tale continues in *Brutal Planet*. Keep reading for an unedited excerpt of that book, coming in July 2025.

BRUTAL PLANET CHAPTER 1

Monsters always come at night. That's especially true on Libertine, first of the Free Worlds. I was climbing the scaffolding on the drill, which was pumping once more. Zaya had made all the repairs. Working helped her deal with the aftermath of having been held hostage by Ashi warriors. There were hundreds of them on Libertine, and the radar we had installed on top of the drilling tower had picked up movement coming toward us from the east.

"What do you see?" Zaya asked.

"Nothing yet," I told her.

"Well, what are you waiting for? Get your big butt moving, Marine!"

I grunted in response. Zaya was not a Marine, but she did enjoy barking orders. I thought she would have made a fine drill instructor.

The top of the drill scaffolding was a hundred feet above the old terraforming platform, which we had made our home after the Ashi bombarded the colonies on Libertine from orbit. The terraforming station had been defunct for a long time, but the structures and gear were still intact. It took some time to get the drill pumping again and the refinery churning that crude oil into usable fuels, but Zaya had a knack for fixing things.

I was only good at one thing - combat, which was why I was in charge of security. The platform was a solid base, with tactical advantages not found in other places. For instance, we had a three hundred and sixty-degree view. No one could approach without being seen or picked up on radar. It was also twenty feet above the ground, which allowed us to retract the ladder and block off the entry section so that it was difficult for intruders to get in. The Ashi weren't the only monsters on Libertine, but they were thirteen feet tall, so having some height off the ground was in our favor.

We had spent a good amount of time further securing the rig with sandbags. We found entire crates of empty bags, which we filled with dirt; there was plenty of that around our home, too. The sandbags were then stacked and secured to the railing around the rig. The Ashi had laser rifles, and sandbags were ideal at stopping the high-energy beams. We had come to call our terraforming platform Refuge. Its technically name was HLT-87, but the beings who built and installed them on Libertine were all dead. And the rig, one of well over a hundred such terraforming platforms, hadn't been used in decades. They required constant maintenance, which was hard to keep up with if a person didn't live on site 24/7.

Zaya and I had found the rig after crashing down on Libertine in an Ashi escape pod. She was on board as a slave. I was there to kill the aliens for bombarding the colonies on the poles of the Free World, which were in the only habitable zones on the planet before the bombs kicked up enough ash and organic matter to reshape the environment. Not far from the rig, a river now flowed. What had once been nothing but sand dunes for hundreds of miles had become grassy fields. There was still a lot of growing to do. Libertine had no trees, no real flora other than grass and the shoots of a few shrubs that were still in their infancy, but the world was more hospitable than it had ever been. I knew because I made periodic flights in the highly advanced MECH armor that I had first come to the planet in.

That was a long story, and one with some very painful memories. I put it out of my mind as I climbed up to the Crows Nest at the top of the drill scaffolding. It was nothing more than a level platform with a rest for the sniper rifle I had slung over one shoulder. From up on high, I had a clear view of anyone approaching the rig, which was not all that rare an occurrence. Along with the Ashi warriors who had escaped from their warships in escape pods just like Zaya and I, there were about seventy or eighty slaves who had reached the surface of the planet. They were aliens from different worlds, each one just desperate to survive another day. Some of them had found their way to the Refuge as well, and we welcomed them. But the Ashi we killed on sight.

When I reached the Crow's Nest, I unslung my Hemlock Stinger. It was a high-powered laser rifle. The weapon itself was little more than a laser focusing cylinder and a long, tantalum barrel. It was ideal for long-range shooting, since the laser blast had no mass and therefore wasn't affected by gravity. Nor did it create friction the way a projectile would. Not that lasers were perfect sniper weapons, they could be rendered useless in a dusty environment. Anything in the air that might contact the beam on its trajectory could cause energy bleed, rendering the blast ineffective. But they were, by far, the easiest to use.

If the Stinger had one drawback, it was the high power requirement. A laser blast strong enough to kill a person at five thousand feet or more needed a lot of juice. The sniper rifle itself was lightweight and easy to handle. The attached battery pack, which was the size of a six-pack of beer and weighed eighteen pounds, was cumbersome and difficult to lug around. I kept mine in a backpack with thick, padded straps, which I had found among the gear left behind on the terraforming platform.

My rifle, which I had carried with me from Earth and across the galaxy to Libertine, was fitted with an aluminum stock and a Vortex adjustable scope with low-light amplification and an infrared rangefinder. The entire weapon was painted matte black as I laid it carefully onto the sandbag rifle rest and scooted everything around the Crow's Nest so that I could look through the scope toward the approaching figures.

"I've got enemy fighters in sight," I said softly.

My words were carried to Zaya via the comlink in my ear, and it relayed her words back to me.

"How many?"

"Hard to tell yet," I said. "Twelve, fifteen maybe. They're bunched up."

"Weapons?"

"For sure," I said. "Not all of them, but enough."

Zaya sighed. "They just keep coming."

"I suppose they will until they're all dead," I responded. "I'm going to let them get a little closer."

"How close?"

"Half a mile, maybe," I said.

"That's too close."

"It's over twenty-five hundred feet," I told her.

"That's not much margin for error."

I could argue, but we had discussed it all before. And Zaya wasn't afraid to speak her mind. In fact, she could be hard to get along with at times. Stubborn, opinionated, and short-tempered, yet she was the only other human on the planet. And, truth be told, the same traits could be said of me, only add to them that I often felt awkward and out of place around people. Social environments confused me, and most people either avoided me, or they mocked me. Until I had been abandoned on Libertine, I had fully believed I was better off alone. That had changed, and Zaya had come into my life. I wasn't one to squander a relationship just because it was difficult.

And Zaya had some valid points. The Ashi carried laser rifles, big ones. But their warrior culture was all about bravado and misguided honor. They relied heavily on their strength, both in numbers and in their physical abilities. They were thirteen feet tall and had hulking physiques, so that made sense. But they had never fought humans before, and we were masters of strategy. The Refuge, for instance, gave us a huge tactical advantage. I could take the MECH and go out to fight the enemy, but why give up the high ground?

The Ashi were big on meeting their enemies face to face, and they liked to be close when they killed an opponent, which was probably why their laser rifles were only effective for a hundred feet or so. They just never felt the need to innovate their weaponry.

But since we had taken refuge on the terraforming rig and beaten back dozens of attacks, the Ashi were starting to take notice. They came at us from different directions and at different times. It was a response to our tactical advantage, and sooner or later, they would find a way to neutralize or overcome it. I wasn't looking forward to that, but I was actively preparing for it.

"You know they're slow," I said.

"Don't get cocky," Zaya replied.

"It's not arrogant if it's true," I said. "They're slow. We're in position. They can't get too close or I'll take them down."

"With only eight shots?"

She had me. I had only carried up one battery, which would power the Hemlock Stinger for eight shots. That might be enough to send the enemy into a hasty retreat, or they might press on. There were definitely more of them than I had the power to deal with.

"I hear you," I replied, nearly choking on the words. "Go ahead and power up the MECH."

"Alright done," she told me. "Now be careful and don't let them get any closer than you have to."

BRUTAL PLANET CHAPTER 2

The Ashi were big targets under normal circumstances. But hitting targets, even big ones, at over a mile away was never easy. Even with the rifle on the rest, the aiming reticle seemed to bounce and weave. Part of it was the drill. I was up pretty high, and since the bombing of Libertine, the weather was more volatile. At night, in the darkness, a person didn't notice the thick clouds moving in. There must have been a storm coming, because the top of the drill scaffolding swayed back and forth. It was only a few inches either way, but that was enough to throw off my aim.

I couldn't blame the platform entirely. Being a big man has its benefits and its drawbacks. Lifting heavy things was easy for me, being completely still was not. I liked a weapon I could get a good grip on, but the sniper rifle required a delicate touch. I snugged it into my shoulder in the hopes of steadying my aim. The Hemlock Stinger didn't kick like a projectile weapon, and therefore, it didn't need a stock. I had added one to my rifle, just a simple fold-down model that helped me get the right feel when taking long shots. But I couldn't press it hard against me, that only made it tremble. Instead, I tried to connect the swaying of the scope's image with my breathing.

"How's it going up there?" Zaya asked.

"Slow is smooth," I replied

"And smooth is fast, yeah, you keep saying that. Doesn't make it true."

"Patience," I said. "Can't afford to waste shots."

The motion of the cross hairs was minimal. I exhaled about halfway, then held my breath. For just a moment, the jittery image I was seeing through the powerful scope steadied, and I pulled the trigger. There was a flash of light, but the rifle didn't move. There was no recoil, and the only noise it made was a soft whine as the light focusing cylinder recharged for the next shot.

In the distance, one of the aliens dropped to the ground with a smoking hole in his abdomen. The Ashi aren't like people. They're tall bipeds that require two hearts to keep their blood pumping. I'm no expert on their anatomy, but I know the important stuff. For instance, their vitals are protected inside a chest cavity that is surrounded by thick bone. Whereas humans have ribs, the Ashi have bones as thick as armor plates. But just below their chest, the stomach has no protection at all. My blast ripped through the alien warrior's stomach and turned a section of his spinal column to vapor, killing it instantly.

"One down," I said.

The other Ashi were in a panic. I'm not even sure how well they could see in the dark. It was the hour just before dawn, and most of the stars were being blotted out as the storm rolled toward us. The aliens reminded me of ants. As a child, I was fond of kicking small ant hills and watching the ants run around in panic. I'm not sure what that says about my mental health, but most of the kids I knew did the same thing. My long-distance shot had set the Ashi into a similar state. Some dropped to the ground, raising their weapons in a futile gesture of defiance. Others turned and ran. I let them go. It seemed that the Ashi were probing out defenses, but they didn't want to die. Others charged ahead. I couldn't fault their valor. It was over a mile of open ground between them and the rig, but they charged ahead. The Ashi were agile for such large organisms, but they weren't fast runners. I settled the crosshairs of the scope down on the lead alien. He, or she, I couldn't discern their gender, barreled across the open ground. Unless they could see in the dark, the runners were taking a chance. The landscape was open, but not without its defects. There were stones, and even small cracks in the ground. The bombing had set off seismic changes that were still having effects on the topography of the planet. There were volcanoes erupting in some areas. It was odd to see them forming from mere holes in the otherwise flat ground. The molten rock heaving up, spreading, forming a new mountain. All the while, the new volcanoes were sending more and more smoke, ash, and carbon dioxide into the air. Libertine was a planet in transition, which made the weather volatile and changed the landscape constantly.

I fired again, taking my time. The second laser bolt sizzled through the night and caught the runner on his hip. It wasn't the killshot I wanted. In my mind, the Ashi were just doing what they were trained to do. I had no idea what their command structure was like, or who might be calling the shot. Had they taken a live and let live mentality, we might have been friends, but the Ashi seemed only interested in one thing: conquest. If they came looking for a fight, I would give them one.

The alien dropped. He would never run again, not without surgical intervention, which, to my knowledge, wasn't possible on Libertine. The colonies had all been primitive settlements, and besides, they were wiped out by the Ashi fleet. I had successfully destroyed two of their three ships in orbit. The third was still up there, but no longer viable. It was in a retrograde orbit, slowly circling down into the planet's gravity, where it would be ripped apart long before it could crash into the surface.

I saw him thrashing in pain. When I had the time, I would finish him off, but there were more Ashi looking to attack us. My second shot had taken down the lead runner, which means that his companions must have seen him fall. A pair of them slowed, uncertain what to do. In my mind, this was the perfect example of a situation where caution was the better part of valor. The Ashi gained nothing by throwing their lives away, and I was in a perfect defensive posture. I held the high ground, had the more potent weaponry, and the only cover for miles around. That meant the Ashi were in a terrible tactical position.

Taking aim at another runner, I breathed out softly, then fired. The laser bolt flashed like lightning and killed the Ashi warrior I was aiming at. His lower body kept moving, while the top folded over the gaping wound in his stomach. Then fell face first into the ground and lay crumpled in the darkness.

Behind me, thunder crashed. It sounded loud and close. A second later, when Zaya spoke, her signal was laced with static.

"Time to come down, Hugo," she said. "We've got a storm moving in."

"Roger that," I said, giving the aliens one last glance through the scope before flicking the safety on and rising to my knees. "I'm not finished yet."

"It'll have to wait," Zaya insisted. "You know how the drill attracts lightning."

She wasn't wrong. The drill, or rather, the metal scaffolding that supported the drill, was the tallest part of the structure. It was made of metal and was the only thing sticking up off the ground for hundreds of miles. The refinery had three different-sized smoke stacks, but they weren't as tall as the scaffolding over the drill, plus they were made of heat-resistant ceramics that didn't conduct electricity.

I slung the sniper rifle over my shoulder and grabbed the emergency cable that Zaya had installed. It was fed through a pulley and had a simple counterweight attached to the other end. There was a loop for one of my boots to go into. With my rifle secure, I stepped off the Crow's Nest and descended. It's faster than climbing, but slower than falling. When I reached the deck, I stepped off and worked the cable hand over hand to lower the counterweight back down. By the time I finished, fat rain-drops were falling.

I went immediately to the nearest gunner's nest. We had constructed several in strategic spots around the platform. They were small, barely large enough for a single person. But they had extra sandbags for cover, and a roof that kept the rain off me. Electrically powered weapons didn't play well in moist condi-tions. The Hemlock's battery and power cord were both insu-lated, but I was a strong believer in taking precautions when it came to things like fighting in the rain.

"What's the radar looking like?" I asked.

"There's a nasty storm rolling in fast," Zaya replied.

I knew that much was true because it hadn't been on the radar when we first spotted the Ashi. Our radar setup allowed me to rest knowing that nothing could approach the rig without us knowing it. I set up an alarm system so that anything moving in the darkness would wake me up. That's how we spotted the Ashi pressing toward us under the cover of darkness, but there had been no signs of the storm then. Had it been day instead of night, we would have seen it approaching. The radar was mili-tary grade and not built to pick up weather. Plus, I had only been able to bring the transmitter from my cave in the mountains. Zaya had built the receiving dish from spare parts she found on the rig. It only showed a radius of about five miles in every direction. It was perfect for defense, but it did us no good when stormy weather rolled in.

The flashes from lightning lit the pre-dawn darkness, and made looking through a night vision scope impossible. The scope amplified light thousands of times, and a person looking through a scope when the lightning flashed could damage their vision.

The storm came charging on. The wind picked up and gusting hard. We were forced to turn off the radar to keep the dish from being ripped off the drill scaffolding or ruining the little motor that rotated it. Zaya had used remotely controlled servos so that the radar dish could be folded up to protect the transmitter. It also turned freely so that it gave little resistance to the wind during a storm.

"How close were they?" I asked.

"Over half a mile out," Zaya said. "I counted four of them still coming our way. Will the storm stop them?"

"Doubtful," I said. "Better batten down the hatches. I'll do what I can, but that won't be much until they're a lot closer."

"Copy, I'll wake the others."

The terraforming rig had five dome-shaped buildings for housing the workers. Four were small apartments, the fifth was a larger common area with a full kitchen and recreational facilities, and furniture for lounging. All four apartments were occupied by former slaves, and the common space would have to be used if more refugees arrived.

Zaya and I had set up a living area in one corner of the rig's workshop. It was basically just a few thin, rubber-coated mattresses on a metal frame next to the radar equipment. I had my weapons there, and Zaya was in charge of the tools. Fixing up the rig was how she spent her days, and she was constantly making improvements.

My eyes swept the dark plain before me. There would be no more carefully crafted shots. It was time for instincts and muscle memory. I held the sniper rifle loosely, the stock snug against my right shoulder, and my index finger just outside the trigger guard.

Lightning flashed, but there were no enemies in sight. I set the Hemlock Stinger down and dashed out into the storm. My boots thumped on the metal deck plates. The wind was whipping hard, the rain almost flying sideways in the gale. I reached the doorway to the workshop, soaked and puffing. Zaya was just inside. She had my Sterner M88 Classic and a spare magazine.

"Just in case," she said.

I took the rifle and wiped the water from my face. Glancing toward the MECH armor, I wondered if it would be better to face the approaching threat with the big guns, but I decided that was overkill. Plus, the MECH burned through ammunition that we couldn't replace. And sooner or later, I was convinced that the Ashi would attack in greater numbers. When that happened, I wanted to meet them in fully mechanized armor with a variety of high-caliber weapons they weren't prepared for.

"Thank you," I said, which I thought was growth for me. I probably would have just grunted in acknowledgement of the gesture a few months earlier.

She had the Jagger strapped around her hips, and my Ambrose Hill XOR rifle slung over one shoulder. It was a heavy weapon with both a four-round projectile machine gun and a grenade launcher in one unit. In truth, it was too much weapon for her, but it fired shock wave explosive rounds that had more stopping power. And Zaya was not a dainty woman. She had survived a difficult life and had a well-muscled, sturdy frame that came from decades of hard labor.

"Careful with that thing," I told her.

"Right back at you," she said.

We dashed back out into the rain just as the first dull rays of dawn made the heavy clouds visible overhead. Not that we were looking up. Lightning shot down and hit the drill scaffold. The resulting thunderclap shook the entire rig, and sparks popped out across the platform. We bent lower and kept running. My nest was closer than the resident domes, but I stayed with Zaya until she reached the big building.

She didn't say anything, and I didn't either, but she looked over her shoulder before dashing inside out of the rain. We were an odd pair. Under different circumstances, we probably wouldn't be together. She was not one to keep her thoughts to herself, and I was the brooding type, who didn't talk much. But we had been through a lot together, and I certainly had a lot of affection for her. I couldn't say how she really felt. I was the only other human on the planet, and I had saved her life a few times. Maybe that didn't add up to true love, but it was enough to forge a bond between us. And her look meant a lot to me.

For most of my life, there had been no one who cared if I lived or died. It seemed like Zaya did, and I was thankful for that. Maybe, if I had thought more about it, I would have drilled down to some less-than-affectionate reasons for her concern, but I wasn't the type to have deep thoughts about relationships. We hadn't killed each other, and neither wanted to leave, which was all I really needed in a partner.

I was cold and completely soaked by the time I got back to the little gunner's nest. The wind whipped through the narrow slits between the sand bags and the roof of the structure with a savage howl. Lightning was rippling through the crowds and occasionally sending thick bolts of blinding energy down into the ground. I had seen what those lightning strikes did to the soil. The silica was melted into chunks of dark, glassy material. We had reclaimed some of it, and Zaya had flint-napped herself a blade that was sharper than my K-Bar combat knife.

The thunder was almost constant, and added to the drumming of the rain on the metal roof over my shooter's nest, there would be no way to hear the enemy if he were right behind me. The light was muddled, too. The lightning combined with the dim sunlight to create a world of gray. All I could really see was the rain. It would have been the perfect time for an all-out attack, but it seemed the rain and howling wind wasn't something the Ashi preferred to fight in.

I sat on a stool, thankful for the shelter of my little nest, but the wind was still whipping the rain sideways. Some of it found the gap between my sandbags and the metal roof, which creaked under the strain of that same wind. I won't lie and say the storms on Libertine since the bombing weren't scary. For over a year, I lived on Libertine in what many would have thought of as a tropical paradise. The entire planet had been a hotbox then, mostly desert, with only hospitable zones on the extreme northern and southern poles. But then the Ashi bombed the planet, and that kicked-started the terraforming into high gear. It also slaughtered countless innocents, which was the reason I had taken the fight to the Ashi in orbit, and why I didn't feel bad killing the warriors even when they were so far away they couldn't fight back. They had used that tactic first, and since the rules were out the window, I planned to kill the Ashi wherever and however I could.

It took a while, almost half an hour, but eventually I saw shadowy forms in the pouring rain. I immediately went to work.

Kestrel Class

Jump Point

Gravity Flux

Modulus Echo

Zero Friction

Planet Fall

Charter

Jack & Roxie

My Lady Sorceress

The Man With No Hands

ARC Angel

Battle ARC

Broken Crucible

Hidden Kingdom

War INC

Carthage Prime

Cronus Team

Skandia Seven

Mercurial

Magnificus Prime

Incursio

Merlin Appears

Runners

Survivors

Infiltrators

Resistance

Conquest

Occupation

Extraction

The Signal

Battle Orders

Base Of Fire

Hard Site

Recall

Evade

Assault

Space Fever

Staying Alive

Fractal Cut

Blast Zone

Action Zone

Covert Infil

Armor Brigade

Havoc Squad

Thunderbird

Ghost Tactics

Quantum Combat

Infinite Threat

Shadow Threat

Evolving Threat

Lingering Threat

Latent Prowess

www.ingramcontent.com/pod-product-compliance
Lightning Source LLC
Chambersburg PA
CBHW051957240626
47153CB00005B/1800